I0728227

Also by David H. Hendrickson

Bubba Goes for Broke
Cracking the Ice
Offside

Writing as D. H. Hendrickson

Body Check
No Defense

"Hendrickson's debut novel paints a gripping account of a courageous young man rising above evil."

— Booklist

"*Cracking the Ice* scores the literary equivalent of a hat-trick: funny, harrowing and finally, heartfelt. This book is a winner."
— Greg Neri, author of *Yummy: the Last Days of a Southside Shorty*,
a 2011 Coretta Scott King Honor book

"One of the most interesting books I've read this year, a one-of-a-kind book."
— Reading in Color

"A compelling, civil rights tale of a young man's coming of age on the ice. Hendrickson personalizes history with unforgettable characters."
— Jewell Parker Rhodes, author of *Ninth Ward*,
a 2011 Coretta Scott King Honor book

"A worthy, if heartwrenching read…. The best of humanity is explored—and some of the worst, exposed."

— Long and Short Reviews (four stars)

"A must read for every adult and young adult alike."
— Pete Webster
UNH Hockey Radio Network

"This is a terrific book and I would recommend it to anyone who likes a great story, hockey fan or not."

— Dan Hannigan
Maine Hockey Radio Network

OFFENSIVE FOUL

a Rabbit Labelle novel

DAVID H. HENDRICKSON

Pentucket Publishing
www.pentucketpublishing.com

Author's Note

Although this book can be read and enjoyed on its own, its events follow those of *Offside*. To maximize your enjoyment, the author suggests that you read *Offside* first.

Although Lynn is a real city with its streets and landmarks accurately depicted, this is a work of fiction. Other than clearly identified public figures and historical incidents, all characters and events portrayed in this book are fictional and any resemblance to real people or incidents is purely coincidental.

For dramatic effect, Lynn English High School is described as including ninth grade, which is true today, but was not yet the case in 1967.

*To my mother,
whose love and shining example
have guided my way.*

CHAPTER 1

Monday, November 27, 1967

The pounding of a half dozen basketballs being dribbled up and down the court echoes through the Lynn English High School gymnasium. Sneakers squeak on the varnished hardwood floor as the seventy or so players trying out for the team, myself included, drip with sweat in the warm, heavy air. We start and stop, pivot and pass, dribble and shoot. The nets swish with every perfectly made shot. Missed shots clang against the rim and fall away, only to be grabbed high out of the air, higher than I've ever seen before.

It's the first day of tryouts. Everyone's hair is cut short as if we're Marines in Vietnam even though the style, of course, is to wear it long like the Beatles. The black kids' hair is short, too. A week ago, my friend Charlie Watkins' Afro was huge. Now his hair is cut close to the scalp like everyone else's. Coach Abrams demands it. He's a legend around here. He and his older brother, Delvin, dominated Lynn English basketball as players more than twenty years ago, back in the team's glory days just after World War II when it made its only serious runs at a state title. He returned as coach about ten years ago, and will probably be the coach until the day he dies, or at least retires. What he says, goes. And he says if you want to look cool like the Beatles, you can look cool sitting in the stands. And no one here wants to be sitting in the stands.

I'm worried that I'll be one of them.

Up in the little hick town of Plainfield, Maine, I was the star of my teams, a tiny point guard not yet even five feet tall but with an accurate shot and more than enough speed and quickness to blast past anyone. I'm wearing the plain white sleeveless jersey and shorts of my summer league team up there, the Bandits, its name stenciled across the chest in big black block letters with a figure below it that looks a lot like the cartoon character Yosemite Sam. We won that championship, and I was named the league's Most Valuable Player.

But this is a whole different league, almost like a different sport. I'm surrounded by players a foot taller than me, some even more than that, though some less, who also jump as if vaulted by trampolines. I'm not in the minors anymore. High school basketball here in the big, bad city of Lynn, Massachusetts, is the big time.

I'm not going to be the star down here, that's for sure, even though there's a separate team for freshmen to go with a varsity and JV. I'm not sure I'll even make the freshmen team. This isn't like football where there were no cuts; if you survived and could keep going, you stayed on the team. There are about seventy guys here doing drills. Even with the three teams, half of us are going to get cut.

Maybe me.

"Hey, hero!" a kid named Rick Cassidy says as he passes the ball to me. The two of us take off down the floor along with Charlie Watkins in a three-man, passing drill, weaving behind the guy we pass to without dribbling.

Coming from anyone else, the "hero" remark would be one of congratulations and maybe even admiration because of my big plays in the Thanksgiving Day football game four days ago. I certainly heard plenty of that today in the hallways and classrooms along with getting many slaps on the back. I'd only played for the junior varsity all year, but in my first varsity action I returned two kicks for touchdowns and completed a halfback option pass to Charlie at the end of the game to help us beat our cross-town rival, Lynn Classical.

Cassidy, however, a lanky, dark-haired sophomore who is already a shade over six feet tall, means "hero" in a sarcastic way. We got off to a bad start at the bus stop on the first day of classes back in September, and he's made it clear ever since that he thinks I'm as useless as a bug. He led the freshmen team last year in scoring and rebounding, as he told me that first day, and he bragged that he'd be the star on the JVs this year and might even get a little time with the varsity. When I, a lowly freshman just barely five feet tall, said that I hoped to get brought up to the JVs, he took it as a personal insult. He hadn't gotten called up; why would a little pipsqueak like me?

Now I can see what he meant. I have no chance at JVs. But I can't take back those three-month-old words and he isn't about to let me forget them.

On his next pass, right after he glances at the coaches who are huddled talking and not paying attention, he fires the pass so high over my head that I have to jump to catch it. Seconds later, his pass comes in hard and low, halfway between my knees and ankles. I almost stumble reaching down for it. He's trying to make me miss the pass and look bad. And he's got a smirk on his thin, angular face as he does it.

His next pass comes in even lower and I have all I can do to bend over and corral it with one hand.

Coach Abrams' whistle blasts. We stop in our tracks.

"Cassidy!" he yells, his face showing sudden splotches of red in the cheeks. He's a tall man, about six-two, with broad shoulders and a crew cut as short as ours, though his black hair is streaked with gray. "What's your problem? Have you forgotten how to pass?"

Rick Cassidy stares at Coach Abrams, then waves an upturned hand at me, but says nothing, as if nothing needs to be said beyond pointing out the source of the problem.

"It's the midget's fault you're throwing it at his feet?" Coach Abrams demands, hands on his hips.

"Coach, he's, um…" Cassidy glances my way, the smirk long gone, looking like a little kid caught with his hand in the cookie jar. "He's a small target," he says feebly.

"Oh, really!" Abrams' look becomes even more menacing. He points to the basket thirty feet away. "That hoop over there is an even smaller target, and if you can't hit it, you can't play the game. I suggest in the future you hit the damned midget in the chest with your passes or you won't be passing the ball to anyone." One eyebrow rises ever so slightly, as if to ask if his point has been understood. "Not that passing the ball has ever been your strength."

A few snickers erupt behind me, and Cassidy's face turns red.

Abrams blasts his whistle with even more gusto than before. "Now get back in line and start the drill all over again. See if you can do it right this time."

This time, Cassidy fires hundred-mile-an-hour, two-handed bullets at me, but they're right at my chest, as if there's a bull's-eye on it, so I don't mind. When we finish, however, and move to the back of the three lines, Cassidy minds. He minds a lot. He glares at me as if it's all *my* fault.

"Think you're a hotshot, don't you?" he says.

Charlie steps between us. "Just play the game," he says to Cassidy, and stares him down. At five-nine, he's giving away a couple inches to the older sophomore, but would dominate any contest of strength. Charlie became my best friend on the football team—in fact, my only friend for a while—even though he's black and I'm white. At first, I was a bit afraid of him because he was so good and also, to be completely honest, because I'd never been around black kids up in Plainfield. There weren't any. But he's a great guy.

Cassidy pokes his head around Charlie just long enough to give me one last dirty look, then goes to the far lane.

"Don't nobody white like you?" Charlie asks.

We both laugh, but my smile evaporates fast. Charlie is a terrific player and even though he's still a freshman, he's sure to join Cassidy on the JVs, if not go to the varsity right away. He's got dazzling moves and fakes that just about make you dizzy. The coaches will never waste his talent on the freshmen team. I, on the other hand, have to be less than a fifty-fifty bet to make any team at all. The last thing I need is someone like Cassidy making me look worse than I already am, and drawing attention to my lack of size.

I suddenly realize the words Coach Abrams used to refer to me. Not by my name or my nickname. Not by the identification number—number 53—scribbled in black magic marker on the square sticker affixed to the back of my jersey. No, he said, "the midget" and even worse, "the damned midget." *Hit the damned midget in the chest with your passes or you won't be passing the ball to anyone!*

Geez. Not the way I want the coaches to think about me.

The damned midget.

I surprised a lot of people, including the football coaches, with my play on the football field the last few months, but you can be "five-nothin', hundred-nothin'" as the head football coach, Coach McDonough, described me—barely five feet tall and a hundred pounds soaking wet— and get away with it if you're quick enough to outrun your opponents.

But height is a pretty big deal in basketball, and I'm without question the shortest one here. There are only two other kids who are even close. And oh my gosh, guys like Charlie can jump through the roof. While I've always used my speed and quickness to make up for my lack of size, there are a lot of players here, not just Charlie, with almost as much quickness and a whole lot more size.

And some of the moves they make! Especially Charlie and another black kid, a short, thin one with skin even blacker than Charlie's named Jamaal Bryant. Seems like no matter who's guarding them, those two can fake that defender right out of his jockstrap. Watching some of Jamaal's spinning moves is enough to make you dizzy. He's another freshman who's sure to make JVs, even though it doesn't look like his outside shot is very consistent. But with his moves, he can get away with that.

That's about the only thing I've got on him. I can consistently hit a fifteen-foot jump shot. Back up in Maine, I did so on a regular basis. Just drained one after another. I never lost a game of H-O-R-S-E where you had to match anything the other guy sank or pick up a letter.

But down here, I wonder if every shot I attempt in a game or practice is going to be slapped right back into my face by a big meaty hand. Heck, sending it down my throat. For as long as I can remember, everyone has called me Rabbit because I'm quick, but my real name is David. And this feels like David versus about seventy Goliaths.

I've always liked to challenge myself, playing for older teams when I could up in Plainfield and always asking my friends to throw footballs or baseball grounders out of my reach so I'd have to dive to get them. So I guess I need to look at these tryouts as my latest challenge. This time, though, I may have bitten off more than I can chew.

*

As soon as I get home, I try to call Anna Levesque. I kind of like her. But the basketball tryouts went late and Mrs. Levesque tells me they're eating dinner, could I please call back in an hour? Disappointed, I say yes and hang up the phone, hoping that tonight my father works extra late so *we* aren't eating dinner an hour from now and I have to wait almost *two* hours.

But of course, that's what happens.

We're down to T minus nine minutes—to use the pretty neat count-down language of the Apollo spaceflights to the moon—when my dad walks in the door, wearing his usual dark suit, white shirt, and tie, and carrying his tan leather briefcase. This means it *will* be another hour before I can call Anna. My father and I aren't still at war over the move from Maine to here in Lynn, not like we were the first few months down here. We've been getting along okay since he apologized four days ago, after the Thanksgiving Day football game, for missing all my games and making it look like he really didn't care about me much at all.

But even though we've both tried to make a new start, I'm certainly not happy to see him now. Why couldn't he have gotten "hung up at the office" for another twenty minutes or longer, just like happened night after night during the football season?

Before I got Anna's phone number.

He can see the disappointment in my face.

"What's the matter?" he asks, setting his briefcase down against the wall and pushing his dark-rimmed glasses to the bridge of his nose. "What did I do?"

"Nothing," I say.

"I'm on time for dinner, just like I promised."

Yeah, that's the problem, is what I think, but I can't say that. So I nod and try to put a smile on my face that I don't feel. "Meatloaf and mashed potatoes."

"Then why did you look like I've just taken the air out of your football?"

This isn't a discussion I want to have. A few weeks ago, my dad wasn't getting home until 8:30 or even close to 9 o'clock some nights because he was trying to make a good first impression with his new boss. He's still trying to do that, but he's promised he'll be home by 7 o'clock most nights now because he wants us to eat as a family and be together. He's really trying, so I can't say what I'm thinking.

So I just say, "I'm fine. Really."

My mother tells me to wash my hands and come to the table. It's going to feel like forever before I'm talking to Anna, who I don't just kind-of-like, if I'm being honest. I like her a lot. She's got shoulder-length blonde hair, maroon-framed glasses, and a really nice smile. She's pretty, but in a quiet sort of way, not like a Brigitte Bardot or a Raquel Welch, movie stars who wear clothes that show off their big chests and expose lots of skin, or like Barbara Eden, who plays the sexy genie who comes out of the bottle in the TV show *I Dream of Jeanie.*

Anna isn't like that. She doesn't wear extra short skirts either, at least not compared to the miniskirts some girls wear that are so short they barely cover…well, they…they, you know…they're really, really short. That isn't Anna. It's not like she's old fashioned or anything. Her skirts are still a little bit above the knees, and they're always nice colors, and she always looks pretty.

Just not miniskirt or Raquel Welch pretty.

Anna pretty.

Her smile melts my heart. When I see it, it gives me a warm glow inside. She's in three of my classes, and was the first person to be nice to me after I moved down here. I finally got the courage to ask her for her phone number last week and she gave it to me. She also said with that nice smile that if I lost the number, it was in the phone book, which even a dope like me can figure out is a pretty good sign.

"So Rabbit, how was school today?" my father asks as soon as we sit down at the table, beginning the same question-and-answer ritual I went through with my mother when she picked me up after tryouts.

I fork a big slab of meatloaf onto my plate beside the mashed potatoes and gravy.

"Fine," I say, knowing what's coming next.

"How did basketball tryouts go?" he asks.

Bingo.

"I don't know," I say. "It's going to be tough. There are a lot of good players."

"That's never stopped you before." He chuckles. "Look at what you did in the Thanksgiving Day football game. You were amazing."

"Yes, you were!" my mother chimes in. She's taken off the plain white apron she wore while she was cooking, hanging it on a hook in the kitchen beside the refrigerator, and is wearing a light brown dress. It's kind of plain, like most of the things she wears, and she never wears makeup or flashy jewelry, and she ties her long, brown hair up in a bun, but I guess she's still kind of pretty in a mom sort of way. But she doesn't know much about sports except for games of mine she's seen.

I try to tell her and my dad that basketball is a very different sport, and my lack of height—being a damned midget, as Coach Abrams puts it—may make me a totally incapable of playing at this level. But they won't listen. They recite the nine touchdowns I scored for the junior varsity just on kick returns, and then the two touchdowns and my pass for the winning two-point conversion in the Thanksgiving Day game, my first actual action for the varsity. In their minds, I'll just do the same thing in basketball.

It'll be a piece of cake.

I chew my meatloaf, which is juicy with a hint of spices and topped with ketchup. "It's not the same," I say. "I can dribble and sink free throws with any of them. Other than that, I'm kind of lost."

"Oh, stop being modest," my mom says with a shooing-away gesture and a smile.

I give a shrug, since they're both going to expect me to not only start at point guard but be a star on at least the freshmen team, if not JVs. And they're certainly going to dismiss any possibility of me getting cut outright until it actually happens.

So I switch the subject. I don't even try to transition gracefully.

"Could I get a phone of my own?" I say. "For up in my bedroom?"

It hits them like a left hook from Muhammad Ali, one they never saw coming. My mom and dad both blink, stunned at what I've said. If they were on the Saturday morning cartoons, there'd be stars around their heads and birds would be tweeting while they staggered about, barely able to stand up.

"What for?" my mother asks.

"It'll be too expensive," my father adds a split second later. "We can't afford it."

"It could be my Christmas present," I say. "Just give it to me early so I can use it right away." When they just stare at me in stunned silence, I add, "Or you could wait. I can wait, but it would be nice to have it now."

"What's wrong with the phone we have right here?" my mother asks, gesturing toward the black phone resting on a small, dark wooden table up against the wall twenty feet away. It's just outside my father's study on the far side of the hallway opposite the bathroom and linen closet.

"There's no privacy," I say. "The two of you are always right around the corner. Either in the kitchen or the front room. Or Dad's in his study."

"What do you need privacy for?" my father demands, the tone of his voice suddenly stern. "There isn't anything you should be saying on that phone that you shouldn't be comfortable saying in front of us."

"If I'm talking to..." I stop, flustered. This isn't going well. I should have rehearsed my words so I wouldn't be backed into a corner like I am now. "If I'm talking to a girl, I don't want the two of you hanging around listening to every word."

"Why not?" my father asks, an angry flush rising into his cheeks. He leans close as if he's an FBI or CIA agent who's caught a Russian spy redhanded. His breath smells of coffee and the meatloaf. "You shouldn't be saying anything to her you're ashamed to say in front of us."

Good grief. They just don't get it.

So I drop it. For now.

But of course, now that I've brought up the topic of privacy, I get even less of it. None of it at all, in fact. When I call Anna twenty-five minutes later, there's dead silence around the corner in the front room where my parents are sitting on the sofa. The RCA black-and-white TV is off, and so are the radio and stereo. I can almost feel my parents' hot breath on my neck as they soundlessly lean toward where I stand in the hallway that leads from the dining room, the both of them straining to overhear my every word. Probably wishing they could somehow eavesdrop on what this evil girl is saying to their son.

Me and my big mouth.

CHAPTER 2

The next day quickly becomes a great day, but it doesn't start out that way. I can't make up my mind what to do. Admit to Anna that when I call her on the phone, my parents are in the next room straining to hear my every word? Or avoid that embarrassment and let her think that the awkward silences on my end and barely coherence sentences when I do talk are because I suddenly can't carry on a conversation as soon as I have a phone in my hand? Or even worse, that I don't really want to talk to her, which isn't true at all.

I can't decide, so I say nothing about it before homeroom, which we share because Labelle and Levesque are close to each other in the alphabet, or right after it as we head for our separate English classes. I figure everything is okay because she still smiles at me in that special way of hers. But I guess I'm not very good at keeping my mouth shut because I spill the beans as we meet up in the crowded and noisy hallway on the way to history class. I'm wearing brown dress pants and a dark blue button-down shirt. She looks beautiful in a yellow dress with white trim around the collar. Her blonde hair falls over the collar, and I can just barely sense her lilac-scented perfume.

Or at least I think it's lilacs. I don't know much about flowers. Anyway, we're side by side, close to each other, her on my left, and we're carrying our books in our outside hand. All around us, students are opening their green lockers, shoving books in and taking other musty ones out, then slamming the lockers shut and locking them.

"It may not sound like it," I begin hesitantly, "but I really like talking to you on the phone."

Anna smiles. "I like talking to you, too. On the phone, and even more in person." Then she frowns. "Why do you say it may not sound like it?"

"It's just awkward at my house," I say. "We only have one phone and it's right between the kitchen, dining room, and front room. So my parents are right there and it just feels like they're trying to listen in, you know?"

Anna nods.

"I asked if I could have a phone in my bedroom for Christmas, but that didn't go well."

"What did they say?"

I groan and shake my head. I give her the rundown and even add that my parents said, "We never had phones of our own when we were growing up." They didn't really say that, but they would have if they thought about it, I'm sure. It's the kind of thing they say all the time. And it matches everything else they said.

But I immediately feel guilty for being anything less than one-hundred-percent truthful with Anna, so even though she's laughing and nodding her head in sympathy, I quickly add, "They didn't really say that last part. Everything else, but I got a little carried away. They didn't actually say anything about not having phones when they were kids." A flash of inspiration hits. "Of course, they couldn't have. Telephones hadn't been invented yet."

Anna bursts into laughter, and I join in. We bump shoulders, and then our hands touch, my left to her right, and…

and…

…for a moment, I freeze just a little, not breathing, afraid to make a mistake, not sure if this is the right time, if there'll ever be a right time, but…

…I take her hand in mine just as she does the same, at first palm-to-palm, and then our fingers intertwine. The skin of her palm and fingers feels soft.

A slight flush creeps up her cheeks and I feel my own grow a little hot, too, but we both smile, at first cautiously, and then with huge, happy grins. Not quite ear to ear, which is what some people say even though that's impossible, but pretty close. She gives my hand a delicate squeeze and I squeeze back. My heart pounds with delight. My head is swimming.

It's my first time holding hands with a girl.

We continue walking, a warm glow filling my chest. I hope Anna feels the same way. We even keep walking past the classroom, not because we don't know where we're going, but because neither of us wants this moment to end. Our friend Jeff Goodwin, redheaded with freckles, dressed in bright, plaid pants, and usually quick with some type of quip, is coming from the other direction and starts to say, "Hey—," then sees our intertwined hands, falls silent, and keeps walking.

"I guess we better turn around," I finally say after we've gone five classrooms past where we want to go. We have to walk quickly to make it back in time and we step inside the room just as the bell rings.

From my seat on the far right of the room, four rows back, I find myself every once in a while looking over at Anna, three seats to my left and one row ahead. Okay, maybe a little more than just every once in a while. One time, she catches me and smiles.

All I can think is, *wow*! My heart races and my head swims. It's a good thing our teacher, Mrs. McPherson, doesn't call on me, because I haven't really heard much of what she's said.

Just…wow!

*

Tryouts that afternoon are like a roller coaster. Rick Cassidy doesn't mess with me like he did yesterday, but no sooner do I start feeling comfortable that I'll make the team than I take a sickening plunge into what feels like disaster.

The air in the gym has become progressively more thick and muggy. Sweat stings my eyes and tastes salty on my lips until I have a chance to lift my jersey and wipe my face dry. But as the jersey gets more and more damp, clinging to my chest, it becomes less and less effective, and the sweat just drips off of me.

I'm not alone. Everyone is feeling it. Coach Abrams is working us hard. Sprints up and down the court. Fast-paced drills. Move, move, move!

He blasts his whistle. "Four lines, one under each side basket!"

The stands have been retracted up against the side walls, so we move away from the glass backboards at each end and crowd underneath the two opaque, white, fan-shaped backboards on each side. "Those of you on this side"—Coach Abrams points to the side I'm on, away from the large series of gym doors that spectators will use later this year—"dribble to the other side with your right hand only. Those of you on the other side, dribble only with your left hand. As fast as you can while in control. Spread out!"

Finally, my kind of drill.

I've practiced dribbling with both hands for as long as I can remember, and speed is my game. So when it comes my turn, I fly up the one side, dribbling with my right hand, almost as fast as I flew up the sidelines in football, and then just as fast up the other with my left hand. Most of the other players either have to slow down at least a little when dribbling with their off hand or lose control of the ball entirely and have to chase after it in embarrassment when it bounces away.

But not me. I'm a regular Bob Cousy out there, and if Coach Abrams needs me to do a behind-the-back or between-the-legs dribble I can do that, too. And with both hands. I may not be able to touch the rim—I can't even touch the net!—but I'll get the ball up court without any fear of an opponent stealing the ball, and I'll lead the fast break and dish it off to a teammate for an easy layup.

If I get the chance.

At least I think so.

But I start to wonder when we switch to half-court scrimmages that take place beneath the four sideline baskets. We break into four groups. First, the fourteen or fifteen older players destined for the varsity form underneath one basket all to themselves. The larger next tier that will be vying for spots on the junior varsity split up beneath two other hoops. These are guys certain to make it like Rick Cassidy, Charlie Watkins, and Jamaal Bryant, as well as those on the borderline, like some of the more athletic freshmen members of the football team: Chris Higgins, CJ Powell, and Mark Evangelista.

Then there are the rest of us—the other freshmen and those presumed to be hopeless long shots at making *any* team—who crowd beneath the last basket. There are about thirty of us in this last group that I'm already thinking of as the "rejects"—we're the bottom of the barrel—and we're playing short stints of five-on-five. We spend twice as much time watching as playing, just standing on the sidelines, hands on our hips, smelling everyone else's sweat and the rubbery scent of the basketballs.

But that isn't what worries me. The problem is you can't run a fast break when there's no opposite hoop to run to. Playing half court, if your team gets the rebound, you have to clear the ball to the foul lane, then you turn around and go on offense, shooting at the same basket. So no fast break.

And playing half court without knocking down the sides to at least four-on-four leaves no room at all. We're packed in like sardines, and as the designated midget, I can't get much of anything done. I'm surrounded by a forest of long arms with no room to get free.

The only coach paying any attention to us rejects is the freshmen coach, Coach O'Donnell. He's the youngest of the three coaches, about thirty years old, thin, brown-haired, and under six feet tall. He watches, scribbles on his clipboard, frowns, and watches some more. It would be better if he were ignoring me now, like the other coaches. In this half-court, sardine game, I'm not even one of the best rejects. But he's watching and without a doubt, he's writing me off as a midget who can't play this big man's game.

I'm no fool. I'm not making this team. I'll be one of thirty or forty guys next week who'll have these ridiculous Marine-style crew cuts, and we won't even be on the team.

Not on any team. It will all have been for nothing.

We'll be the butt of every joke. I'll be "the shorty with the short hair" or something stupid like that. We'll be like the scarlet-letter woman in that old novel, only our letter of shame will be our haircuts, at least until they grow out. We had the audacity to think we could actually make it, but we got swatted away like a shot taken anywhere near Boston Celtics center Bill Russell. I can only imagine what a smart aleck like Rick Cassidy will say. Every time he glances over here at the "rejects" basket and sees me, he just smirks.

My emotional roller coaster has plummeted into the abyss.

It isn't until the final drill of the practice that I get to redeem myself, and my dark cloud lifts. We're shooting free throws, this time evenly distributed at the six baskets, the four we've been using on the sides and the two primary ones with glass backboards. If you miss, you're exiled to center court where an increasing number of players gather and watch those who haven't missed yet.

By the time I've made seven in a row, it's down to just four other guys and me and we've been herded to the glass backboard basket closest to the locker room and away from the gym doors where spectators enter for games. Everyone else gathers around in a semi-circle and the five of us keep going. Three of them are older kids, all guards about six feet tall from the varsity: Joe Thurman, a black kid who's the team's acknowledged superstar, a Spanish kid named Luis Ramirez, and Alan McLeod, a red-headed white kid. Then there's Charlie and me.

I take the ball, dribble twice, take in a breath of air and exhale, bend my knees, and shoot, giving the ball backspin off the tip of my fingers.

Swish.

Charlie, who looks like a different person without his big Afro, gives me a nod and a barely discernable smile at the corners of his mouth. Then he makes his, too. Nothing but net. Ramirez misses his free throw, and McLeod's shot goes around the rim and out, so it's down to just three of us. The superstar senior and the two freshmen, Charlie and me, one a future superstar and the other a midget with probably no basketball future at all.

Thurman looks at me and smiles, as if I'm the funniest thing he's seen all day. He sinks his free throw and one-hands a soft bounce pass to me.

"Hey, kid," he asks, still smiling. "This the only way you can get off a shot?"

That taunt may be even more of a bull's-eye than the nine perfect swishes he's made with the ball, but I just grin back, shrug, and move to the line.

Dribble twice. Breathe. Bend the knees. Let the ball spin off my fingertips. *Swish.*

Charlie misses on his tenth attempt, and it's down to Thurman and me. We keep going until we've hit twelve straight. Thirteen. Fourteen.

He raises his eyebrows and nods in approval. He may still have a slight smirk on his lips, but at least as far as free throw shooting goes, I'm a worthy rival.

"I can go all day, kid," Thurman says.

Back home—what I still think of as home, up in Plainfield, Maine, the hick town I came from where everyone was my friend—I would have made a snappy rejoinder.

"I can go all night," I would have said to Donnie Boudreau or Jimmy Chaisson or Scooter Seavey, and we all would have laughed, because they knew I could keep going and going, long past every single one of them.

But this isn't Plainfield, just like Dorothy in *The Wizard of Oz* found she wasn't in Kansas anymore. This is the big, bad city, and I've gotten knocked around enough—football hero or not—to know to keep my mouth shut. So I just smile, nod, and shoot.

Dribble twice. Breathe. Bend the knees. Let the ball spin off my fingertips.

I miss on number sixteen. It goes around the rim and out. Thurman makes his shot.

I smile. I can't be unhappy with this result. David went against the Goliath of the varsity and at least lived to see another day.

I don't think to put my hand out in congratulations until Thurman has already turned to join his varsity teammates, a group of which I'm not a member and probably never will be. Shaking hands is another thing I would have done back in Plainfield, but it's probably a good thing I didn't try it here. I probably need to show I belong in a whole lot more than just the free throw shooting drill before the varsity superstar is going to be shaking my hand.

*

I open the door to my mom's light blue Ford Fairlane and slide in the front, well-worn bench seat that extends from side to side. She's been waiting along with all the other parents parked inside the semicircle driveway that curves around to the school's entrance and back out. She hands me a fluffernutter wrapped in wax paper that crinkles as I unwrap it. It's a sandwich made of peanut butter and marshmallow fluff, a white, thick, and sticky goo made here in good old Lynn, Massachusetts. Between us, lying on its side on the tan-colored, canvas-backed seat is a chrome thermos with cold milk. Sandwiches like this became a tradition after football practices because I was always ravenous and dinner was delayed because my father worked late.

"Thanks," I say, biting into it, the peanut butter crunchy and the fluff sweet. I wash it down with a gulp of the cold milk.

After first asking about school, she asks how tryouts went.

"Some good, some bad," I say, and between bites of the sandwich describe the ups and downs, going from a dead certainty that I won't make the team to battling Joe Thurman to the end of the free throw shooting contest.

"That's wonderful!" she says, delighted to hear about the free throws while seeming not to have heard how lost I was in the half-court five-on-fives. "Almost as good as the star senior! I'm so proud of you!"

"Mom, that was just the free throws."

She waves a hand of dismissal at what I've just said. "Stop worrying. You're a *great* basketball player."

She doesn't get it. The only basketball games she's ever seen have been of me back up in Maine when I was winning MVP awards. She's never seen a pro or college game, or any game down here. I love her—she's my mom—but she has no idea what's she's talking about.

"Mom, I'm not a *great* basketball player. Bill Russell is a great basketball player," I say, referring to the Boston Celtics center, who blocks shots like no player ever before him. He won two national championships in college, an Olympic gold medal, and an NBA championship every year in the league except one time when he had a broken ankle and couldn't play and then last year when Wilt Chamberlain's team finally beat him. "That's a great basketball player. Wilt Chamberlain, Elgin Baylor, and Jerry West are great players. Bob Cousy was a great player until he retired. In high school, Joe Thurman is a great basketball player. I'm not great. I'm not even close."

"Oh," she says, waving yet another hand of dismissal as she stops at the light at Maple Street. "You will be."

"Mom, you don't understand. Height is a much bigger deal in basketball. And some of these guys can jump to the moon."

She cautiously asks, "The blacks?"

"Well, yes, but there'll only be a few of them on each team," I say, recalling how back in the fall Rick Cassidy said almost half the team was black, exaggerating just to intimidate me. "But some of the white kids can jump pretty good, too. Better than me and I'm way shorter than all of them. *Way* shorter than almost everyone. There's a kid on the varsity who's six feet five inches tall! That's almost a foot and a half taller than me. Joe Thurman is almost six feet tall and he can do *everything*. You should see his moves. His speed. His leaping ability. He's amazing."

"He's…black?"

"Why do you keep saying that?" I ask. "Yes, he's black. He'd be amazing if he were purple."

"Of course. I was just…just trying to picture everything." Her eyebrows shoot up. "What about Charlie from the football team? Charlie… Watkins."

Charlie became my best friend on the football team at a point when I didn't really have any friends there. He and I played the same positions, flanker on offense and cornerback on defense, and at first shared nothing more than our common positions and a few words out on the practice field. He was so good I even asked him to do some extra one-on-one drills with me, but he declined. Maybe because he didn't trust me back then. I never asked.

But we became friends after I convinced my mom to give him a ride home one day when his mother couldn't pick him up. At first, Mom didn't want to—she was scared of him and his huge Afro—but I practically forced her to turn around and we took him home even though he lived on the other side of the city. We became friends, and after Jimmy Keenan sucker-punched me on the way out to the practice field, Charlie and Jessie Stackhouse—a friend of his and a star black *hockey player*, if you can believe that—walked out each afternoon together with me.

None of that prepared Charlie and me, however, for the day his mother was giving me a ride home and two Hells Angels pulled up beside us at a stoplight, their chrome-plated Harleys roaring. Blocked in on all sides, we could only sit there helplessly, doors locked, while the leather-jacketed bikers tried to kick in our doors and windows. Then, when that didn't work, one of them, his tangled black hair hanging down to his shoulders and his beard scraggly, pulled out a gun and pointed it at me.

The stuff of my nightmares. The black barrel of that gun. His trembling finger on the trigger.

Going through something like that together forms a special bond. We've never talked about it since, but it's there. Unspoken but real. If he's at all like me, he still has the occasional nightmare, though perhaps not every night like the first few weeks after it happened. Some nights—and some days, too—I still see that gun pointed at me. I still shrink away from that drugged-out biker, the pupils of his eyes dilated, his shaking finger just the tiniest fraction of an inch away from blowing my brains all over Charlie and the insides of his mother's car.

I wish there were some kind of soap that could scrub terrifying images like that out of my mind forever, but there isn't. It's the reason why my breath quickens and my heart skips a beat each time a car I'm riding in stops at that light just two blocks away from where my mom and I are now.

"Charlie's an amazing basketball player," I say. "He's going to be on JVs. I'd be surprised if he doesn't even get some time on the varsity."

My mother frowns. "But he's a freshman, right? Like you."

"Yes, but he's really, really good. By his junior or senior year, he'll be great. Maybe even better than Joe Thurman is now. I'm just okay."

"I'm sure you'll be great, too, dear."

I wish I were so sure. I take the last bite of the fluffernutter and wash it down with a gulp of milk.

*

Dinner time is almost an exact duplicate of the night before. When I first try to call Anna, her family is having dinner. Then I get within five minutes of being able to call back, and my dad marches in the door, and we spend the next forty-five minutes eating.

But worst of all, when I finally do get to talk to Anna, my parents are once again just around the corner in the front room where it's suddenly hushed, the TV shut off so my parents can hang on my every word. There isn't even a rustle of the newspaper my father is supposed to be reading. Of course, there's no need to rustle it while turning the page if you're just staring at the same words, not reading at all. I almost wonder if they're holding their breath so the mere sound of breathing won't interrupt their eavesdropping.

Midway through the five-minute conversation with Anna—that's my time limit to avoid accumulating too many message units on the phone bill—I get an idea that should fix the problem. I don't say anything right then because I don't want to be overheard, but I can't wait to discuss it with Anna tomorrow.

"You're smiling," she says. "I can hear it in your voice."

"I'm always smiling when I talk to you," I say, thinking it's a pretty good Romeo line if I don't say so myself, at least for a guy like me who's never had a girlfriend before.

As Anna laughs, I think that my line is also pretty close to the truth when we're actually together. It's only when I'm on the phone with her and I've got my own version of J. Edgar Hoover and the FBI wiretapping the phone—at least, that's how I feel about my parents' eavesdropping— that I find myself occasionally scowling and if not that, at least glancing at the partial wall that separates me from them in the front room.

"I'll tell you tomorrow," I say.

"Oooh, tell me now," Anna says. "Please?"

"I can't," I say, guessing the suspense is killing my parents even more than it's killing Anna. "First thing in the morning."

"Promise?"

I promise, and a minute and a half later, right on time, I end the call with, "Have a good night, Anna."

"You, too, Rabbit."

Something about her saying my name makes me feel good all over. I know it's silly, but I can't help it. Everyone else on the planet can say my name and it's just, "Yup, that's me."

But when Anna says it, it's…special.

I hang up the phone with a big grin on my face. I just stand there for a few more seconds, probably looking really dopey as if I'm basking in the glow of something special, and then my mom comes rushing out of the front room.

Obviously, she heard me hang up the phone. Of course she did. She was hanging on my every word. She looks at me with a nervous curiosity.

"What's so funny?" she asks.

"Nothing," I say.

"It doesn't look like it."

"I'm just happy," I say.

It's the truth, but it's also the kind of thing that'll probably drive my J.-Edgar-Hoover parents nuts, especially because I'm sure they also heard my promise to tell Anna something special tomorrow. What could it be? Why am I happy? How does that fit into everything else I said in the half of my conversation with Anna that they overheard?

And I suppose it makes me even happier that it'll drive them nuts. Not that I'm trying to be mean. It just seems like an appropriate punishment for their snooping.

And if they think this is bad, wait till tomorrow.

CHAPTER 3

That's hilarious!" Anna says, breaking into laughter when she hears my plan as we walk together to homeroom the next day. She's dressed in a navy-blue dress and faintly smells, once again, of lilacs. Her eyes sparkle behind her maroon-framed glasses. "Ingenious!" she adds.

I'm beaming. "So you'll do it?"

"Of course," she says, but then almost instantly her face clouds and her eyes widen just a bit. The sparkle has gone out of them. "But what if… what if your parents get mad? I don't want them to hate me."

"They're not going to hate you," I say. "They're not going to hear a word you say, unless, that is, they really do have our own phone wire-tapped, FBI-style." I smile. "And that would cost money, so my father would never go for it. He's the one insisting we talk for only five minutes to keep the phone bill down. So if they're going to be angry, it'll only be with me, and trust me, that's something I got used to the last few months."

I think of all the fights I had, especially with my father. Not Muhammad Ali–kind of fights, although the former heavyweight champion isn't fighting at all right now. He's in jail because, according to my father, he's a draft-dodging coward, willing to fight in the boxing ring for money, but not willing to fight for his country in Vietnam. No, my father has never punched me, but over the past few months he sure gave me a couple hard slaps while we were hollering at each other.

That's in the past now, at least both of us hope so, as does my mom. But trouble never seems too far away from me and my father. Maybe that's how it is between teenagers and their parents, although it never used to be like this when we lived in Plainfield, Maine.

Things were easier then. Simpler. There didn't seem to be much to fight about.

Down here, there's always something. Maybe this phone privacy disagreement will be the next one. But I doubt it.

"I don't think they'll be angry," I say. "In fact, I'm sure they won't be. Maybe a little embarrassed because it'll show them they aren't being fair. But not angry. I'm going to make it so outrageous they can't possibly believe it. And if it's so obviously unbelievable, what can they be angry about?"

"I don't know," Anna says hesitantly. "I guess so."

*

That afternoon at tryouts, we go through all the same drills, but when it comes time to break into four groups scrimmaging half-court beneath the two baskets on each sideline, I find myself elevated from the last group—the rejects, the bottom of the barrel—to the third. Apparently, my performance in the free throw shooting contest at the end of yesterday's practice caught the coaches' attention, and I've separated myself from the pack of also-rans.

That's good, but I still have a tough time dealing with the size of the other players in a half-court, five-on-five game. There are no fast breaks where I can use my speed and even when I can burst past the player who's guarding me, it still feels all clogged up inside and there's no room to drive to the basket. The better players like Charlie Watkins and Jamaal Bryant, not to mention my not-so-good-buddy Rick Cassidy, are at the number two basket, but this third group is still a significant step up from the last one.

Fortunately, I notice that a kid named Jerry Epstein, a skinny, white lefthander, has a good jump shot from fifteen feet out on the baseline. A freshman, he's kind of awkward, has a slow release and can't jump hardly at all, so he has trouble getting his shot off, but if he's open, he's pretty accurate.

"Go to your spot on the baseline," I say to him after the other team sinks its shot. "Be ready."

Another player on our team inbounds the ball after first bouncing it to the nearest defender who "checks it"—makes sure his team is ready—then bounces it back. The ball comes to me on the right above the key, outside the foul lane, twenty feet from the basket. My defender, who's all arms and must have me by a good nine inches, is playing me tight, too tight since I'm not about to launch a shot from twenty feet out.

I fake left, then drive right. I've got a half step on my defender right away, but he immediately gets help from Jerry Epstein's man, Randy

Thorpe, a big but sort of flabby, slow-footed lineman I know from the football team. My path to the basket is blocked. It's really all clogged up down low because two of our guys are already down there, bringing their defenders with them, but that's fine with me. I drive right up to Thorpe, Epstein's original defender, then look to the left and pass to the right where Epstein is waiting on the baseline. He's all alone and even though it feels like it's hours before he cranks up his shot, he gets it off before anyone gets near him.

Swish!

He looks at me, gives a little grin, and nods. I nod back and say, "Good shot."

When we get the ball back, we run the same play. My defender isn't the brightest bulb in the chandelier, so his response to me blasting past him last time is to try to play me even tighter. It's the exact opposite of what he should do. He should back off a little, play me to drive, and see if I'm going to try to beat him with a twenty-foot shot.

So I make him pay. I blast past him yet again and Thorpe, Epstein's defender who's an even dimmer bulb in the chandelier, comes after me again, like one of Pavlov's dogs who automatically starts salivating when it hears the bell it associates with getting fed. Thorpe just can't help himself. He comes over with his two hundred pounds of sweating bulk to block my path, but once again he's left Epstein open. Another no-look pass to Epstein produces the same result.

Swish!

Epstein's grin is larger this time. Who doesn't love to hear that sound of their shot dropping cleanly through the net?

The Dimwit Twins, as I've begun to think of my defender and Randy Thorpe, allow us to do the same thing yet a third time without making an adjustment. And then, unbelievably, a fourth.

A shrill whistle blasts.

"Comeau! What's wrong with you?" Coach O'Donnell yells at my defender. "You, too, Thorpe! How many times are you going to let Labelle and Epstein run the same goddamned play?"

The Dimwit Twins just stare at the coach.

"Thorpe, were you playing football without a helmet this year?" Coach O'Donnell yells, arms spread wide in disbelief. "If a guy like Epstein hits three straight shots *from the same spot*, shouldn't that tell you not to leave him alone for a fourth?" The coach turns to Comeau. "And you! If you were playing with half a brain, Thorpe wouldn't have to cover for your sorry ass. Look at Labelle! Look at him! I bet he isn't even five feet tall."

I actually am five feet tall. Not five-one or five-two, I'll admit. I barely pass the five-foot mark, but I do pass it. I can't hardly say anything, though, not in a gym full of guys so much taller than I am. It would be like someone saying, "I bet you don't even have an IQ of twenty," and you respond, "I do so have an IQ of twenty!"

So I say nothing, but feel as if I've suddenly sprouted horns on my head since everyone is staring at me. Comeau looks confused, as if he isn't sure what he's supposed to see in me.

"What's his name, for crying out loud?" Coach yells.

"Labelle?" Comeau says feebly.

"It's *Rabbit*! Rabbit Labelle! Everyone knows his name from the Thanksgiving Day football game!" Coach O'Donnell shakes his head with exasperation. "What does the name Rabbit tell you?"

Comeau just stares, wide-eyed, like a deer caught in a car's bright headlights. I feel bad for him.

"It tells you he's quick!" Coach says, sounding angrier and angrier. "And even if you didn't see him in the football game, and even if you didn't know his nickname, you still should guess that speed is his game just from looking at him. So you *back off*! Until he hits a couple in a row from twenty feet, don't go that far out to press him. He'll just blow right by you. Like he did four freaking straight times!"

Coach O'Donnell takes a deep breath and looks at the ten players gathered around him in this section of the floor and then the rest waiting on the sidelines. "I'm not just picking on Comeau here. I'm trying to make a point. You've got to use your brains in this game. You have to size up your opponents strengths and weaknesses. If your initial guesses are wrong, don't make the same mistake over and over."

He goes on for a bit longer, but everyone gets the point. I'm happy my play caught his eye, but his loudly delivered scouting report puts an end to my collaboration with Jerry Epstein. It was good while it lasted and increased both our chances of making the team, but with Comeau backing off me and Thorpe sticking to Epstein like sweaty glue, I have to try other options and although I do a few good things, nothing clicks like those four straight plays with Epstein.

At the end of practice, my downward spiral continues. I fail to make the final group of free throw shooters, making only five straight and missing on the sixth. When Joe Thurman, who I went head-to-head with yesterday, sees that I'm not there, he says with amusement, "No midget this time?"

*

That night after tryouts, I don't even try to call Anna before my father gets home and our family eats dinner. I suppose I'm setting a trap for my parents, which kind of sounds bad, but if that's what it is, I want both of them to be around for what I've got planned.

I want both of them to be snooping on my conversation with Anna.

So after we've eaten and I've helped out with the dishes, I pick up the black-handled receiver and on the base of the phone put my finger in the slight hole for the first digit to her phone number and swing it around clockwise almost full circle. Then, standing there with my thigh almost touching the dark wood table on which the phone rests, I dial the next number and the next until I've entered the entire number. While the phone rings, I stare down at the plain white memo pad atop the Lynn area phone book and yellow pages, a black pen on each side. The tomato and cheese smell of the night's meal, lasagna, is still in the air. Just like the last two nights, the TV is off and my parents are hushed around the corner in the front room.

Not making a peep so they can listen in on my every word.

Anna answers the phone, and we say our hellos. This time, she's the one who sounds nervous and awkward, not me. I can tell from the quiver in her voice and the barely audible sound of her breath that her heart is pounding. She has her doubts about this, but not me. I feel cool as a cucumber, as if I'm standing at the free throw line and only need to sink one of two to win the game. I'm a little excited, of course, but mostly because I'm sure this will end the snooping.

I've never once gone fishing, but I suppose this is what I'm doing now. I put the worm on the hook and cast into the waters of the front room where my parents are just waiting to snap at the bait. I turn to face the front room and speak in a voice no louder or softer than I use on the phone with Anna.

"So can you get the getaway car for Friday night?"

Even as Anna giggles, I hear a muffled gasp from the front room.

"Are they going for it?" she asks.

If I were answering her question, I'd say, "Hook, line, and sinker." My parents haven't just nibbled at the bait. They've devoured it. But I stick with the script.

"No, it can't be a red Corvette," I say. "That's too noticeable. Every cop in Lynn will be after us."

Anna's uproarious laughter has put a gigantic smile on my own face, one that will instantly give me away if my parents come around that corner, but that will be fine. I'll have made my point.

But they don't come around the corner. In my mind's eye, I see them sitting rigid and wide-eyed on the sofa, my mom gripping my dad's arm so tight she's pressing her fingernails into his flesh, hurting him just a bit. And he's probably angry, the storm clouds building on his face, fury in his eyes.

Until, of course, they both recognize the total absurdity of what I'm saying and realize I'm using this harmless prank as a way to get them to stop snooping on me. They'll look at each other in dawning realization, roll their eyes and shake their heads, and whisper something like, "He got us!"

For the briefest instant I wonder if they could possibly believe what I'm saying, but that foolish concern vanishes even more quickly than it arose. The possibility of me dunking a basketball even though I'm not an inch taller than five feet is more believable than this nonsense about a getaway car. And if I really did have any serious misgivings that this prank is a bad idea, well, that cat is out of the bag, as my mom often says. It's too late to back out now.

Besides, I really do think I need to make this point, and stop my parents from listening in on my conversations. I've never, ever gotten in trouble before, so they should trust me. I'm no criminal. They shouldn't make me feel like one by acting like J. Edgar Hoover.

Full speed ahead.

"We need something that will blend in," I say. "A red Corvette is the worst possible choice. A beat-up station wagon would be best. As long as it's reliable."

"They can't possibly be going for it," Anna says. "It's so totally unbelievable. You're too sweet."

"We don't want some jalopy that'll be stalling out at the wrong time," I say, plowing ahead with the script.

Then it hits me what Anna just said. I heard it, but I didn't really *hear* it. "What did you say? Say that again."

"They can't be going for it."

I groan. "No, not that. The other thing."

"Your parents should never believe anything bad about you," Anna says in a soft, warm voice. Then she says the magic words. "You're too sweet."

A huge smile fills my face. Before I can respond, she says almost the exact same words one more time. "You are *sooo* sweet."

"You are, too," I say, really meaning it but wishing I could be saying it with her right beside me. I'd hold her hands. I'd look through her glasses into her warm brown eyes. Maybe even take the glasses off so I could see those eyes better, like they do in the movies.

I've totally forgotten about the script now. Forgotten about my mom and dad listening in. All I can think about now is Anna, wanting to be with her, hold her hands, see that pretty smile, and hear her voice.

Only Anna.

Then something in the front room falls to the floor, landing on the rug with a soft *thunk*. Something like one of the books on the coffee table. That would be right in front of the sofa where my parents are sitting, unless, of course, my words have gotten them out of their seats.

That noise, followed by a rustling in there, startles me out of my reverie. It ruins what had been a wonderful moment: Anna calling me sweet.

I half-heartedly return to the script. "It doesn't matter that I don't have a license. Driving without a license will be the least of my concerns."

"You should probably stop there," Anna says. "Don't give your parents a heart attack."

"You're right," I say. "That was my plan, too." My words answer Anna honestly and at the same time keep up the ruse.

"So how will I know what happens between you and your parents?" Anna asks. "I can't wait until tomorrow at school. The suspense will be killing me."

I stop. I hadn't thought of that.

I guess I was so sure this would go well—my parents would instantly realize they were wrong and I was right—that there'd be no reason for Anna to worry. But isn't that like assuming every basketball shot you take is going in, or every time you touch the football you're going to run it for a touchdown?

You want that mental confidence. If you think your shot is going to clang on the rim and fall out, it probably will. But it's ridiculous strategy to assume a one-hundred-percent shooting percentage with no plan for getting the rebound if you miss. I've been so sure this shot would go *swish*, nothing but net, that I've got no teammate under the basket for the rebound, no way to handle an explosion with my parents.

And the idea that any shot involving your parents admitting they're wrong and you're right is an automatic *swish* is a foolish one. Looking at it that way, that kind of shot is like a desperation one you take from half court with the buzzer about to sound. But I've let the shot fly and the best I can do is scramble after any rebound myself.

I look at the clock on the wall, then turn my back to the front room and say in a whisper, "I've got a minute and a half left out of the five I'm allowed," I say. "If everything is okay, I'll call you back."

"But what if it isn't?" Anna says, anguish in her voice. "Oh, Rabbit!"

"Then you'll read about me in the newspapers," I say.

"That's not funny!"

I *was* trying to be funny. Not ha-ha, knee-slapping funny, but at least end on a light note.

So much for that idea. So much for this whole idea, I start to think, getting a sense of real foreboding, as my English teacher, Miss Minter, would say. I've been sure this would be easy, nothing harder than sinking a free throw, an automatic *swish*, but the near-panic in Anna's voice has thrown a bucket of ice cold water in my face.

For the first time, I consider that this could end disastrously.

"Down to a minute," I say. "I'll call if I can. Bye!"

I think I hear Anna swallow hard, although maybe that's just in my head, then she softly says, "Bye."

I hang up.

I step toward the front room, intending to confront my parents right away, and if, against all logic, they really are panicked, put them instantly out of that misery. But they've apparently shot right out of their seats, or maybe they had silently gotten out of their seats earlier, and moved right to the corner to try to catch every word.

Whatever the case, we all round the corner at the same time, and I crash into my father. My mother is right behind him, and one look at her ashen face makes me feel awful.

"*What's going on?*" my father thunders, grabbing my bicep with his hand. He squeezes hard with a pincer-like grip. "Tell me now or I'll tan your hide so hard you won't be able to sit for a week. Tell me!"

"Nothing is going on," I say. "I just—"

"It's drugs, isn't it?"

"No—"

"*Tell me!*" my father shouts, shaking my arm, his face red with fury and, I realize to my amazement, *fear*.

"You can't possibly think—"

"If you think for one minute, young man, that we don't know what's going on—"

I lean in until I'm inches from my father's face and yell right back. "*You don't know anything!*"

He leans back and slaps me. It stings, not so much the tingling of the skin on my cheek, which surely is turning crimson, but even more, feeling the power of his rage.

"Don't you talk back to me, young man!" he says, and behind his glasses I see the black pupils of his eyes glare at me. "We are *not* going to have that kind of behavior in this house. I won't tolerate it! I don't care what Dr. Spock says. Spare the rod and spoil the child. I'm afraid you've become quite a spoiled little brat!"

"Andre!" my mother finally interjects.

My father turns on her. "You heard him!"

My mother, white-faced, nods. "Rabbit," she says, her voice shaking, "what's going on? Tell us."

"I just wanted some privacy when I'm talking to Anna."

"That girl is no good for him," my father says. "She's a bad influence. Look at what's happening to him!"

Fear leaps into my throat at these words. How can he be blaming Anna for something that was totally my idea, and something I had to coax her to participate in? I remember now her words, *I don't want your parents mad at me*, words I instantly dismissed based on the logic of the whole situation.

But there's no logic involved now.

And I seem to have made my parents think that Anna is the enemy. Even though she's the best part of my life.

"This has nothing to do with Anna," I say.

"We heard you on the phone planning some getaway with her, something you needed to hide from the police," my father says.

"And you believed that?" I ask, incredulous. They didn't just swallow the ridiculous story hook, line, and sinker. They swallowed the whole ridiculous boat!

They stare back at me.

"It's what you said," my mother says, looking suddenly confused.

"When have I ever gotten in trouble?" I ask. "When have I ever given you reason to think I'd get in trouble with the police?"

After a few seconds of dead silence, my father feebly says, "There was that Jimmy Keenan thing at the dance."

Now I'm really angry. No, not just angry. *Furious.*

"His friends tricked me into going outside where they ganged up on me and he beat me with a baseball bat! If Coach Callahan hadn't stopped him, Jimmy Keenan might have beaten me to death! That's my trouble with the police? That's reason to believe I'm doing something with a getaway car?"

"Well..." my father says, glancing back to my mother as if hoping she'll say something in support. "Okay, you have a point there, but—"

"I expected the two of you to come out of that room laughing at the absurdity of what you heard, never believing it for a second, and then you'd admit you should stop snooping on my conversations as if you're the FBI!" Now I'm not just angry. I'm hurt. Offended. Outraged. "If you believed in me—I'm a good person who has never gotten in *any* trouble—that story should have made as much sense as Martians coming down and stealing our car to rob a bank!

"For crying out loud, I'm still two years away from getting a driver's license, and yet you believed that I was arranging for some getaway car to avoid the police? I didn't make up a borderline believable story that would really get you worried. I made up the silliest thing I could think of. Something you would never, ever believe.

"But you jumped right at the possibility of me doing it all."

I feel a crushing weight on my chest, knowing that my parents had so little faith in me. I never would have believed that.

"We worry about you, Rabbit," my mom says, her eyes filling with tears. "We know this isn't like Plainfield and so we worry."

A few weeks ago, I would have pounced on those words and snapped at my father and said again how much I hate it here in this often scary city, torn away from all my old friends back in Plainfield, Maine, and the safety of its peaceful, rural life. Said something like, "Why did we ever leave?"

But right now I only feel sadness. Sadness that my parents would believe the most wildly improbable, awful story I could make up about myself. Sadness at seeing the tears in my mom's eyes.

Then my father explodes.

"You think you're pretty smart, don't you?" he says, stabbing me in the chest with his index finger. "Think that was a pretty clever trick you played on us?"

That's exactly what I thought yesterday. I thought it was an *extremely* clever trick that would make my point. It would force my parents to see things my way. Teach them a lesson, I suppose you could say, although I'm sure smart enough not to use a phrase like that with them. Parents want to be giving the lessons, not getting them, and most of the time I understand. They know things I don't know.

Just not this time. There was no reason for them to insist on snooping in on my phone calls. This time I was right. They had a lesson they needed to learn.

But do I still think it was a clever trick? Do I still think I was pretty smart to come up with it? Heck, no! I'd have to be dumb as a brick to still think that after the way it's totally blown up in my face.

And then my father makes it even worse.

"Young man, you're grounded from using the phone for the next *year*!" he shouts.

"Andre!" my mother says.

My father glances back at her. "Okay, a month."

"Andre, that's—"

"Okay, a week," he says, his face flushed. He stabs at the middle of his glasses, jamming them back up to the bridge of his nose, then glares at me. "But not one second less! You're going to understand that use of this phone is a *privilege* we grant you, not some unalienable right granted by the Constitution!"

I stare at him dumbfounded. I'm so stunned and angry I can't think of words to say. So he keeps right on yelling.

"It's high time you start appreciating things around here!"

I lash back, my tongue finally unglued.

"Maybe it's high time *you* start appreciating that I'm a good son!" I yell, every bit as loud as my father has been. "The only problems we have are problems *you* cause!"

He slaps me again hard across the face. It stings, but it doesn't stop me for a second.

"Go ahead, slap me again!" I taunt. "It's the one answer you have when you know you're wrong! Like in sports, the best defense is a good offense. You've got no defense for what you did, so just whack me again."

"Don't you *dare* sass me like that!" he says, and slaps me. "You're grounded for a month! No phone for a month! I don't care what your mother says." He pauses for a split second, cocking his head as if considering something, then nods to himself. "And you're to end your silly relationship with this girl, whatever her name is. It's over as of right this instant. You're too young to be in a relationship in the first place, and she clearly is no good for you. It's over!"

I shake my head, and even as my mother exclaims my father's name, I say, "No!"

He slaps me yet again. "Don't you *dare* defy me!"

My mom grabs his arm to stop him from hitting me again as I speak, and that's probably a good thing, but I really don't care.

"You're a horrible father," I say, practically spitting out the words. "I hate you!"

CHAPTER 4

The next day, Anna is waiting for me as I approach my locker before the start of homeroom. I had run by her locker first, the two textbooks I had homework in last night pinned against my side, but when she wasn't there I figured she might be here. The long hallway—end-to-end it extends the length of three football fields—smells faintly of pine disinfectant. It's half-filled with students either getting things out of, or putting things into, their lockers, or walking to and from them. There's a constant buzz of conversation punctuated with the rattle of a locker being opened or the slam of it being shut.

Anna is as pretty as ever in a black, pleated skirt and a light blue sweater, her two textbooks and a notebook crooked in her left arm against her chest. I can smell just a hint of lavender on her. Really nice. But her face is just a little pale and her eyes are filled with concern.

"When you didn't call, I was up all night worrying," she says. She cranes her neck forward just a little and hesitantly asks, "Bad?" even though I'm sure she knows the answer.

"Take the worst you can imagine and multiply it by ten," I say. "Then multiply that by a hundred."

"Oh, no," Anna says, wincing, her free hand going to her mouth. "What happened?"

"He slapped me across the face a few times when I got hollering at him, but I don't—"

"You hollered at your father?"

"We both got hollering quite a bit."

"But your father?" Anna asks. "I don't think I've ever hollered at my father. In fact, I'm sure I haven't. He'd kill me."

I give her a long look, then think back to how things were before our family moved here, before my father and I went to war over that. Back then, I never hollered at him. Never talked back. Things were good. I thought he was a good dad and he thought I was a good son. Maybe even a great son. And he was at least a pretty good dad, even if he missed some of my games for his job and never seemed to have the energy anymore to do anything with me, like toss the ball around in the backyard like we did in the old days.

Still a pretty good dad, though.

But everything changed when he tore us away from Plainfield, Maine, where I was friends with everyone and the worst you could say about the place was that all the manure in the fields really got to stinking sometimes, and he brought us down here to Lynn, Lynn, City of Sin. He subjected me to all that has happened since just so he could take a promotion. He even hid the phrase, "Lynn, Lynn, City of Sin, never come out the way you went in" from my mom and me, so we wouldn't fight the move the way we would have if we'd known what we were getting into. He knew there would be problems, and he dragged me here anyway.

And things have never been the same.

Maybe I am a rotten son for talking back and even hollering. Maybe it's all my fault. I guess I really shouldn't holler at my parents, ever. Six months ago, I never would have.

But now I feel I have to stand up for myself all the time. It's always a battle. It used to be easy, but now it isn't easy at all. Sometimes it can be so hard.

We "made up" after the Thanksgiving Day football game, when he tearfully apologized for not getting to any of my games and thinking only of his job. And I thought maybe things might get back to how they used to be between us or at least close to it. He wouldn't be in the backyard throwing the football to me or anything. Those days are over, and not just because our backyard down here is so small you can't really play a decent game of toss.

But I thought things would be peaceful again between the two of us, and we'd like being around each other again. We'd both respect each other and love each other like I thought a father and son ought to do.

So much for that idea. The peace between my father and me lasted less than a week.

"It's almost like my father and I are the United States and Russia," I say to Anna. "We can agree to a peace treaty, but the nuclear warheads are still pointed at each other. It only takes a single disagreement and we're ready to launch the warheads and blow each other up."

Anna looks at me somberly. "That's awful."

"It wasn't always that way," I say. "But last night was the worst."

"Are you okay? You look…well, you look okay on the outside, but I can tell just from looking at you that you're not okay at all. Not on the inside."

She can read me like a book.

"I can't talk to you on the phone for the next month," I say.

Anna's eyes bug out behind her glasses. It might even be comical, something we could laugh over, if the situation weren't so awful. "You're kidding! A month?"

"My father—God, how I hate him!—first he said a year, he was so angry—"

"A year?"

"He was so angry, his face so red with rage. It was like he was so furious he couldn't even think straight. So at first he said a year, then after my mom said something, he knocked it down to a month, and then a week."

"A week? I thought you said it was a month?" Anna says.

"Then we got hollering at each other and it went back up to a month again. I'm 'grounded on the phone' for the next month."

"Well…" Anna says, and takes a deep breath. She looks so sad. I wish I could wipe that sadness away, wipe out everything that has happened. And wipe out the last thing I have to tell her, the thing that is making my heart hammer and my palms feel sweaty, the thing I'm taking forever to say because I don't want to have to say it.

"…we'll just have to make the best of it," Anna says. She purses her lips and raises her eyebrows. "Right?"

I swallow hard. "There's something else."

A surprised look comes over her face, then fear creeps into her eyes. "Something else?"

I go to swallow again and for a while it feels like I'm stuck mid-swallow. But eventually it completes, though a bitter taste fills the back of my throat.

"They want me to break up with you."

"No!" Anna looks at first astonished and then like she's going to cry. She closes her eyes and looks down at the ground.

"That's what I told them," I say quickly. "I told them I wouldn't do it."

It's as if Anna hasn't heard the words. She keeps her head bowed and shakes it.

"I'm not breaking up with you," I say. "I don't care what they do to me." A thought pops into my head from an old history class. "They can even go all Spanish Inquisition on me. I'm not breaking up with you."

She looks up at me, tears streaming down her face. "You are so sweet, Rabbit. *So* sweet. But you can't defy your parents."

I'm still holding the two textbooks I brought home last night, my locker still unopened, but with my free hand I brush away her tears. Her skin feels so soft even as I smear the wet tears across it.

"Yes I can, and I will," I say. "I'm not giving you up. I told them I wouldn't break up with you. I refused. Then I told my father that he was a terrible father and I hated him."

Anna gasps and her eyes grow wide. "*You said that?*"

"And I meant every word."

"But…but saying that had to make him furious. If he's angry, doesn't that make things worse? Won't he be even tougher on you now?"

"What more can he do? Kick me out of the house?"

She bows her head and begins to sob. "Oh, Rabbit, this is…it's awful!"

I wrap my free hand around the back of her neck, not knowing or caring if this is against school rules and some teacher might report me. I hold her trembling body against me.

*

We're almost late for homeroom. We break into a run when the bell rings while we're still twenty yards away, and we get inside the door just in time and rush to our seats before Miss Matthews takes attendance. The smell of freshly sharpened pencils fills the air.

Two girls near the door stare at Anna, perhaps seeing the remnants of the tears in her eyes or that they are just the slightest bit red and puffy from crying, and glare at me with sour, disapproving looks. I suspect they've concluded we've had our first fight, adding two plus two and getting fifteen, then assigning me the bad guy role. A week ago, after I was the hero in the Thanksgiving Day football game, they were giving me dreamy looks and smiling.

Now, I'm suddenly a jerk.

Or maybe that's all in my head. I'm so messed up right now I might be seeing things that aren't really there. Either way, I really don't care what anyone thinks except Anna.

It bothers me that she's taking this so hard. I'm not very good at handling any woman or girl who cries. My mom can get to me almost every time by crying, although there have been one or two exceptions. And even my dad's tears after the Thanksgiving Day game—the only time I can ever remember him crying—helped thaw our frozen relationship, at least for a week, although his words of regret and request for forgiveness certainly made the biggest difference.

But seeing Anna cry was even worse. It broke my heart, even though that sounds sappy and melodramatic, to see such a sweet, otherwise happy person so unhappy. I guess it's just another piece of evidence that shows how special she is to me.

As if there were any question.

I think I'm in love with her. Head over heels in love with her. In fact, I don't just think it. I *know* it. I'm not sure if I can actually say those words to her quite yet:

I love you.

We've just started going out, after all. In fact, we haven't even really been on a date. It's all just been spending time together here at school and talking on the phone. Can you be in love even before you've gone on your first official date?

And what if you say the words and the girl doesn't say them back?

That would be awful. I think Anna would say the words back to me, but what do I know? She's my first girlfriend ever. I don't know anything about girls. Maybe the words *I love you* would scare her away, make her think I'm getting too serious, too fast. Maybe it's best if I wait and let *her* say the words first. Is that just being a chicken? I don't know. I'm mixed up about almost everything. All I know is that she's wonderful and I can't stop thinking about her.

I *love* her.

And yet my father thinks he can get me to break up with her. Never in a million years. Never in a million, billion years. If he thought things got bad between us before, with our fights about him dragging our family down here, all of that will be like a day at the beach compared to the World War III that's going to happen if he really tries to make me break up with Anna.

Yeah, I'm ready to launch the nuclear warheads in the relationship with my father. In Social Studies, Mrs. O'Rourke talked about the theory of Mutually Assured Destruction, and how the deterrent that keeps our side and the Russians from launching our weapons is that if either side strikes, the other will retaliate and both countries will be obliterated under a nuclear cloud. To strike first is to assure mutual destruction. Mrs. O'Rourke noted that the acronym for Mutually Assured Destruction was quite appropriately, MAD.

Well, I'm mad. MAD, even.

Perhaps last night's demand that I break up with Anna was just a threatened nuclear strike on my father's side. Perhaps he'll realize his mistake and back off, although he usually takes a long time to see he's making a mistake and even longer to acknowledge it.

But if he really follows through and launches that warhead, I'm going to respond and launch all of mine.

We'll have Mutually Assured Destruction.

*

At tryouts, I have to put everything out of my mind except basketball. I've spent the day getting angrier and angrier at my father for everything. With every passing minute, I even grew more and more resentful that the first time I embraced Anna and wrapped my arms around her was not a sweet moment, but instead to console her after she heard of his attempt to separate us, her tears dampening the collar of my shirt.

I hate that.

I'm pretty much ready to also blame him for the ongoing Vietnam War, for the Civil Rights riots last summer, and for the lunch room running out of chocolate cake for dessert. If something is wrong, it has to be his fault.

But you can't play basketball with all that rotting mental garbage clogging up your brain. And this is the biggest day of tryouts. The coaches post the team at the end of tomorrow's session, but everyone says they pretty much decide tonight and just use tomorrow to double-check. I can't afford to play anything but my best. So I take the deepest breath before stepping out on the gymnasium floor with the other seventy or so guys trying out for the team, and push all that other junk—everything but basketball—out of my mind.

For the first time, we scrimmage full court, at least partially. We still don't use the full length of the court and play a single game end to end, but at least we abandon the four groups playing half-court beneath the four side baskets, an approach that takes away all fast break possibilities and minimizes all the quickest players' speed. Now, we're continuing to use the four white, fan-shaped baskets on the side instead of the two with glass backboards at the ends, but we're playing two simultaneous games of a shorter form of full court, playing cross-wise on the court instead of length to length. It shortens the court, but now a rebound can result in an outlet pass to one player and if that player is me, I can race to the other end on a fast break.

This is my game. It's my best chance to show what I can do. The best players, the ones who are competing for positions on the varsity and those who are locks to make JVs like Charlie and Jamaal, are playing in the other game, soaring high in the air and making flashy moves most of us on the lesser side can only dream of, but that's all right with me. There are still plenty of good players over on this side, and if I can't prove myself here in a full-court, fast break game, then I'm not making the team.

At the beginning, guys trying to show off for the coaches dribble themselves even if they're slow or bad with the ball instead of making the outlet pass to quicker guards. The opposing team gets back in time or even steals the ball away or causes the player to bounce the ball off his foot or make some other turnover. But if this happens and a faster player had been open up ahead waiting for a pass, one of the coaches blows his whistle and its shrill screech brings the game to a halt. He hollers at the offending player, telling him to get the ball up court or to pass the ball to someone who will.

Soon, the other four guys on my team—we're all wearing bright orange fishnet pinnies over our jerseys so both sides can tell each other apart—realize that if they pass me the ball and hustle up court, I'm likely to set them up for an open shot or a layup. If I have the layup myself, I take it, but more often than not, one or perhaps two defenders are back. I love setting up a teammate by driving to the basket, attracting the defensive attention, and then dishing a pass off to an open teammate. If the player moves well without the ball, I try to catch him midstride to the basket and he can lay it right in.

It doesn't always work perfectly. Sometimes I expect the player to do one thing and he does another. Or he misses the shot. Not everyone over here is going to make the team. In fact, almost all of those who are getting cut are playing here. And even those who will make it are still learning each other's game. But my team of mostly freshmen, including Jerry Epstein and the bulky, slow-footed, and occasionally dimwitted Randy Thorpe, does pretty well.

By the time the final whistle sounds and we all head to the locker room, I feel confident I've taken a huge stride toward making the team. I've been able to show what I can do in the partial full court games, taking advantage of my speed and ball-handling skills in the open court, and I actually win the free throw shooting competition this time, outlasting everyone, even Joe Thurman, who misses on his thirteenth attempt.

Soaked to the skin with sweat, my jersey clinging to my chest, I feel a warm sense of satisfaction. I'm tired and need a shower real bad, but it's a good tired.

It isn't until I'm getting dressed after my shower that my mind careens back to my father.

*

"This can't go on," my mom says.

We're riding home from tryouts, and she's finished the usual run of questions—How did school go? How were tryouts?—while I've wolfed down a chicken salad sandwich she made to "tide me over" until we have dinner with my father. Chicken salad on Wonder Bread is one of my favorites. My mom makes it with little bits of celery that crunch as I eat them and plenty of the juicier dark chicken meat. If it weren't for dinner, I could eat three of these sandwiches.

But even though I appreciate the ride home since there are no buses this late and it's a two-and-a-half mile walk, and I certainly appreciate the sandwich and was sure to say thank you when she handed it to me wrapped in crinkling wax paper, all the rest of my answers are only a single word or two.

My mother is a partner, willing or unwilling, with my new, but old, enemy: my father. I know she's caught in the middle, kind of, and typically tries to soften my father's punishments. This time she even kept him from continuing to slap me, but push has come to shove, as she likes to say, and she has sided mostly with my father. On a TV crime show like *Dragnet*, she'd be called an accomplice.

I love her, I really do, but she has sided with the enemy. So my answers are short and delivered in a sullen monotone.

"How did school go?"

"Good."

"How did tryouts go?"

"Good."

"You'll make the freshmen team at least?"

"Dunno."

Stymied, she falls silent for a minute or two, then reaches back to the far more pleasant football discussions we had over the past few months.

"Charlie Watkins is really good?"

"Yup."

"Rabbit!"

I know why she's exasperated, maybe even angry. Any other time, I would have said *something* other than my one-syllable, sullen "Yup." I would have said that Charlie isn't just good, he's exceptional. He blasts past defenders, scoring almost at will, and at the other end he can stop all but the best seniors. He'll be the team's star by the time he's a junior, no question about it. Maybe even next year.

And then I might have told her about Jamaal and all his twisting and spinning moves. Sometimes I think he's trying to copy Earl "The Pearl" Monroe, the flashy NBA rookie who plays for the Baltimore Bullets and is already scoring more than twenty points a game. Last Sunday on TV, I saw Monroe do this crazy reverse spin dribble where he was dribbling with his right hand, and without slowing down hardly at all or palming the ball, he spun clockwise 360 degrees, cupping the ball still with his right hand enough to continue the dribble. He left his defender guarding nothing but air, looking foolish.

Jamaal can't do that move. I don't think anyone but Earl the Pearl can do it—that's why they call the move "The Pearl"—but Jamaal is like a high school version of that NBA star. A whirling dervish, the TV announcer called Monroe, and that's Jamaal. A whirling dervish. I'll bet before he graduates, Jamaal will be doing "The Pearl" all the time. He'll figure out how Monroe does it, then practice it for as many hundred hours as it takes.

I could say all of that, but I don't. Not to the enemy's accomplice.

"What?" I ask, as if I don't know.

"This can't go on."

I stare out the window.

"Did you hear me?" my mom says.

"Yup," I say.

"I don't know what to do," she says, and I can tell from her unsteady voice that she's about to cry.

I don't have to look. I know.

So I give her more than a one-word answer, because I can't stand to see her cry. But it's not what she wants to hear.

"I'm not breaking up with Anna," I say. "Dad can beat me into a pulp if he wants to, but I'm not breaking up with her."

"Rabbit—"

"And a one-month phone ban is totally unfair," I say, my anger and resentment tossing aside my sullen one-word answers. Now that I've gotten going, I don't want to shut up. I'm like a stuck faucet that, once it's opened, everything gushes out and it can't be closed. "I never thought you two would actually believe I was part of a crime. I mean, really! And not because I can't even drive. What really hurts is…*where was your faith in me?*"

Now I'm the one with the shaking voice. I'm the one fighting back the tears. I'm not a little baby, but the thought of my parents' betrayal—and that's what it is, for both of them to have thought I'd be arranging for some getaway car to avoid the police, *a getaway car!*—takes hold of my heart and tears it in two.

And for them to follow that betrayal with their the-best-defense-is-a-good-offense attack on my relationship with Anna crushes me.

"Rabbit—"

"If anyone should get a one-month punishment, it's *you two*! You should be ashamed of yourselves!"

"Enough of that!" she yells. "Enough! Enough! Enough! I won't have you talk back to me like that. I won't take another minute of your insolence. Not one! Just you wait until your father gets home." Her fingers grip the steering wheel so hard they turn white. "This is *exactly* why he slaps you. I hate it when he does it, and I've tried to get him to stop, but you just won't quit. You feel you can say anything and get away with it. What are we supposed to do with you?"

CHAPTER 5

As usual, I'm sitting on the side of the dining room table that faces the kitchen, my father on one end to my left still wearing the dark suit and tie he wore to work and my mother at the other in a dark blue dress. I'm still in my school clothes, dark dress pants and a button-down blue shirt. We're eating together as a family, as my mother insists. Tonight, it's green peppers stuffed with hamburger and rice in a tomato sauce, all on top of mashed potatoes, usually another one of my favorites.

But we sure don't feel like much of a family. I stare down at my plate, cut a piece of the pepper, and shovel it into my mouth, barely noticing the sharp, tomato smell, the juiciness of the meat, and a flavor I would have savored some other time.

Tonight, it might as well be a hard, stale piece of bread.

Other than the clinking of the silverware on our plates, the wall clock behind me makes the only noise.

Tick…tick…tick….

Tick…tick…tick….

Tick…tick…tick….

None of us looks at each other. No one says anything. There will be plenty said after the meal. My mother assured me of that following my outburst in the car.

"Just you wait until your father gets home," she said back then, her fingers gripping the steering wheel so hard they turned white.

But she also insisted that we first eat dinner as a family, as if it's some final meal before an execution.

Presumably mine.

That's okay with me. If the tension hanging in the air is supposed to make me nervous, terrified of my certain punishment, it isn't working.

I don't care.

What more can they do to me?

*

We've gathered in the front room for my execution. I can hardly say I enjoyed my last meal, but I do have a full belly. The tomato, hamburger, and onion smells from dinner linger in the air. My parents sit together on the sofa, the same one where they concluded last night that I was arranging for a getaway car, but not a red Corvette so as to avoid detection by the Lynn police.

Even though I've never even sat in the driver's seat of a car. Even though I'm two years away from a license. Even though I've *never* been in trouble before.

Yeah, the most believable story ever.

I'm sitting in the tan lounge chair—my electric chair with its arms ready for strapping me in. Normally, it's almost in a straight line with the sofa, only angled a little, but it's been set at a right angle so I can face my parents.

My father pushes his glasses to the bridge of his nose, takes a deep breath, and shakes his head. "I don't know what's happened to you. You used to be such a good kid. We're so disappointed in you."

He looks at me, expecting an answer. So I purse my lips and give him one.

"I feel the same way," I say.

My father blinks in surprise, and my mother's eyebrows shoot up.

"Good!" he says. "We're on the same page. You're disappointed in your behavior?"

"No, I'm disappointed in *yours.*"

My parents' jaws drop. Their eyes widen in shock. My father's narrow in red-hot rage.

Maybe I shouldn't have said it. A part of me *knows* I shouldn't have said it, even if it's true. This isn't helping my cause. But I couldn't hold back the words, and as usual, I keep them coming.

"I'm disappointed," I continue, "that for no reason at all you're trying to force me to break up with Anna, a very sweet, nice girl. She had nothing to do with the whole 'getaway car' story. I made the whole thing up. In fact, she tried to talk me out of it until I told her it would be okay, that you'd never, ever believe such a crazy story. It would be *impossible* for you to believe such a thing about me.

"I'm *so* disappointed about that," I continue, my righteous anger building. "How could you have believed such an outrageous story? Why didn't you immediately recognize it for what it was? If the story had instead been about me being a serial killer, would you have believed that, too? If it had been about me being a cannibal, would you have believed that and gone looking for the bones of my victims buried in the backyard?

"What would it have taken for your reaction to have been, 'No, that's not Rabbit, he's a good kid,' instead of immediately assuming I'm guilty?"

"We were just so shocked," my mother says. "We couldn't believe our ears."

"You *shouldn't* have believed your ears!" I say. "That's the point!"

"Watch your mouth!" my father snaps, and looks poised to jump over the coffee table and slap my face. Put me in my place. "Do *not* talk back to your mother!"

I spread my hands wide, palms up, in frustration. "If I'm not going to be allowed to defend myself, then what are we doing here? Just strap my arms to the electric chair here"—I slap my forearms down onto the lounge chair's arms for emphasis—"and pull the switch."

"Enough of that!" my father says. "This is not a democracy. We are your parents and what we say goes. You do not get to run your mouth off and say whatever you want to us. We provide for you and care for you. It's our job to make sure you grow up right and stay out of trouble even if you aren't always happy with our decisions. You *will* abide by what we say, and you *will* respect us."

I'm about to snap back with a reply that respect must be earned, not demanded, and how can I respect what he's done these last few days? But out of nowhere, Anna's words from this morning, when I told her I'd said to my father that I hated him and thought he was a terrible father, come back to me.

Saying that had to make him furious. If he's angry, doesn't that make things worse? Won't he be even tougher on you now?

I blink, stunned every bit as much as if I've been doused with a bucket of ice water. I realize, perhaps too late, that my "talking back"—my insolence, as my mother put it this afternoon—is making it so my parents can't even see my point.

Can't even see that *I'm right.*

All they hear is the anger and disrespect in my words. None of the logic behind it. Yes, I have to defend myself, but if I say every angry thought that comes into my mind—even when I'm right—and more importantly, express it in words they find threatening, then all they hear is the threat. And it makes things worse.

Of course, I'm a dope for not knowing this all along and not realizing it until, as my mother would say, the horse is out of the barn. But maybe it's not too late.

I take a deep breath and try to focus my mind on saying what I need to say in a way that works for my parents and isn't just more raw meat for the snarling lion of my anger.

"I apologize for mouthing off," I say. "I'm sorry. I've said things I shouldn't have said." I look into my mother's eyes. "Mom, I love you, and I'm sorry." I'm about to add the "respect" word, because it does apply to her, except for this episode, but I can't use that word with my father. And if I say it to my mother and not to him, the glaring omission will be all that gets noticed. So I just turn to my father, but not before seeing my mom's eyes pool with tears. "Dad, I love you, and I'm sorry.

"I hope you both will accept my apology and we can discuss this calmly and without hostility." My anger and frustration still boil beneath the surface, but I feel I've clamped a lid on it. "I want to get along with both of you. Like we used to." My voice even wavers on this last note. Anger and frustration aren't the only emotions I'm feeling.

My father's face softens a bit, though he's a long, long way—a million miles away—from my mother, who looks like she wants to spring off the sofa and come hug me.

"But just like it hurt you when I mouthed off, it hurt me when you jumped to the conclusion that I—"

"It's not the same!" my father says, hardness back into his face. "You seem to think that a parent and a son are equal. They're not. This is not a democracy. End of story."

"I apologized for my mouth. Can you apologize for not believing in me?"

My mother nods, and says, "Yes!" as she wipes away the tears, but my father's jaw juts out and, behind his glasses, his eyes narrow.

"It's not for a son to demand apologies from his parents," he says. "I apologized once, last week, in a moment of weakness."

"A moment of *weakness*?" I say, my head starting to explode. "So you meant none of it?"

"Stop it! No more talking back!" my father says. "That was a poor choice of words. Don't nitpick what I say. That isn't what I meant." But even as he continues, I wonder, my fury only barely contained, if that wasn't *exactly* what he meant. "That apology was sincere, and I stand by it. But it seems that that one apology has given you the expectation that we're going to apologize for any little offense, even one that *you*"—he points at me—"instigated with an alarming story intended to embarrass us. You should be ashamed of that! Ashamed of yourself! So no, I won't apologize for reacting to something that *you* started."

I can see annoyance on my mom's face. I can guess he's every bit as stubborn in refusing to apologize to her in their arguments.

I start to shake my head in frustration, then realize that will only incite my father's anger even more. Even though I'm close to not caring—let the jerk get as angry as he wants—I remember again Anna's words. *If he's angry, doesn't that make things worse?* So I take one last stab at a peaceful discussion, and getting my parents to see what is most important to me. I look at my mother since it's easiest to stay calm and focused that way.

"Okay, but what about me talking to Anna on the phone?" I say. "Until I give you a reason to distrust me, why can't you give me some privacy?"

"Talking to her on the phone?" my father asks, his voice rising at the end in disbelief. "I told you to break up with her, and that's exactly what I expect you to do. What *we* expect." He takes hold of my mother's hand, as if trying to show solidarity between the two of them, but she looks away, clearly uncomfortable. She doesn't agree with him at all, I'm sure, but she can't say so. She can't *undermine his authority*, as he would put it. So she says nothing while he continues on, getting angrier and louder with every word.

"When we tell you to do something, you *do* it! We are your parents and what we say goes. No questions asked. It's high time you stop acting like a pampered little *brat* who thinks he can make his own rules. You will *stop* challenging our authority, and you *will* break up with this girl. Don't you *dare* ignore me, young man!"

I sit there and stare at him. I had thought he'd surely come to his senses and drop that demand, especially after I made clear that Anna had nothing to do with my disastrous getaway car story. But he hasn't budged an inch. He hasn't listened to a word I've said. Oh, he's heard it all, but as my mother would say, it's gone in one ear and out the other.

Almost anything I say now is going to make things worse. Except to say that I'll break up with Anna. And I will never, ever agree to that.

Ever.

I so much want to lash out at him, let him hear exactly how I feel. Punish him with my words. But I think back yet again to Anna's words, and try desperately to hold onto my composure, even as it wants to slip away and give in to my anger.

I take a deep breath and try to calm my emotions. Try to collect my thoughts. Think of how I can say what needs to be said in the best way possible. If there even is a best way.

"I've always tried to be a good kid," I say, looking into my mother's troubled brown eyes. "And I promise to try a lot harder to stop mouthing off. I'm sorry about that, and I will get better." I take a deep breath. "But if the two of you insist on trying to break up Anna and me, what you're going to break is the relationship between *us*." I put my hand to my chest and then gesture in their direction. "Between you two and me. And you're going to break things between us that can't be put back together." A childish comparison pops into my mind, so childish I hesitate to use it, but it fits. "Like Humpty Dumpty. We'll never put it all back together again."

"Don't you threaten us!" my father yells.

I close my eyes and try to stay calm even though I want to scream back at my father. Not everything is a threat. Not everything is a challenge to your authority. I am not a spoiled brat. I'm just trying to keep you from launching this nuclear warhead because if you do, I will launch every last one of mine, and we will most certainly have Mutually Assured Destruction.

MAD.

I *won't* break up with Anna. And if somehow you drive us apart, I will never, ever forgive you.

Ever.

In thirty or forty years, I will come to the cemetery where you are buried and I will still, after thirty or forty years, spit on your grave.

It's a horrible thought and maybe thinking it means I'm every bit as much of a horrible son as you seem to believe I am. But if you insist on winning this battle, we will have Mutually Assured Destruction.

Count on it.

So I make one final attempt. I know his anger and his stubbornness won't allow him to back down. Not now. Right now, he's so angry he can't even see straight.

But perhaps my mom, who I am sure is on my side about breaking up with Anna even if I've offended her with my big mouth, will help him see how disastrous a war over this will be. She can get him to calm down. Talk some sense into him. It probably won't work—he's got an even thicker skull than mine—but it might.

I have to at least give her a chance.

"I'd like to propose a twenty-four-hour cooling-off period," I say. My father's face starts to cloud over so I look to my mom. I suppose most of my message is to her anyway since my father really isn't listening, and she's going to have to be the one to get him to change his mind. "We can all think about everything involved here, and you two can talk about it between yourselves."

Since it'll be hard for my father to back off from his demand—he'll view that as tantamount to admitting he was wrong to make it in the first place—I try to eliminate that demand and force him to make it a second time, if he really thinks it's the right thing to do, if it's really appropriate and fair.

And he can't *possibly* think that, can he?

"Can we come back tomorrow night with a clean slate, as if there have been no angry words between us, and no punishments established or demands made?" I ask. "We start over, remembering how much we love each other. Start over with a clean slate. Then you'll tell me what you've decided."

My father appears ready to shoot that down, but my mom jumps in first.

"That sounds like a great idea," she says, shooting to her feet even as my father looks at her with annoyance. "Tomorrow night, then."

*

She comes up to my bedroom an hour or so later. She closes the door behind her and leans on it. I'm sitting at my desk, the bed behind me and dresser off to my right. My gray desk lamp with its adjustable, crane-like arm spills light on math homework that on any other night would have been done long ago. I've been hunched over it, reading the same words of the problem over and over.

It's been as if my IQ has suddenly dropped to about two.

I look up at my mom, who smiles weakly.

"Your father loves you," she says. "He really does. You know that, right?"

I feel like saying, "He's got a strange way of showing it," and maybe even add in a sound effect of him slapping my face. *Whack!* There's even a part of my brain ready to mock him. *I'm the boss! Don't challenge my authority!* And of course his favorite phrase, "This is not a democracy!" to which I'm ready to add, "It's Russia and I'm Joseph Stalin! Prepare to die, peasant!"

But I'm supposed to be keeping my mouth shut. No more mouthing off. I'm supposed to stop being, as my supposedly loving father puts it, a spoiled brat.

So I try to put on my most angelic face and smile, even if it is a weak, plastic one.

"I know," I say, but honesty—or perhaps it's the spoiled brat cooped up inside—insists that I add, "I guess."

"As a parent, he has to guide you on your way to becoming an adult," she says softly. "That involves establishing rules and meting out discipline when rules are broken. It isn't easy. He isn't perfect."

Really? I feel like saying. *Geez, I think he's the most perfect parent ever. Each time he slaps me, that's what I think. Or when he tries to make me break up with Anna. Couldn't be better!*

But I hold my spoiled brat tongue.

"He's also under an extraordinary amount of pressure at work," she says. "If it weren't for us, he'd probably stay there until midnight every night."

I wish he would, I think. *You and I could work out any problem.*

But I just nod.

"He asked me to call Anna's mother and see what she thinks."

My back stiffens, and a wave of fear washes over me. It's bad enough that my father is actually trying to break up Anna and me, but it makes me sick and embarrassed to think her mother is going to hear about it, and find out what a horrible father I have, and think that I might be anything like him—I'm his son, after all!—and think less of me because of all of this.

I'll be a ridiculous kid with ridiculous parents. I've never met Anna's mother, so this will be her first impression of me.

It'll be so humiliating.

Anna's mother will ask Anna about it, and maybe then Anna might think…what will she think? That I'm pathetic? Not worth the trouble? Just a dumb hick with dumb hick parents who won't even let their kid— their *really good* kid!—talk on the phone with his girlfriend.

"Your father thinks you're too young to have a girlfriend," my mother says. "He thinks you're rushing things. And I think he may be right."

Without thinking, I give her a look that stops her dead in her tracks. I can't believe it! She's on his side! This isn't just a matter of her not wanting to contradict him, to *undermine his authority*. She thinks he's right!

My mother is the enemy.

Maybe not the worst of the two. That role is clearly my father's, but she's just admitted that she isn't even partly on my side. My heart sinks, and a bitter taste fills the back of my mouth.

She's the enemy.

"You!" I shake my head in disbelief. "I always thought you were—"

"You're awfully young," she says defensively. "You're only fourteen. Neither of us had a boyfriend or a girlfriend anything close to that young."

"That was"—I stop myself before saying that it was during the Dark Ages, which would be another case of me mouthing off, of me being *a spoiled brat*, so I soften my words as much as I can—"that was your generation. It's different now. Plenty of kids my age have boyfriends and girlfriends."

"Just because other kids do it, doesn't make it right," she says, and I know her next words before she even begins the sentence. Predictably, she adds, "If all your friends jump off a cliff, does that make it right for you to do it?"

"There's nothing wrong with us going out," I say. "We haven't even gone on our first date. We just spend time together at school, and then talk on the phone at night." Then I correct myself. "We *used to* talk on the phone at night."

"Your father doesn't understand that, either," my mother says. "He figures if you've spent all day with each other, why do you need to talk on the phone at night?"

"Because we want to!" I say, mystified at the dumb question. "We like talking to each other. I tell her about basketball tryouts and she tells me about her band practice. Or whatever. We talk about lots of stuff. It's what a boyfriend and girlfriend do." And when my mother shows no reaction, gives no *Of course, you're right* response, I ask, "Didn't you and Dad talk on the phone when you were going out?"

She flushes. "Not so much, actually. Your father wasn't..."

I wait for her to finish. Wasn't the talkative type? Wasn't the romantic type? Wasn't *a normal human being*?

But she stares down at the floor and doesn't say anything.

"Mom, I don't want to lose you."

She looks at me sharply. "What's that supposed to mean?"

"This is important," I say. "Please don't be like Dad and start talking about me challenging your authority or making threats or anything like that. I'm trying to be honest here. I'm not trying to be"—I practically spit out the next words—"a spoiled brat.

"But if you and Dad try to make me break up with Anna, we'll never be the same again. Dad and I have had problems sometimes, but I think that mostly you and I are okay. We love each other. We respect each other. We can talk to each other.

"But if you make me break up with Anna, all that goes away." My mother's face turns ashen, but I keep going. "It really will be like I said. Humpty Dumpty. We won't ever be able to put it back together again. I'll always resent what you did. I'll never again respect you the way I do now."

My mother purses her lips. Her eyes pool with tears. "You two." And I know she's talking of my father and me. She shakes her head. "I don't know what I'm going to do."

I look at her and with all the love in my heart, I say words that I hope help her decide.

"Do the right thing."

CHAPTER 6

I meet Anna in front of my locker, where she's wearing a cat-that-ate-the-canary grin. She's also wearing a light orange sweater that might not look that great on anyone else—I've never thought of orange as a good color for any kind of clothes, but it looks great on her—along with a navy blue skirt.

Shows how much I know about clothes.

And unless it's all in my head, she's also wearing a different, more citrusy perfume, perhaps coordinating it with the orange sweater. Do girls really do that, try to match a perfume with a sweater? The more time I spend with Anna, the more I realize that I don't know anything about girls.

I am dumb as rocks.

But compared to that grin of hers, I barely notice her clothes and perfume at all. I immediately wonder if it's because my mother called hers and it went well. Really well, based on that grin. I have no idea myself because neither of my parents said anything this morning, apparently deciding to wait until tonight to discuss it.

The longest, most agonizing waiting ever for the other shoe to drop.

"Hey," I say, not wanting to bring up the embarrassing and potentially disastrous possibility of my mother calling hers unless it actually happened. Realizing I've uttered a greeting no better than what the dumbest of dumb jocks would come up with, I hastily add, "You look really nice."

"Thank you," Anna says, beaming. "You do, too."

I'm wearing just an average blue, button-down shirt and dark pants, the kind of thing I wear every day to school. It's so undeserving of a compliment that I halfway wonder if Anna is making fun of me, but that is so unlike her I respond the only way I can think of.

"Thanks," I say, since I can hardly say something like, "I don't look special at all, certainly not compared to you."

But then I realize that I *can* say that. In fact, I *should* say that since she really does look, and smell, that nice, and it is—I think—the kind of nice thing a guy should say to his girlfriend, at least once in a while. I've never heard my father say anything like that to my mother, so that gives me another reason to say it. So I do.

"I don't look special at all, certainly not compared to you."

She blinks, straightens up a bit, and beams even more brightly at me.

"Thank you, Rabbit," she says. "You are so sweet."

I figure we could discuss who is sweeter, but right now I want to know, need to know, if our mothers have talked. So I just spill the beans.

"Did your mother get a call from mine?" I ask.

Anna's big grin vanishes. "No. Not that I know of." She cocks her head. "Why? Was she supposed to?"

I tell her, giving her the *Reader's Digest* condensed version, like that magazine does every month when it includes shortened versions of novels. It would take all of homeroom, our first period classes, and maybe more to give her the whole blow-by-blow account of last night. So after first thanking her for her words that helped me keep my cool, I get right to the proposed discussion between her mother and mine.

"Oh, Rabbit," she says. "I'm getting you in so much trouble." She looks down and shakes her head. "They really want us to break up?"

I feel a stab in the pit of my stomach. "Is that what your mother will suggest?"

"No!" Anna shakes her head hard enough to send her shoulder-length blonde hair tossing back and forth. "At least I don't think so. My mother's cool. But…you know how parents can get when they start talking to each other. If your mom were real persuasive, she could push my mom in a direction she might not naturally go. I just don't know. I never even thought about it."

"My mom isn't pushy, if that's the only worry," I say, feeling a little bit better. "She just doesn't like to disagree with my father. None of this would be happening except for my father."

"Maybe they'll talk today," Anna says. A look comes into her eyes. "I'll call her. Right now. I'll make sure she says the right thing."

And she turns to dash off to the pay phone down the hall.

"Meet me at homeroom," she says over her shoulder, leaving me still wondering what that sly grin on her face had been about before things got serious.

*

She gets to homeroom late, but hands Miss Matthews a pass from the principal's office. Walking toward her seat, she glances my way, smiles, and nods. Then she gives me a wink.

I don't need a translation to figure out that's good news.

I hold my breath until the bell rings, then slide up next to Anna and begin walking with her toward her first-period class. We're taking different sections of English and mine is in the opposite direction, but I've got to hear what she has to say even if it makes it so I'll have to sprint back in the other direction for my class, dodging other students in the crowded and noisy hallway as if I'm running back a kickoff, cutting in and out of open gaps toward the end zone.

"What did she say?" I ask.

"You've got to go to your class, Rabbit! I don't want you to be late because of me. It's bad enough your parents—"

"Just tell me what she said," I say. "I don't mean to interrupt—sorry!— but just tell me. Or I really will be late."

"Your mom hasn't called yet," Anna says, "but if she does, it'll all work out okay. Trust me."

"You're sure?"

"Yes, now get going before you're late!"

"Just one more question," I say, and Anna rolls her eyes in exasperation, sure I'm going to get into trouble. "Why did you have that big grin on your face this morning?"

"I have a surprise for you," she says, back to beaming again. "Just a little one, but I think you'll like it. At least, I hope you do. I'll give it to you next period. Before History starts."

I stand there and smile with probably the dopiest look on my face ever. *A surprise! Even a little one!* That familiar glow of happiness fills my chest as it so often does when I'm around Anna.

A surprise. Wow.

"Now get going!" Anna says. "If you're late, I'll…I'll throw it away."

With my smile still a mile wide and my heart pounding, I say, "Bye!" then spin and race for my class, my two textbooks tucked under my arm like a football.

*

I wait outside history class for Anna, the strong smell of what must be an egg salad sandwich radiating out from a nearby locker. I move to the other side of the classroom door, which helps a bit. I shift my weight from one foot to another as the flow of other students goes past me. I've come from a much closer classroom than Anna's, so I expected to easily beat her here, but while I wait the seconds tick by slowly…

…slowly…

…slowly.

A surprise.

I can't wait to find out what it is.

Come on, Anna! Come on!

I'm like a little kid before Christmas. *What could it be?* And then: *Why didn't I think of a surprise for her?*

It feels like forever before I finally see her coming from more than a classroom away on the left side of the corridor. I race toward her, trying to flatten myself up against the lockers as I go against the flow of the foot traffic, bumping into people who aren't watching where they're going.

"Sorry…" I say to the first one I bump into, and then "Sorry…" and "Sorry…" to the others until I'm finally next to Anna.

"So?" I ask expectantly, and for a moment I think that instead of being like a kid at Christmas I'm really like a panting puppy dog with its tail wagging, waiting for its owner to give it a bone or throw a stick for it to run after.

"Go fetch, Rabbit!" Anna would say, and then after I brought the stick back to her, she'd scratch behind my ears and give me a treat.

Good grief, I hope that's not how pathetic I look. I should calm down and not look so puppy dog anxious, but I still can't help myself. *A surprise from Anna!* I had trouble concentrating all through English and Miss Minter's discussion of gerunds and participial phrases because all I could think of was Anna and her surprise.

What could it be? If it cost money and now I need to get something for her, I'll never get a penny from my parents, not the way things are right now.

But Anna just smiles and cocks her head. "Were you late?"

"Nope!" I say, trying to calm my racing heart and seem less like the panting puppy dog. I smile. "They don't call me Rabbit for nothing."

She reaches into her navy blue pocketbook—I belatedly notice that it matches her skirt—and she produces a four-by-eight-inch white enve-lope. "I wrote you a letter last night." The cat-that-ate-the-canary grin is back. "I figured since we couldn't talk on the phone, I'd write you a letter. Just a short one, kind of like a five-minute phone conversation."

She holds it out to me shyly, looking closely for my reaction.

"Wow!" I say, so thunderstruck that I can't think of anything else to say. So I say it again. "Wow!"

I take it, and without even getting it close to my nose I detect on the envelope the faint fragrance of lilacs. Anna's usual perfume. What must be the biggest, dopiest grin creeps across my face.

"What a great idea!" I say. "How did you think of it?"

"I was just thinking of you last night, and..." she smiles and shrugs "… and it popped into my head."

A guilty feeling comes over me. "But I don't have anything for you."

"That's okay."

"I'll write you tonight, I promise."

"Deal," she says with that pretty smile that melts my heart at least a little every time.

"Can I open it now?" I ask, and without thinking, I eagerly begin to tear it open before she grabs my hand.

"No!" Anna says. For a brief moment, I'm afraid she's going to take the letter away. Instead, she says, "You can't read it now. It's for tonight when we'd be talking on the phone. Read it then."

The bell rings and we file into the classroom, Anna first and then me, looking at the back of her pretty, oh-so-smart head.

And I wonder what she ever sees in me.

*

For a while, all I can think about is Anna's letter inside that white envelope that now has a half-inch tear in the one corner where I'd started to rip it open. It's tucked inside the front cover of my history book, but I can still smell Anna's lilac perfume on it—unless that's all in my head—and based on where my attention is focused, I might as well be waving it in front of my face.

A letter! One that Anna has written to me. What does it say?

It doesn't help that she's sitting at the desk just to my left, only five feet or so away, both of us three rows back from the front. Her being so close makes it even harder to stop thinking about the letter.

What does it say? What does it say? What does it say?

Mrs. McPherson, our stuffy, white-haired history teacher, drones on up by the blackboard about something that happened hundreds of years ago, but I can think of only one thing.

What does it say? What does it say? What does it say?

I usually like History, but I'm not learning a thing today, and it's all my fault. *Actually, it's Anna's fault*, I think, amusing myself. *If she weren't so sweet, I'd be able to concentrate a lot better. Yeah, it's all* her *fault.*

Not exactly knee-slapper funny, but it puts a small smile on my face.

Anna glances over, sees me smiling, and gives me a quizzical look. But I just shake my head, feeling my face grow warm.

Suddenly, it dawns on me that I need to write a letter, too. Not tonight, like I promised, but today before we both leave school. It won't be fair for me to have one to read tonight while Anna has none. And it's such a great idea. I have to do my half.

I'm almost prepared to tear a sheet of paper out of my notebook and write it right there in history class, but I remember one time a year ago back up in Maine, Kristie Mapes got caught passing a note to her friend and the teacher took it and read it out loud to everyone. It was about a boy she liked, a friend of mine named Jimmy Chaisson, and Kristie got so embarrassed, burying her face in her hands, it looked as though she wanted to have the ground open up and swallow her. I don't want to get caught and have that happen to me.

So I wait until after lunch when I have a study hall period in the cafeteria. The air still smells of that day's special, chicken fricassee over mashed potatoes, which was pretty good as cafeteria food goes, although I couldn't bear to eat the tasteless string beans. Wooden tables about ten feet long and four feet wide are set end to end, forming a dozen long, extended rows where groups of guys and girls, almost never mixed, sit. Some study or read a book, others play a card game called kitty whist. If I don't have homework, I usually read, mostly books and magazines about sports but sometimes ones about the Civil Rights movement, a subject I've found compelling ever since reading *Black Like Me* last summer, a time when I'd never even met a single black person.

But I'm not going to read or do homework today. I take an empty seat halfway down a row, close to my friends Jeff Goodwin and Paul DiSimone. They're a study in contrasts. Jeff has red hair, freckles, and is always firing off a wise crack while Paul has a thick mop of black hair and rarely gets a word in edgewise, at least not as long as Jeff is around. They're sitting on opposite sides of the table playing what they call table football. One of them folded a piece of paper over and over into a tight triangle, about as thick as ten sheets of paper and its sides about two inches long. Now they're flicking it with a snap of a finger, trying to get it just right so it goes to the other side of the table and hangs off the edge without falling off. That's a touchdown, which Jeff just scored. So now he goes for the extra point. Paul forms a goalpost with his fingers and Jeff stands the triangle upright and tries to flick it through the uprights.

Except Jeff flicks it hard and high and the triangle hits Paul square in the nose. Jeff bursts into laughter.

"Hey! You did that on purpose!" Paul says, touching his fingertip to his nose.

"Damned straight!" Jeff cries with glee. "Bull's-eye right in the schnoz! Now go ahead and pick it!"

With only a single empty seat separating me from the two of them, I try to think of what to write. I'm trying to make it look like I'm doing homework, my notebook opened to a blank sheet of paper, since I'm not about to admit to these two what I'm really doing. Which, of course, catches their immediate attention.

"Whatcha doing, Samson?" Jeff says, referring to my basketball-team crew cut, as he's done the last day or two, having switched from "Hero," which was my nickname the first few days after the Thanksgiving Day football game. In the three months I've known him, he's also called me, at times, Frenchie, Rabid instead of Rabbit, and whatever else strikes him as being funny.

"What's it look like I'm doing?" I say.

"Looks like you ain't doing nothing but stare at a blank piece of paper," he says.

I don't like to lie, but I don't have much choice. "It's an English assignment," I say because even though Jeff and Paul are in most of my classes, they aren't in Accelerated English. And then I add a layer on top of the lie, trying to shut him up.

"If I make the basketball team, I may be pretty busy so I want to get a jump on this one." And since Jeff really only understands sarcasm—it's like his primary language and English is a distant second—I add a zinger. "So if the two of you can get back to your intellectual game of table football and leave me alone, I might get some of it done."

"Touché…" Jeff says, and I know what's coming next because it's almost his corny trademark. "Turtle," he says, referring to the popular Saturday morning cartoon show, *Touché Turtle*.

I look back down at the blank sheet of paper and wonder what to write. If only I knew what Anna wrote, then I'd have an idea of what to do myself. I wouldn't copy it, of course, but it would be like a map that showed me where to go. It would point me to the path to take. Instead, all I see are tangled thickets and thorny bushes. Nowhere to go.

No clue what to write.

Is this what writers call writers' block? If so, I've got it bad. I stare and stare at the paper, afraid that whatever I come up with, it'll be stupid and I'll embarrass myself to Anna.

Finally, for some reason I don't begin to understand, I decide to write a poem. Not Shakespeare or a sonnet or anything fancy like that, which I don't know anything about. Just a silly, sing-song poem, the kind of thing I think they call a limerick. Why I decide this when I can't even come up with any two regular words to put together, I'll never know. But I just start.

There once was a girl named Anna.

Okay, what next? What rhymes with Anna?

Banana…Ghana…Nana…

Good grief, that's awful. A fruit, a country, and a relative. What am I supposed to do with those?

There once was a girl named Anna.
Whose nose looked like a banana.

It's so awful it's almost funny. I shake my head and try harder. What else rhymes with Anna?

Hannah…Bandana…Vanna.

That's even worse. Two of those three are just other girls' names. I'm pathetic. Why did I ever try to write a poem, even a dopey one, a limerick, if that's what it's called?

I am such a moron.

I think a little harder for other words that rhyme with Anna, but realize I've hit a total dead end when my brain takes the exaggerated Bostonian accent some kids down here have—an accent I hardly ever notice now— and translates piano to "pianah."

There once was a girl named Anna.
Who learned to play the "pianah."

Oh my god, I am such an idiot. *Pianah!* That's it. Forget the rhymes.

The limerick idea was a really dumb one. Study hall is almost half over and I've got nothing to give Anna. Time to just write regular stuff.

But what?

If only I could peek at what Anna wrote. Just get some idea of what to say.

But I can't. I've promised. Not until tonight. Not until we'd normally be talking on the phone.

"Look at him!" says a voice that seems to be coming from far, far away.

I jerk my head up and see Jeff laughing at me, and Paul following suit.

"What?" I ask, annoyed.

"You should see yourself in the mirror," Jeff says. "One second you've got this dreamy-eyed look on your face, and then the next it looks like you're ready to jump off a cliff. What kind of English homework makes you look like all goofy that?"

Jeff stands up quickly, and from two seats away cranes his neck to try to peek at my notebook.

I slam the notebook shut.

"What's wrong with you?" I say. Jeff recoils, but I'm not done yet. "Can't you give a guy any privacy? You're as bad as my parents!"

I stand up as if I'm about to leave the table and go to another one, which I've half a mind to do. But Jeff throws up his hands in defense.

"Sorry, man," he says. "I was just messing around with you. Just having fun."

I'm about to tell him to have his fun at someone else's expense and then leave the table, but I don't. He has a wounded look on his face, a freckled face that's usually so alive with laughter, and he has such a sorrowful look in his eyes.

So I let him mostly off the hook.

"Forget it," I say. "Just…just don't be snooping on me."

I sit down and figure this will probably make him want to snoop on me even more and figure out what I'm trying to hide. But at least he keeps to himself for the rest of the study period, playing a much more subdued version of table football with Paul, while I actually come up with a few words for my note.

Finally.

Not very good words. The letter is probably really stupid and embarrassing. I should probably throw it out, but I won't. It's all I could come up with. I just thought about Anna, and with Jeff and Paul keeping their distance, let the thoughts spill onto the paper.

Dear Anna,

I'm not really sure what I should be writing. I know you've written something really neat. This was a really great idea.

I wish my parents and their stupid rules didn't bring us to this, but you've made it a good thing, at least as good as we can have without being able to actually talk to each other on the phone. My mother would say that you've turned lemons into lemonade. She has a million sayings like that. You've got to take the good with the bad. A penny saved is a penny earned. Stuff like that. And lately, this one: Obey your father!

Ugh!

I'll find out how bad things are going to be tonight. Maybe they'll even admit that they're wrong and I'll be able to call you, but the odds of that happening are probably right up there with me being able to come to your next band practice and play perfectly every note on the tuba.

I don't play the tuba. Haha.

It really isn't haha, though, that my parents are making things tough for us. It's going to be awful having to go the entire weekend without talking to you. Well, hopefully this letter and the one you wrote for me will make it easier for us to get to Monday.

See you then!
Rabbit

*

I give her the letter before our last class together in the afternoon. She's waiting outside the classroom door, books cradled in her left hand tucked against her chest, as other students two and three abreast on both sides walk by, the buzz of everyone's conversation filling the air. She sees something in my face that tells her something is up. I guess I'd be the world's worst poker player since I'm not very good at covering up my emotions. Everyone else at the table would know right away if I was bluffing.

I'm not bluffing now as I walk toward her, my two textbooks and my notebook tucked against my leg. I'm both bursting with happiness and anticipation at being able to give her the letter—which I hope she'll think is the ace of hearts or at least a king or queen—and at the same time terrified that what I've written will sound stupid—a deuce or a three or a four—especially compared to what she's written. I suppose I'm the one who should write the better letters since I'm the one in Accelerated English, but it doesn't work that way. Anna's still really, really smart, and I think girls are better than guys at this kind of thing. Although maybe that's just an excuse because sometimes I'm such a dope.

"What's up?" she asks, seeing the wide grin on my face that I can't suppress.

I'm about to just hand it to her shyly, the same way she handed me my letter, but my struggles writing it, including the little spat with Jeff, prompt me to make a bigger deal of it than that.

"Ladies and gentleman," I say in a circus announcer voice once I'm next to her, the both of us up against the wall just outside the classroom. "The Amazing Rabbit will astound you with a trick seen only once before in the halls of Lynn English High School, and that being just this very morning."

Anna puts her free hand to her mouth, laughing softly, and leans just a little closer to see what I'm going to do.

"The Amazing Rabbit will not pull a rabbit out of his hat," I say, "since he has neither a rabbit nor a hat. But what he does have is something he has created out of thin air for his fair lady. It isn't very good, and it's probably really stupid, but he did create it out of thin air." I reach into my pocket and pull out her note, the sheet of paper folded into the same tight triangle as Jeff and Paul's pretend football so it won't open until she untucks the edges. It has "Anna" written on the front and the back.

With a bow and a magician's flourish, I hand her the note. "For my fair lady."

She beams. "How did you…when did you do this?"

"A magician never tells his secrets," I say, then add a split second later, every bit as bad a magician as a poker player, "In study hall."

She takes the little triangle, reaches her free arm around my neck, and pulls me close in a hug. I smell her citrusy perfume and the strawberry scent of her hair that nestles against my nose. I feel the warmth of her cheek against my neck. My head swims and my racing heart seems ready to explode.

The embrace only lasts a second or two before she pulls away and looks at me, her face flushed, as I suspect mine is as well. "Thank you, Rabbit. That was so sweet."

It's one of the happiest moments of my life.

CHAPTER 7

As I head toward the gym for the final day of basketball tryouts, the dust-filled hallways smell musty with only the slightest trace remaining of the morning's clean, pine disinfectant scent. I'm tempted to open Anna's note. Technically, school is over and the sealed envelope has been burning a hole in my pocket all day. I feel like a kid the day before Christmas, holding an amazing present but unable to open it.

But Anna said, "Tonight when we'd be talking on the phone," so I honor that. It would feel dishonest to open it now.

But I want to! The suspense is killing me. I can't wait!

And I hope she likes the letter I wrote to her. Maybe I shouldn't have done the whole magician thing. That probably raised her expectations that it's really good. I should have just handed her the triangle and said, "This is really stupid, but it's the best I could do."

But then maybe I wouldn't have gotten that hug, and smelled the strawberries in her hair and felt the warmth of her cheek against mine. I wouldn't trade that for anything. So I'm glad The Amazing Rabbit made his appearance.

It's going to be a *long* wait until Monday.

*

At the end of the tryout, Coach Abrams tells us that there are three sheets of paper posted on the wall outside the doors to the locker rooms. They hold the names of the players who have made the three teams: varsity, junior varsity, and freshmen.

"I want to thank you all for trying out, even those of you who didn't make it," he says, standing at center court, a whistle looped around his neck and a basketball crooked under his arm. Sixty or so sweating players are gathered around him in a half circle, all down on one knee, so at six-foot-two, he towers over even the tallest of us.

Each day, a couple players have dropped out. Today, the decision will be made for more than a dozen more. Maybe close to two dozen. Their season ends today. I hold my breath that I'm not one of them. I think I've done enough to make the team, but you can never be sure, especially at my size.

"There were some tough cuts," he continues, running a hand through his gray-streaked crew cut, "especially seniors because this is your last year and you can't play JV. It's varsity or nothing. Thank you for your effort, and I'm sorry it had to end this way. I hope you'll continue to support this team as a fan, even if you can't help us on the floor."

"As for you who made the team"—he scans the anxious crowd of players around him—"I want you on the court tomorrow morning at ten ready to work hard. We're going to play fundamental basketball, and we're going to make this year's team the best one we've ever had. Got it?"

We all yell, "Yes, sir!" and if everyone else is like me, they just want Coach to wrap up the speech so we can find out if we made the team or not.

Perhaps sensing that, he says, "Shower up!" and turns to leave.

There's practically a stampede to the wall where the team lists are posted on three sheets of white lined paper, although a couple players take their time, walking slowly and with confidence. Players like Joe Thurman, who hasn't merely made the team but will be varsity captain.

Not me.

I race over, and skip over the varsity list on the left and the JV one in the middle. There's no point in even looking. I go immediately to the sheet on the right listing the freshmen team and am ready to whoop with delight at the sight of my name.

Rabbit Labelle.

What stops me are the crestfallen looks of those who didn't make it, including a few older kids, clearly seniors, who stare in disbelief. For them, it's over. Their hopes…crushed.

I can't let loose my own jubilation without rubbing salt in their wounds. Plenty of others do, but I can't ignore the hurt in the other players' eyes.

So I'm about to silently, respectfully, push through the doors to the locker room, when I see Charlie Watkins staring at the list in shock. Beside him, Jamaal Bryant swears softly.

"You gotta be kidding me," Charlie says under his breath.

I look up to the JV list and see—

His name isn't on it. Neither is Jamaal's.

All the other names I would have expected on that list—Rick Cassidy, Chris Higgins, and Mark Evangelista along with a few names I don't recognize—are there. Even Jerry Epstein, the lefty I set up for all those jump shots a couple days ago, is on the list even though he takes about fifteen minutes to get his shot off and can hardly jump more than a couple inches.

But not Charlie or Jamaal.

I instinctively look at the varsity list, because if they didn't make JVs then they've *got* to be there, but they aren't on that one either. Only after scouring the other two lists multiple times do I turn to the freshmen sheet and see their names there.

Charlie? On the freshmen *team? Jamaal, too?*

My jaw drops. There must be a mistake. I look again and then triple-check to make sure that my eyes aren't deceiving me.

"Charlie—" I say, not having any idea what else I'm going to add.

But he just shakes his head, his eyes filled with pain and anger. "Not now, man."

Jamaal swears even more vociferously, shaking his head and gesturing toward the list. I stand there as if paralyzed.

"Don't say a damned thing," Charlie says, and pushes through the doors to the locker room.

*

I wait for Charlie after I take my shower, then we walk side by side from the locker room to our rides, me on his left, our gym bags slung over our shoulders, our footsteps echoing down the long, empty hallways. His close-cropped hair is still damp, as is my crew cut. Our thick winter jackets, mine dark gray and his black, are open, not yet zipped against the cold outside. We're still warm, almost sweating. At least I am.

"I don't understand it," I say. "It doesn't make any sense."

Charlie's face is hard, his eyes distant and cold.

"Wait up!" I hear from behind us. Jamaal catches up to us, and falls in step on Charlie's right. The two of them look as if they're in shock.

"Can you believe it?" he says, looking at Charlie, and I realize for the first time that Jamaal speaks in a soft Southern accent. I've never spoken with him before, and though I must have heard the accent when he was swearing while looking at the team lists, it didn't register because I was so stunned at what I saw. I recall now someone saying his family moved here this summer from either North or South Carolina. Or maybe it was

Georgia. Someplace like that. "The freshmen team?" he asks. "Are you kidding me? It's just 'cause we black!"

He glances my way, looking unsure what to make of me. I'm pretty sure he wishes I'd just go away and leave him and Charlie alone.

"Makes no sense to me," I say, although I wonder if I should really just keep quiet or even leave so the two of them can be alone. But Charlie is my friend and I want to be here for him and in some way try to help. And maybe help Jamaal, too, even though I don't know him from Adam, and he doesn't know me. "I guess you've just got to play so great that you give them no choice," I say. "You can do it. Both of you. Force them to move you up."

Charlie stares at me, looking as if he's trying to decide whether or not to tell me something. He gives a brief nod, perhaps to himself, and says, "I don't know if I can play for that man."

"Coach O'Donnell?" I ask, referring to the freshmen team coach, who hasn't seemed half bad.

Charlie looks at me like I'm stupid. "Abrams. He calls the shots. Even on the JV and freshmen teams."

"Oh." Charlie's right, or at least that look of his is right. I am stupid. "But what's so bad about Abrams? I mean, other than cutting you guys from JVs, which is ridiculous, and the haircuts?"

"Man, you didn't see 'cause you was on the other court. No offense, but you wasn't there. I'm not meaning to put you down, but..."

I get it. I was on the lesser court. And for a while when we were scrimmaging half court, I was stuck with the last group, a million miles from the kids Charlie and Jamaal were playing with. Fact is, I missed a lot of Charlie and Jamaal scrimmaging. I didn't need to see much to be as befuddled by them not making JVs as they are, but I'm sure I missed a lot.

"Don't worry about it," I say. "No offense taken."

Charlie shrugs. "Well, there were times I'd make a move on a guy, clear myself for a shot, and he'd call out, 'Work the ball around, Watkins! Fundamentals, Watkins, fundamentals!' As if I don't know my hoop fundamentals! He didn't blow the whistle and stop play or nothing. That's why you didn't even hear it. Sometimes, he just shook his head and gave me a dirty look. I'm scoring baskets, but he still saying stuff like that and give me the look. One time he even said, 'This ain't a playground, Watkins!'"

"Yeah, said that to me, too," Jamaal says, his Southern drawl lengthening out words. *Yeaahhhh.*

"A playground?" I ask, mystified at the comment.

Charlie grimaces. "*Playground* is a code word for black basketball. *Fundamental* is a code word for white."

"*What?*"

"Listen, man, you're a good guy," Charlie says. "But sometimes you are *so* naïve. I bet you just stopped believing in Santa Claus and the Easter Bunny."

"I'm not *that* bad."

"Close, man. Close." We've reached the big bank of three double doors to go outside to our rides, but we've stopped. Our parents can wait. "What I'm trying to tell you," he says, "is that when a guy like Abrams says 'fundamental basketball,' he's talking about white basketball. Pass the ball around a lot. Don't do anything flashy. And when he says 'playground basketball,' he's referring to black basketball, but like it's a bad thing.

"Dunking the ball is black. That's playground ball. Bad. Beating a guy one-on-one is playground. You should have passed the ball around instead for fifteen minutes until the damned defense fell asleep of boredom, then you scored. If you weren't able to box a guy out for a rebound but out-jumped him instead, that's playground. Guys like Abrams can't say 'white' and 'black' without sounding like George Wallace down in Alabama, so they use the code words. But that's what they mean.

"Abrams don't like me and Jamaal because we play too black. He picked white guys for that JV team that can't hold either of our jock straps. Guys like Jerry Epstein. I mean, are you kidding me? Jerry Epstein? If I played him one-on-one, I'd beat him twenty-one to zero!"

I nod in agreement. It's not an exaggeration. Jerry Epstein would never be able to get a shot off. Charlie would block every one.

"I'd wipe him out, too," Jamaal says. "Man, he can't do nothing!"

"And Randy Thorpe?" Charlie says. "He's two hundred pounds of blubber. He was a good tackle on the football team, 'cause he didn't have to run. But he can't get up and down the basketball floor! He's got no game! How's a guy that out of shape, who can't do nothin', get picked ahead of me?"

"The great white whale," Jamaal says.

"They white! That's all it is!" Charlie says. "And they play white. All of them on the JVs do. They play Abrams basketball. White basketball. I cut my 'fro as short as all you white guys to make him happy." He gestures toward Jamaal. "Him, too. But we still play black and Abrams don't like it. Decided he had to put us in our place."

"Yeah," Jamaal says, and shakes his head.

I stare at Charlie, open-mouthed. I can't believe what I've just heard.

"Wouldn't usually say all this to a white boy, but you different," Charlie says. He eyes me and perhaps interprets my wide-eyed astonishment as disbelief. "You think I'm making this up? Why you think the NCAA outlawed dunking? It was making the game too black. White coaches—and almost every coach be white—don't like it. Have to keep the game white." He gestures toward me. "No offense intended."

I shake my head *no*. I'm too stunned to be offended. Too stunned to respond. My head is still swimming. It all makes sense, but…but I'd have never imagined it. Never in a million years. I've been blind to it all. I must be as naïve as Charlie says, even if I don't believe in Santa Claus or the Easter Bunny.

"Coach Abrams just like the rest of them," Charlie says. "Got to keep the game white with his *fun-da-men-tals*. Don't believe me? Pay attention when he talks. You'll see."

I nod, as if in a dream, and we begin to push through the doors. But before we're even half outside, a voice calls out from behind us.

"Hey, Watkins! Bryant!"

We turn around and there's Joe Thurman, a gray gym bag over his shoulder. He's only a couple inches taller than Charlie, but he has an authority about him that towers over all of us.

"Got a sec?" he asks, but with a look that expects only one answer.

Charlie gives it to him. "Sure. What's up?" Jamaal nods and looks on expectantly.

"I saw Abrams didn't pick you guys for JVs."

"Yeah," Charlie says, downcast.

Thurman seems to belatedly realize I'm there, the square peg in the round hole. "You mind excusing us?" he says to me.

"He's cool," Charlie says. "We was just talking about it."

Thurman looks at me, then back at Charlie. "You friends with the midget?"

Charlie nods and points a thumb at me. "Name's Rabbit. Rabbit Labelle. Know him from football. We…we been through some stuff together. You can trust him."

Thurman nods, but looks as if he doesn't quite believe it. "I'll take your word for it." He looks around, presumably making sure no one else is within earshot, gives me an extra wary glance, then goes ahead. "You didn't hear me say this, but…"

He looks around again.

"It's total BS that you didn't make JVs," he says to Charlie and Jamaal. "Both of you. *Total* BS!" He points to Charlie. "Hell, you should be on the varsity. But that's how Abrams works. Messes with your head. Tries to turn you white." Realizing what he's said, Thurman looks at me. "No offense."

I shake my head. I'm not offended. More *ashamed* that I'm white. Embarrassed.

"Don't let him get to you, man," Thurman says to Charlie. He turns to Jamaal. "You, too. Both of you'll be on JVs before you know it. And after that"—Thurman grins—"Watkins, you're gonna be the next me."

Charlie smiles for the first time since he saw his name missing on the posted list. "Thanks, man. Appreciate it."

"Bryant, I don't know what you're gonna be," Thurman says. "Man, some of those moves of yours. You're gonna be special, too."

Jamaal grins. "The next Earl the Pearl."

Thurman laughs. "Don't let Abrams hear that. He'll cut your ass."

They all laugh, then shake hands in that way black people do—hooking their thumbs together in something I think is called a Soul Shake—and Joe Thurman pushes through the door. The cold December air blasts in our faces. We pull our jackets tight, duck down, and head for our parents' cars.

"Hey, Charlie," I say when he gets about ten feet away. "Hang in there."

He nods, but I can guess what he's thinking.

Easy for you to say.

CHAPTER 8

Irush up to my room, taking the stairs two at a time even though I'm carrying three textbooks. There's nothing I can do to help Charlie or Jamaal, at least not until tomorrow's practice, and I've got Anna's letter burning a hole in my pants pocket. I put my books on the desk that's up against the left wall, and make no move to straighten the stack when the top one topples halfway off.

I listen to make sure my mom isn't coming up the stairs after me, then pull out the letter and flop facedown on the bed. I prop myself up and sniff the envelope, feeling like those wine connoisseurs in movies that hold their expensive wines to their upturned noses and say things like, "It's got a delicate bouquet."

Anna's envelope has a delicate bouquet, so I don't tear it apart recklessly. I'll want to keep it. I open it eagerly and as quickly as possible, but try to tear the back away from the flap with as little damage as possible. I pull it out and unfold it, my hands shaking just a little and my mouth dry. I read it, a big smile on my face.

Dear Rabbit,

I hope you like this little surprise. It isn't as good as hearing your voice on the phone and listening to you laugh, but maybe it'll make it easier to go without that.

I'm not really sure what to write, but I'm just going to put down whatever pops into my head, kind of like we're on the phone together. So this letter might bounce all over the place, like one of those Superballs that bounce like crazy, if you've seen the commercials on TV.

I guess I'll address the elephant in the room, as my mother likes to say. Whoever has an elephant in the room? Based on what I saw at the circus one time, where the clowns had to follow after the elephants with a shovel and scoop up their you-know-what, I sure wouldn't want an elephant in my room and then be expected to clean up after it. Haha!

Wow, I'm trying to write a nice letter to you and what happens? I'm talking about elephant poop. I should probably throw this out and start all over. But I'll just do the Superballs thing and bounce like crazy away from the elephant poop.

In any case, if you never heard the "address the elephant in the room" phrase—maybe my mother is the only one who uses that—it means that if there's something obvious that needs to be talked about, like an elephant in the room, you just need to talk about it and not pretend it isn't there. 'Cause you can't really pretend there isn't an elephant in your room for very long.

Our elephant in the room is your talk with your parents tonight about us. I hope you're able to get things straight with them. I'd hate to think that I could have done anything to avoid these problems. I probably should have told you not to do the getaway car prank, but I never thought that any-one, much less your parents, could think that someone of your sweet nature was involved in a getaway car that needed to be hidden from the police. Still, I feel a little guilty about that, even though it's probably because, as my mom says, hindsight is 20-20. I just hope for both of us that everything gets worked out okay between you and them. Our parents can either make our lives easy or miserable. and I hope your parents make things easy.

But enough of that. Enough of that smelly, wrinkled elephant.

I sure hope you made the basketball team! It was so exciting to watch you play football, making everyone else look like they were slow as molasses. I would love to watch you play basketball, too, and not just the last game or two of the year like with football. If only I'd known earlier how much fun it was to watch you play!

Tonight I'll be at band, like usual, practicing for our holiday concerts, which I've told you about. I've already got all my parts memorized and can do them in my sleep, but I like to practice and am also working on some harder pieces, too.

Please don't feel that you have to come to any of the concerts. Don't feel obligated at all. I really won't kill you if you don't show up for any of them. I'll only think about it. Haha.

But really, only come if you want to. I think you'll like it, but maybe I'm biased. We're sounding pretty good, except for the guys playing trombone that are always goofing off, using their slides to knock down other kids' music stands.

Well, I better stop here. If I drone on any longer, I'll put you to sleep. Maybe I can even already hear your snoring over here at my house. Haha.
I can't wait to see you on Monday.

Your girlfriend,
Anna

I hold the letter to my chest and close my eyes. I love the whole thing, every single word of it.

But *especially* how she ended it. *Your girlfriend, Anna.*

I hadn't known how to end my own letter. I was afraid to put "Love" since we've just started going out, and I'm terrified to use the L word first and maybe say it, or write it, too soon and scare her away.

Even if I feel the L word. Even if I think I'm…I'm *in love* with Anna.

There. I've said it again. *I'm in love with Anna.*

I'm in love with her.

I love Anna.

She is amazing.

She wrote, *Your girlfriend, Anna.*

I'm in *looooooooovvvveee!*

My heart is bubbling over with giddy happiness. My head is swimming with delight. Is there another, even sappier, way to describe how I feel? I don't know.

Sappy, sappy, sappy. That's me. I'm sappy in love with Anna!

Saaaapppy!

Is that silly? Is it just puppy love like I've heard adults dismiss relationships between teenagers? If so, then I'm Anna's puppy!

Woof, woof, woof!

Oh God, I am so silly. But silly in love.

L-O-V-E!

How is love spelled?

Anna!

Give me an A.

Give me an N.

Give me another N.

Give me another A.

What have you got?

Anna!

Say it again.

Anna!

What have you got?

ANNA!

Oh my God, if it were actually possible to read minds, and someone read mine, I'd die of embarrassment. I'm kind of embarrassed reading my own mind, knowing that I am certainly the most sappy, love-struck boy who has ever lived.

But I can't help it!

Your girlfriend, Anna.

All I can see in my mind's eye is her smiling face and those soft, playful brown eyes behind her glasses. All I can hear is the sound of her sweet voice, and the sound of her joyous laughter. All I can smell is the lilac scent of her perfume and the smell of strawberries in her hair. All I can think of is what it will feel like the first time I kiss her soft, sweet lips, and taste, perhaps, a hint of spearmint upon them.

Your girlfriend, Anna.

Wow!

I read the letter over and over, each time with even a little more delight, until my mom calls me down for dinner.

*

My giddy happiness drains away, the very life sucked out of it, as we eat a quiet, somber dinner of spaghetti and meatballs. I usually love pasta and salivate at the smell of tomato, peppers, Parmesan cheese, and garlic, but I know the big discussion—which has become in my mind *The Big Discussion*—looms afterward.

My father hasn't spoken a word to me other than a grudging hello. Not even the usual "How was school today?" or a request for an update on the basketball tryouts. Mom asked as soon as I climbed in the car for the ride home and was overjoyed at the good news, but my father seems to have forgotten that today was the day the team would be announced. It's clearly the furthest thing from his mind. His jaw juts out belligerently. His cold, stony face seems filled with barely suppressed anger, even rage. Perhaps it's just drained of all emotion, but I don't think so.

He has the look of an executioner.

He's going to give me the death sentence. Not me personally, but our relationship as father and son. It was so great just six months ago, but that relationship got arrested and thrown in jail when he decided to move us here, and even though it got released on bail when he and I made up after the

Thanksgiving Day football game just eight days ago, that bail got revoked and new charges were filed with everything that's happened this week.

He's going to strap that relationship into the electric chair, apply the electrodes to its temples, and pull the switch.

Fry everything we ever had. Burn it into a crisp.

I can see it in his face. I can feel the molten-hot hatred for me that comes off him in waves, like heat shimmering off an asphalt road on a baking hot summer day.

In another half an hour or so, as soon as we're finished with dinner and we have *The Big Discussion*, he and I will be finished forever. It fills me with an overwhelming sadness.

"Rabbit, tell your father the good news," my mom says, as I stuff half a meatball in my mouth.

I chew it, barely noticing the tomato taste, and watch my father for a reaction. But nothing shows on his stony face. I suspect the only thing my father would consider to be good news would be my acceptance of his demand that I break up with Anna.

And he's never going to get that.

But I do answer my mother's question. It's with more of a monotone than I'm sure she'd like, but it's all I can muster.

"I made the freshmen team," I say.

My father grunts in what I guess is a sign of approval, then nods. He swallows his food, pushes his glasses to the bridge of his nose, and says, "Congratulations."

Our Cold War just gets more and more frigid. So I reply with an equally frosty, "Thanks."

The wall clock behind me continues its slow countdown to the execution.

Tick…tick…tick….

Tick…tick…tick….

I stare down at my plate and, while twirling a thick clump of spaghetti on my fork, I try to push all thoughts of my father out of my head. It doesn't work. Trying to forget about him is like what Anna said about ignoring the elephant in the room. You can pretend the elephant isn't there, but you can't fool yourself forever. Eventually, you have to admit it's there.

It's hard to imagine I was so euphoric just fifteen or twenty minutes ago, reading Anna's letter, and now I'm so miserable. The tension in the room is so thick it makes the air feel heavy. I try to think instead of Anna and the note. *Your girlfriend, Anna.* The hint of a smile tugs at the corners of my mouth. No one can ever take that away.

And as I shovel the twirled up spaghetti into my mouth, thinking of her, I'm reminded of that scene in the Disney movie *Lady and the Tramp* where the two dogs both slurp in the same strand of spaghetti until they realize it, their eyes just inches apart, and they suck another inch of spaghetti and then another until their lips are about to touch.

"Rabbit," my mother says, breaking me out of my reverie. "Why are you smiling?"

I see in her eyes that she has latched onto my apparent smile like a drowning swimmer clinging to a life preserver. She is desperate to break the cloud of tension and hostility. But I can hardly explain what I was thinking. If we were still the family we were six months ago, I might admit to thinking about the *Lady and the Tramp* scene, and then ask if one of these days Mom could drop Anna and me off at the movies.

But that isn't happening in this house.

My mother looks to me for an answer, pleading for one. For a brief instant, I forget the question. Then I have to crush that hope of hers.

"Nothing," I say.

Her shoulders slump, and that flicker of light in her eyes goes out. She stares down at her plate and looks like she's fighting back tears.

I feel bad. I know she hates it when I shut her out, but I can't admit to what I was thinking.

Or can I? Can't I say at least a little something?

What can it hurt?

"I was thinking about Anna," I say. "It made me smile. She does that for me."

My mom's face softens and though I don't dare look at my father, I think I've said the right thing. So I keep going. "At first I said, 'Nothing,' because I didn't think…" I give a slight shrug of the shoulders. "I didn't think I should talk about her."

Mom gives a slight nod. She understands.

But my father…just sits there, stone-faced.

The executioner.

*

I take my seat in the front room chair, set at a right angle to my parents, who sit on the sofa. At least they do at the beginning, but as soon as my father sits down he bounces back up again. For a moment, I think he really is going to tan my hide. But he just stands there, feet spread apart, and crosses his arms.

"If it were up to me, young man, we would be having a very different discussion here," he says, and shoots an angry glance at my mom. "A *very* different discussion. You would not get away with defying my authority—*our* authority—and you would break up with this girl this very instant or you would be grounded *for life*!

"You would be grounded until you submitted to our parental authority. You wouldn't leave this house except to go to school. No special events whatsoever. You would withdraw from the basketball team."

My eyes bug out at this one. Make me quit the basketball team? I never even thought about that possibility.

What has happened to the father I once knew? Who years ago played catch with me in the backyard? Who as recently as six months ago joyfully attended whatever sporting events of mine didn't conflict with his job? Who talked to me every night about how the Red Sox were doing, or the Celtics, or in football, the Giants?

Who just eight days ago, after the Thanksgiving Day football game where he saw me play down here in Lynn for the very first time, pulled over onto a side street and tearfully asked me to forgive him for thinking only of his job and hardly at all about me?

What happened to him? Has the pressure from his job made him crack? Or have *I* done this to him? Is it *my* fault?

Have I created a Frankenstein's monster of a father because it's *me*, not just him, who is so different than six months ago? Six months ago, I was carefree, never worrying about much of anything but whether my friends and I could get a touch football game going over behind Donnie Boudreau's house and whether the manure in the fields would be ripe, its smell almost comically overpowering in our nostrils. The only problems I caused my parents were whether they could keep up with me, whether my mom could get to all my sporting events from basketball to track to baseball. The worst scolding I would get would be to clean my room.

But that was before everything changed. Moving here subjected me to things I never saw up in the northernmost part of Maine, in Aroostook County, where there are more cows than people. So yes, I've changed. Maybe I *am* Frankenstein's monster. I don't think so, but what monster thinks he is? I think I'm still a good person, but I've had to change to survive. I'm six months older physically, but maybe six years older in other ways. I've had to develop a hard shell around me that never was there before.

So no, I don't think I'm a monster. But maybe that's what my father sees in me. He sees the hard shell where before everything was soft and carefree. He sees, to use my mother's word, my insolence, my refusal to accept his "whatever I say goes" commands. I defend myself and don't just accept what he says as gospel.

Because I've seen that he was wrong before. He was wrong before and he's wrong now. And where before I'd never say a peep, now I mouth back. Now I challenge his authority, or at least he sees it that way, because he's no longer like the almighty Wizard of Oz. I've seen behind the curtain.

And so, as far as I'm concerned, whatever he says *doesn't* go. Yes, he's my father and I'll accept that *most* of what he says, goes.

But not all of it.

I'm not just going to take what he says as gospel, no matter what it is, and do it. I'm absolutely, positively not going to break up with Anna. That is *never, ever* going to happen.

I'm sure he wishes I were still the thirteen-year-old kid (almost fourteen) I was up in Maine—"thirteen going on three" as he used to put it. Now, he sees a totally different person. Perhaps he really does see me as a monster, or as an insolent teenager about to become a monster.

I terrify him.

That sudden knowledge hits me like one of his slaps across my face. It stings and saddens me. I'm sure his love is buried beneath that terror. In fact, that love is what fuels that terror. He wants to make sure, he *needs* to make sure, his only son doesn't become the monster he fears.

"It's only because of your mother," my father says, giving her a stony glare, "that I'm not tanning your hide and taking every last measure, including kicking you off the basketball team, until you submit to our authority." He noisily draws in a deep breath of air through his nose, his nostrils widening. He slowly exhales. "But your mother has convinced me as forcefully as she possibly could that it would be a mistake."

He holds up his index finger. "For now, I'm taking that advice, although I have serious, serious misgivings about it." He shakes his head. "It won't take much for me to change my mind. And if I do, you'll know it, young man. You'd better hope I don't.

"I still make the final decisions here." He stabs himself in the chest with his index finger. "What I say goes. This is not a democracy. And even it if looks like the two of you have outvoted me here, that is most certainly not the case! I am still the *man* of the house. I am still the final authority." He glares at my mom, and I wonder how hard it must have been to convince him to back down, how much of his anger she'll still have to endure. "I'm not exactly sure what's gotten into your mother, acting like she wears the pants in this family. But this is a *one-time* concession I've made."

He holds his index finger aloft. It shakes with his rage. "*One time!*"

His face remains stony, but a crimson flush has come to his cheeks even as my mom's face has turned ashen and she averts her eyes.

"So here's my ruling," he says. "It holds until the next time you talk back. Until the next time you misbehave. Until the next time you so much as *think* about defying our authority." He takes in another noisy, angry breath of air through his nostrils. "You do *not* have to break up with this girl." He gestures dismissively with his hand. "Anna, or whatever her name is."

My hopes had been growing as he'd made it clear he was going to listen to my wonderful, wise, and kind mother, but now I rejoice. My father hasn't lived up to the worst of my fears after all. He hasn't acted as the executioner, killing our relationship forever. He hasn't spat in the face of Mutually Assured Destruction and launched his own nuclear warheads, forcing me to retaliate with my own.

We won't destroy each other. At least not yet.

Of course, it won't be like six months ago. All peace and harmony and mutual respect. No tension at all.

That genie is out of the bottle.

But we'll still be a family. We'll coexist. Maybe even better than that.

"Until you're much older, the relationship goes no further," he says. "You see her at school and at school events. You can talk to her on the phone for five minutes a night after your punishment ends in two weeks.

"But nothing more than that. Absolutely not. Over my dead body. At this age, you're certainly not going to be going on any *dates*."

My heart sinks a bit at this, but I can't really be surprised. It could have been a lot worse. And maybe after all the tensions subside, he'll lighten up a bit on the date ban.

"You'd better thank your mother for this," he says. "This wasn't my idea at all."

Before I can say a word, Mom says, "Tell him about the phone."

I think she must not have been listening closely because my father already talked about it. But based on his reaction, there's more. He flushes with anger, or perhaps embarrassment although I can't imagine why, and juts his jaw out defiantly. Once again, he breathes noisily through his nostrils and jabs at his glasses to press them back up to the bridge of his nose, jabbing so hard I wonder if he'll wind up with a pair of black eyes.

"The punishment remains two weeks," he says, then glares at my mother for what feels like an eternity. He shakes his head in obvious disgust. "However, we will look into getting a longer cord for the phone so it extends into my office if I'm not in there. Or maybe even into the bathroom."

"To give you privacy," Mom adds brightly even as my father looks like he wants to spit on the floor. "And until you give us reason to do otherwise, we won't listen in on your conversations."

"Thank you!" I say to her with sincere gratitude. And as her eyes pool with tears, I add, "That's great! I really appreciate it."

And I do. Seeing my father's bottled rage tonight, I can't imagine how much this has cost her. She instinctively avoids conflict, especially with my father, so sticking her neck out for me had to be more difficult than I can imagine.

With my voice starting to break, I say, "I love you. Mom."

"I love you, too, Rabbit."

She stands and I can tell she wants to come over and hug me, but I'm not done yet. I can't leave it like this, with words of thanks and love and kindness spoken only to my mother. I don't like the person my father has become, but I think back to what Anna wrote in her letter.

Our parents can either make our lives easy or miserable. I hope your parents make things easy.

My life won't quite be easy now, but it won't be miserable either. And I need to do whatever I can to push things closer to the "easy" end of the spectrum. To try to repair some of the damage in my relationship with my father.

I want to think we haven't burned all our bridges behind us. So I turn to him. There are words he needs to hear.

"I know this was difficult, Dad," I say, and at the sound of the word "Dad" his face softens just a bit. It's a word I've used sparingly in recent months, but I use it deliberately this time. I know it can't be like the old days, but I want us to put the warheads away for good. I want us to stop fighting. If it can't be easy anymore, at least it doesn't have to be so hard. "Thank you. I love you, too.

"I know I've changed in the past few months, and some of it isn't good." I almost add, "but I'm not a monster," but just thinking those words gets me a little choked up now, so instead I just say, "Like I said the other night, I'll try harder to watch my mouth. I love you both."

Mom rushes over to me, almost knocking over the coffee table in the process. Tears stream down her face. I stand up, and she wraps her arms around me. I hug her back just as hard. I smell her talcum powder and feel the wetness of her tears on my shoulder. Her body shakes and maybe mine does a little, too, because she isn't the only one who is crying.

After what seems like a long time, but might have only been a few seconds, my father comes over and awkwardly joins in the embrace.

It isn't perfect, but it could be a lot worse.

CHAPTER 9

At breakfast the next morning, the smell of coffee is in the air. Pancakes sizzle on the stove. My father is dressed in his suit, a freshly starched white shirt, and tie. He's going in to work even though it's Saturday. I'll be surprised if he doesn't bring more work home in his leather briefcase to work on tomorrow. That's how it's been since we moved down here. But the simmering rage barely bottled up inside him is gone. He doesn't meet my eyes for more than a second before looking uncomfortably away, but I'm not facing a stone-faced glare.

Progress.

Although there seems to be an icy coldness directed toward Mom. I can't exactly put a finger on it, but it feels like the temperature in the room plummets twenty degrees when he looks at her as she comes in from the kitchen with a stack of pancakes. She forces a smile that he doesn't return, then looks away.

"Are you sure you only want two, Rabbit?" she asks, focusing on me instead.

"Yeah, I don't want to be stuffed for practice," I say. I try to lighten the mood. "It might not be a good idea to barf all over the gym floor during the first practice."

My father laughs a little too hard. "That wouldn't be a good first impression," he says, and then chuckles some more and sips his coffee.

It's awkward, but he's trying. It's hard to imagine any way that things wouldn't be at least a little awkward between us after last night. Heck, after the last few days. We've put away the warheads, but the memories of them locked and loaded, ready to launch, are still fresh. I guess Anna would call them an elephant in the room, but I'm hoping the memories and the warheads are elephants that are leaving the room and for good.

Maybe the elephants have already left the room and all that's left is their poop. The thought amuses me, and a broad smile crosses my face. My father sees it, apparently assumes it's because of his "first impressions" crack being a big hit with me, and actually smiles.

A real, live, warm smile. Not a forced grin or an awkward chuckle while trying to make conversation. A genuine smile. One with warmth. He almost beams. I'd forgotten what that looked like on him. The thought flashes across my mind: *Who is this human being and what has he done with my fire-breathing dragon of a father?*

Score one for Anna. Of course, I'll never let my father—my dad!—know that it was her elephant comment and not his weak wisecrack that amused me, but it has broken the ice at least a little.

"Yes indeed, first impressions are important and vomiting your breakfast isn't the way to do it," he adds with a chuckle and another loud sip of his coffee, proving that he's no Bob Hope or Henny Youngman in the humor department.

But he's my dad and he's trying. I've got to give him that. So I nod and slather butter on my two pancakes and douse them with the real Vermont maple syrup that he insists on instead of "that awful Aunt Jemima stuff." I take a bite and the hot pancakes almost melt in my mouth. They taste *so* good. I wash them down with some orange juice.

"Um…Mom?" I begin tentatively.

"I made a third one for you, just in case," she says with a coy smile.

I laugh. "How did you know?"

"Mothers always know," she says, warm and loving.

A look bordering on hatred flashes across my father's face, there for only an instant and then gone. But it was unmistakable and I can tell Mom saw it, too.

He recovers, though, and with another awkward chuckle says, "I guess some things are worth the risk of vomiting on the gym floor."

*

Fifteen minutes later, Dad slips into his long, black winter coat, grabs his tan leather briefcase, and heads for the front door. Although December second is too early for a true mid-winter arctic-cold blast—the kind that freezes you to your bones—the temperature has plummeted into the teens, so he buttons up his coat before opening the door.

"If you can stick around just half an hour," Mom calls out from around the corner in the kitchen, "you can take Rabbit to practice."

I'm clearing the dishes from the table and can see them both, although they can't see each other, blocked out by the front room and kitchen walls. Mom has raised her eyebrows, hopeful. My father looks like he's bitten into something sour.

"No can do," he says, coldly and without emotion, his face blank. "You'll have to take care of it." He looks to me. "Sorry, I've got to run." He glances at his wristwatch, a cheap, silver-colored Timex he's had for as long as I can remember, and taps it. "Time is money."

Cutting off any further discussion, he ducks out the door, sending a blast of cold air in behind him.

Mom shakes her head and inhales deeply. "You know I'm happy to take you, right?"

"Sure."

"I just think it would be good for the two of you…oh, I don't know… if you two spent more time together. Idle time, you know?"

"Yeah."

"Time you could talk about, oh, I don't know. Anything. The Red Sox. Football. The Celtics. The space program and whether we're going to beat the Russians to the moon. The Vietnam War. Anything, you know?"

"Yeah, sure." I put the sticky plates covered with a thin layer of left-over syrup into the white plastic dishpan already filled with warm, soapy water. I look into her troubled brown eyes and grin. "But maybe not the Vietnam War."

She bursts into laughter, gives me a playful cuff across the back of the head, and for at least the moment, her troubled look gives way to merriment.

"You're a little rascal, you know that?" she says, and snakes an arm around me for a hug.

"Yup," I say, and we both laugh.

I know that she harbors concerns about the Vietnam War, that a lot of boys not much older than me are coming home in wooden coffins from a place halfway across the world that doesn't seem to matter. And my father sees it in exactly the opposite terms. He talks about the "domino theory" and how if we let the Communists take over Vietnam, they'll be invading Hawaii before we can say Ho Chi Minh. And then it'll be California, although to hear him talk sometimes about "all the hippies and peaceniks out there," the Communists have already taken over that godforsaken state and the sooner an earthquake happens and all those commies fall into the Pacific Ocean, the better.

"But if you really think I should hear what he has to say about the war," I say, shifting into full-speed teasing mode, "we should set aside the time for it. That and Dr. Martin Luther King and the Civil Rights struggle. I could tell him all about Dr. King's latest book, *Why We Can't Wait*. And maybe *The Autobiography of Malcolm X*, too. I bet he'd *love* to read both of them. We'd have a blast discussing them calmly at the dinner table." As I dish out the sarcasm—I've read both of those books, but my father would burn my copies if he knew I had them—the smirk on my face grows and grows. But I'm not done. I apply the clincher. "And then he and I could talk about equal rights for women."

Mom clamps a hand, suddenly soapy from the dishwater, over my mouth and says, laughing, "Enough out of you, young man."

Even though I'm spitting out soap for more than a few seconds and can taste it even longer than that, it's a perfect moment, one that fills my heart with love and a sense of peace.

My father and I have a ways to go, but Mom and I are right where we should be.

Halfway home.

*

I scrape the thin layer of frost off the windshield to Mom's Ford Fairlane, and we head off to practice. Even though it's sure to get much worse in the coming months, it really has gotten cold outside, and inside the car isn't much better. It takes the car heater forever to start blowing anything but frigid air even worse than what's already there. Every breath generates a white cloud in front of our faces.

The heater's still blowing cold air as we pass St. Mary's Cemetery, which extends for a good quarter of a mile along Lynnfield Street, and I'm glad I've dressed in my thickest winter jacket and gloves. The heater doesn't kick in until we reach the stoplight at Wyoma Square.

Fauci's Pizza is on the corner on our right, and I think of bringing Anna there someday and trying out the place. I've heard other kids say the pizza is really good and that it's cut up in squares instead of slices. I never heard of cutting pizza in squares. Would that make Fauci's a good place to take a girl like Anna or a bad place? I don't really know. What about Nickey's Pizza, just a couple hundred yards back?

"Rabbit?" Mom says, pulling me out of my date-with-Anna daydream, one that unfortunately can't become a reality for at least a while.

Maybe a long while.

The light has turned green and Fauci's disappears behind us as we continue onto Broadway, an extension of Lynnfield Street but one with a new name and a grassy median strip separating the two lanes on both sides.

"Yeah," I say, since she seems to need me to acknowledge her, or more likely, indicate that I'm really paying attention, before she'll continue.

"I'm counting on you to live up to your promise last night," she says. "It's important." She glances over to make sure I nod, and then returns her attention to the road, less than half as filled with cars as on a weekday, her two gloved hands gripping the steering wheel.

"I know," I say to underscore my nod. "Thanks again for standing up for me. Thanks for standing up for *us*. I'll never forget it."

She shakes her head and her eyes get a faraway look. "I've never seen your father so angry. Ever."

"I thought he was going to kill me for sure," I admit.

She looks at me sharply. "What?"

"Well, not really kill me. But I thought I was going to get a whipping. And I thought he was going to tell me I had to break up with Anna, and I was going to refuse, and all Hell was going to break loose. The warheads were going to fly, Mutually Assured Destruction."

"Warheads? What are you talking about?"

So I explain it to her.

She somberly nods. "That came closer to happening than I want to think of. Awfully close." She swallows hard. "Scary close. I had to—"

Her eyes widen, as if shocked by her own words. She shakes her head.

"What did you have to do?" I ask softly, afraid of what I might hear. I feel a sudden sick feeling in the pit of my stomach.

She shakes her head and turns onto Chestnut Street. "Nothing."

"Mom."

She shakes her head.

"Tell me," I say.

"Nothing," she says. "Really."

"Mom, when you lie, it's written all over your face. Tell me."

"Rabbit, enough!" she says, but I can tell she's giving in, at least a little. Her shoulders slump, and she shakes her head, this time in resignation. She glances over at me, then back at the road. She sucks in a big gulp of air.

"Okay, you do need to know this much," she says. "Last night, your father wasn't furious with you. Oh, he was angry. Very angry. But that rage you saw wasn't meant for you. It was meant for me."

"Oh, Mom," I say.

An awful inspiration hits, like lightning striking a tree and splintering it into charred halves with a gaping hole in the center, and I'm sure I'm right. Somehow, I don't know how, I suddenly know what she had to do to persuade my father, to *force* him, to back down. I had sensed that it had cost her to stand up for me, but I never imagined how much.

"Oh, Mom," I say again. "You had to threaten to leave him."

Her neck whips around and she stares, wide-eyed, at me. "How did you—"

She shakes her head as if to clear it and gets her eyes back onto the road. She glances back at me, then back at the road. She swallows hard and shakes her head.

There's nothing she can say. The secret is out.

And there's nothing I can say, either.

I can't believe what I've done. I told my mom to do the right thing and so she actually told my father she'd leave him if he launched those warheads. She'd leave him and take me with her.

And now he hates her for it.

I was convinced the relationship with my father would be blown to bits and we'd never get it back together again.

Humpty Dumpty.

But without meaning to, I dumped that awful load on my mom. Is her relationship with my father now over? Did the two of them launch their warheads? Have they mutually assured the destruction of their marriage?

All because of me.

Humpty Dumpty for sure.

CHAPTER 10

My first official basketball practice is pretty uneventful until the very end, although the way my life has become such a soap opera, I guess the gym would pretty much have to blow up to match everything else that's been going on. Instead, we go through a lot of the same drills we've done before, but whenever the drills aren't purely individual ones, the varsity players do them with each other and the same for the JV and freshmen players.

I can see from the angry looks on Charlie and Jamaal's faces that this is one more reminder of the slap they took across the face when Coach Abrams relegated them to the freshmen team. When they're doing the drills with us, they're like what my football coach, Mr. McDonough, called a man amongst boys. They're so much better than us, they're almost wasting their time. I'm angry for them, but that's not going to make a bit of difference.

Finally, Coach Abrams blows his whistle and gathers us all around him in a semi-circle. He motions us to all get down on one knee, and slowly moves his gaze from one side to the other, looking down at all of us.

"Can any of you gentlemen tell me what happened last night?" he asks.

Many of us look at each other, wondering what he might be getting at, but we draw blanks.

"You posted the list of who made the team," Joe Thurman, the varsity star and team captain, says.

"That's true, Joe," Coach Abrams concedes, "but that's not what I'm looking for. Think bigger than Lynn English. Think as big as possible."

I wonder if he's getting at some country that's testing nuclear weapons. Maybe Red China or the Soviet Union, or maybe us. But I suspect that's all popping into my head because of what's happening to my family. Coach Abrams probably isn't talking about nuclear weapons.

"Who's the biggest player in the NBA?" he finally asks.

"Bill Russell," someone says, referring to the Boston Celtics center who has got to be the most outstanding team player ever. Nine NBA championships with the Celtics and counting. But as amazing as Bill Russell is, there's someone who is physically even larger. Russell is six-ten, 220 pounds. Wilt Chamberlain, however, is seven-one and 275 pounds, the single most imposing physical player ever. One year in the NBA, he averaged more than fifty points a game. Another year, he averaged twenty-seven rebounds a game. No one could stop him. Still no match for Russell because of all those championships, if you ask me, but Wilt the Stilt is undeniably the biggest player of them all.

And I read in the paper what he did last night.

"Wilt Chamberlain," I say, and Coach Abrams points a finger at me and nods. But I'm not done. "He missed an NBA record twenty-two free throws last night."

"Exactly!" Coach Abrams. "Imagine that. A professional basketball player missed twenty-two free throws in one game! Twenty-two! I guess for him, they weren't free at all. And that's one of the reasons he's only won a single NBA championship. Only one, despite all his points and rebounds, all his blocked shots and assists. He has a weakness that he's never addressed.

"I tell you, back when I was a player, I worked on my weaknesses so no opponent could exploit them. Same thing with my older brother, Delvin. We wouldn't tolerate a weakness like Chamberlain's—twenty-two missed free throws in a single game!—and that's why the Lynn English Bulldogs of my day were as tough to beat as any team in the state. We didn't beat ourselves with unaddressed weaknesses and poor fundamentals. And you don't get more fundamental than free throws.

"Well, we are going to become a great free throw shooting team. The foul line will be our friend. Free throws will become truly *free* for this team! And that means for every last one of you, not just Joe and the midget."

He points to me and I feel my ears burn, though not only because of Coach Abram's constant references to me as "the midget," as if I don't actually have a name. More than that, I wish the coach hadn't singled me out at all, no matter what he called me. Maybe it's my experience on the football team dealing with Jimmy Keenan's jealousy and how he alienated me from the rest of the team, but right now I'm just hoping to blend in. It's hard to do that when the coach points you out ahead of everyone but the team star. I can feel the seniors resenting me already. And I have to wonder what Charlie and Jamaal think about Abrams mentioning me while burying them with the rest of us freshmen.

"But beyond just free throws," Coach Abrams says, "we, unlike Mr. Wilt Chamberlain, are going to work on our weaknesses. We are going to work on them until there are none left for our opponents to exploit. Every night, we will be the most fundamentally sound team on the court.

"We will pay attention to every last detail. You will double knot the shoelaces on your sneakers, so they cannot become loose and trip you at the worst moment. If you think this is a silly detail, it's one preached by Mr. John Wooden, who has won three of the last four NCAA championships at UCLA, including two undefeated seasons. You will use the backboard for every layup. Years ago, one of my players never used the backboard and in the closing seconds his easy layup went around the rim and out, costing us the game. So you will use the backboard!

"You will also keep your hair cut as short as the Marines serving our country oversees, and not like your silly rock-and-roll idols. Exceptionally long hair can get in your eyes at the wrong time, and even moderately long hair can result in sweat dripping on your hands, causing you to lose control of the ball.

"We will not turn the ball over! We'll be patient and work the ball around until there's a high percentage shot. This isn't the NBA. There's no twenty-four-second clock. You want to play one-on-one while your teammates stand around? You can do it on the playground. Not on my team. Work the ball around!

"And no showboating! You want to look flashy for the girls? Do it on the playground. Not here. Am I understood?"

My gut clenches. Work the ball around? I have trouble in that half-court style of game. I need to be racing up and down the court in fast breaks, using my speed and minimizing my height disadvantage. And what does Coach Abrams mean about showboating? I'm sure that doesn't mean we can't do the things that made Bob Cousy famous: behind-the-back dribbles, behind-the-back passes, no-look passes, and that kind of thing. Sometimes the behind-the-back dribble is the way to get loose from a tight defender. A behind-the-back pass can be the only way to get the ball to a teammate for an easy shot. A no-look pass fakes out the defender. The Cooz is a legend around here because he used those things to help the Celtics win all those championships before he retired.

He's the player I try to emulate. If Abrams is telling me I can't try to be like Bob Cousy, that's making me play with one hand tied behind my back. Not literally, of course. But it limits what I can do on the court, it reduces the ways I can help the team. Even though I've heard that Coach Abrams doesn't pay attention to the freshmen team, this is still potentially disastrous news for me.

As if I needed something else to go wrong.

But that can't be it. Everyone loves the Cooz. So what exactly did Abrams mean?

Belatedly, I think of Jamaal and him trying to be the next Earl the Pearl. Everything about Earl the Pearl is flashy. Not just that crazy reverse dribble move, but some of the awkward-looking shots he seems to make up at the last second. He sinks them, but you wonder how he does it. He makes Bob Cousy look positively boring. If Abrams is handcuffing both Jamaal and me, Jamaal is being given an extra set of chains.

We do finish the practice with free throw shooting, presumably so we won't be like Wilt Chamberlain and miss twenty-two of them in one game, but a couple of our bigger, more clumsy guys on the freshmen team, whose coordination hasn't caught up yet with their recent growth spurt, look like they could give Wilt a run for his money.

*

After practice, I'm walking through the empty hallways with Charlie, Jamaal, and the other black guy on the freshmen team, a kid named Tim Peterson, who's already six-one and also has exceptionally long arms, but is so uncoordinated he can't play a lick. He's always tripping over his own feet and he's so reed-like thin, all elbows and knees without hardly any muscles, he's not even a good rebounder. All he can do right now is block shots, and he's no Bill Russell at that either. But like former Celtics coach Red Auerbach once said, you can't teach height, and if Tim puts it all together, he could go from pretty much useless to a big contributor. I'm sure that potential is why the coaches kept him.

I suppose it looks even more strange for me to be with three black teammates than when it's just with Charlie or with Charlie and Jamaal—Rick Cassidy gave me an odd look and shook his head when the four of us left the locker room together—but I don't care. I don't know Tim hardly at all, but Charlie is pretty much my best friend, and Jamaal seems like a fun guy to be around, what with his Southern accent and his obsession with Earl the Pearl. Turns out, last year Jamaal lived near the college where

Monroe played and saw lots of his games. He really does want to be the next Earl the Pearl.

"He averaged over forty-one points a game last year," Jamaal says of his hero in that Carolina drawl, pronouncing year like *yee-aah.* "And man, that wasn't like Wilt averaging fifty points, getting all those easy points under the basket because no one but Russell or Thurmond could match up with him. None of us can dream of being unstoppable because we that big." He pauses. "None of us, of course, except Rabbit."

We all laugh, mostly because I'm so tiny but also because we thought—I was sure—he was going to say Tim because he's the tallest of us all. Jamaal isn't just good at faking people out on the basketball court. He can do it talking, too.

"The Pearl," he continues, "is unstoppable because of his moves and 'cause ain't no one knows what he's going to do. Most times, not even himself. He just shake and bake!"

I can only wish for moves like that. I sure know what I'll be doing this summer during the long, hot days of vacation. I've got to get *a lot* better. And I will. It may not be good enough, but it won't be for lack of trying. Then what Coach Abrams said pops into my head.

"Are you concerned about what Coach said about playing flashy and showboating?" I ask.

Jamaal makes a dismissive gesture. "Nah, coaches always say that stuff. But if it helps win games…they don't say a thing."

"I don't know," Charlie says. "You heard what Joe Thurman said. Abrams try to turn guys like us white. It's why he stuck Jamaal and me on the freshman team. No offense." He glances at me and I nod. Tim does, too. The two of us know that we're where we belong.

"I guess you just have to prove he's wrong in the first couple games," I say. "He'll have to move you guys up."

Charlie gets a grim look on his face. "He better."

We fall silent until we walk past the wooden phone booth on our left.

"Hey guys," Charlie says. "You all go ahead. I gotta make a phone call." He ducks inside and sits, but doesn't bother pulling the door closed. My jaw drops as I watch him hold the black handset to his ear, slip a dime into the chrome-colored slot, and dial a number.

Anna. I could call Anna.

Charlie sees me staring, and waves me on. He mouths the words, "All set." We shared a few rides home after football practice when one of our mothers weren't available, so he's letting me know he's all set for a ride, I don't need to help him out.

But I stand there transfixed, as if the battered, dark-stained pine planks that form the booth are some sort of religious statute to be worshipped at. I knew it was here, of course. I walk by it every day. It just never occurred to me to use it.

I need to talk to Anna. Need to hear her voice. Tell her everything that's happened.

"I'm all set, man," Charlie says, holding his hand to cover the receiver. "You need a ride?"

I shake my head dumbly, but don't move until he frowns. When I realize he's looking at me as if horns have sprouted from my head, I quickly turn back to Jamaal and Tim, who are looking at me funny, too. I wonder if they're suspecting that I only want to be with them as long as Charlie is around, which isn't the case at all. Sometimes I'm like a blundering bull in a china shop. Whether it's my parents or my friends or Coach Abrams, I can't seem to do anything right. The only exception is Anna.

Anna. I've got to talk to her. Hear her voice. The delight of her laughter.

Jamaal and Tim turn their backs and walk away.

"Wait up," I say, and chase after them.

Jamaal gives me a look with a raised eyebrow as if to say, *Don't feel you got to do me any favors.*

A blundering bull. That's what I am.

"Sorry, man," I say, and I find myself talking in Jamaal's Carolina drawl. Not *man*, but *mayhan*. Shifting back to my own way of talking—I sure hope he didn't think I was mocking him!—I say, as we continue to walk, "I just hadn't really noticed the pay phone there before." And when both Jamaal and Tim look at me like I'm nuts, I try to explain. "I mean, I knew it was there, I just never thought of using it to make a call."

Jamaal laughs and shakes his head. "Yeah, that's the last thing I'd ever think to use a phone for." He and Tim laugh, but it's an awkward "us versus you" laugh. I feel my face grow hot. I'm sure they think my blundering bull stupidity isn't because I'm a fool—which I know for certain that I am—but instead is because my foolish words are trying to cover up something associated with our racial divide.

"What I mean is," I say, and stop because I don't know what to add. Finally, I blurt out, "It's a girl."

And that one word—girl!—explains everything. Their faces, tight with what I guessed was disbelief and perhaps mistrust, relax.

Girls. No explanation needed. They both smile.

But I still feel the need to explain. "I hadn't thought to call this girl from the pay phone until I saw Charlie stop."

"You don't have a phone at home?" Tim asks in surprise, and for the briefest instant I wonder if there's a racial angle there, too—*a white boy with no phone?*—and then I dismiss it, and tell myself to quit looking for racial angles everywhere. Sometimes a question is just a question.

"My parents..." I say, shrugging, not really wanting to say anything more.

And then I realize I don't have to. Jamaal and Tim nod in understanding.

Girls. Parents. Two words that explain all.

"I think I might call her when Charlie's done," I say. "The girl, I mean. So I'll see you guys tomorrow."

Jamaal laughs. "That'll be a sight to behold."

I frown. I don't get it.

"Tomorrow's Sunday," he explains. "Ain't no white faces in our church."

Bull in a china shop. Just a blundering bull.

*

I wait fifty feet away from the phone booth, shifting my weight from one foot to another, nodding at the groups of teammates that pass, at least at the ones that acknowledge me. I'm well out of hearing range of the phone so there can be no question of me listening in on Charlie's conversation. I don't want to be a snoop like my parents, or even look like one.

"You okay?" he asks when he emerges, clearly surprised to see me there.

"Yeah, I just…I just realized that I needed to make a call."

Charlie nods and heads for the front doors. My heart pounds as I take a dime from my right pants pocket. Anna's letter remains in the left one. I duck my head into the booth and close the rickety door. It smells of old wood.

Suddenly, I imagine Charlie, who has gotten to know my mom, ducking his head into our car and saying something like, "Rabbit will just be another minute or two, Mrs. Labelle. He's just making a phone call."

A bolt of electric fear shoots through me. I'm not supposed to call Anna for the next two weeks. Sure, this isn't our house phone, which is what my father certainly intended to prohibit. There was no mention of pay phones at school.

If he had launched the warheads and tried to break up Anna and me, I'd drop my dime into the slot in a heartbeat. I wouldn't care. I'd take

-94-

advantage of the loophole in a rule set down by a hideous dictator I had every intention of defying.

But he didn't launch the warheads.

Because Mom stood up for me. Put everything she had on the line. *Everything.*

I slide the phone booth door open and poke my head out.

"Charlie!" I yell, and he turns around. "Don't say anything to my mom."

He nods and for a second turns to go, running his hand through his close-cropped hair. But then he comes hustling back, frowning. "You in trouble?"

"I'm…it's complicated," I say, shaking my head. "I'm fine, really."

"You don't look fine," he says, his eyes narrowed. "What's up?"

"It's…it's a girl," I say. "I'm not really supposed to—"

"Anna? Anna Levesque?" he asks, the tension in his face and body loosening as I nod.

I'm surprised. "How did you know?"

"I ain't blind. I seen you two together in the hallway." He grins. "Two lovebirds."

My face grows hot and I shrug. "Yeah, I guess."

"So you okay? I can leave you alone to call your sweet thang?"

Your sweet thang. I like the sound of that. Anna, my sweet *thang.* Yes, she is.

"Yeah, I'm fine. Just don't say anything because I'm kind of…well, I'm grounded as far as using the phone."

"*You?* Grounded?" he asks, incredulous. "What for? Jaywalking? You're an angel."

"It's complicated."

Charlie nods. "Okay, man. Long as you're sure you're okay."

I nod. "Yeah," I say, and Charlie leaves.

I stare at the phone. Anna's number races across my mind. I want to talk to her so bad it hurts. I *should* be able to talk to her. The two-week ban is so unfair.

Except…

What if Mom finds out? What if I call and Anna's mother picks up? She probably will. She's always picked up the phone first, then handed it to Anna. And if Anna's mother answers, do I just hang up in a panic? Do I ask for Anna and risk that her mother calls mine at some point and spills the beans?

Or, God forbid, calls my *father*?

My mom's words flash back to me. *I'm counting on you to live up to your promise.*

And I realize I can't call Anna, even though I want to so bad it hurts. Hurts deep in my gut. Hurts all the way into the center of my heart.

Because I *love* her and it's killing me not to hear her voice.

But I can't call.

Not just because I might get caught. But also because I can't break the promise my mother is counting on me to keep.

I can't betray my mom's sacrifice.

"Oh, Anna," I say out loud. I shove the dime back into my pocket and head for the front doors, the echoing of my footfalls sounding as lonely as I feel.

*

I climb into Mom's car, still thinking about how great it would have been to hear Anna's voice. To tell her about everything that has happened. Yesterday afternoon when I last talked to her feels like another century.

"How did it go?" Mom asks. The heater is blasting away so it feels almost sweltering hot after coming in from the cold outside. I also notice there's no sandwich waiting for me, wrapped in wax paper. No smell of chicken salad or the crunch of the celery she chops into it. No fried egg, the yolk broken so it doesn't drip all over my clothes. No sticky-sweet fluffernutter. Even though I know we'll be eating lunch today alone and the sandwich after practice is only for weeknights when we have to wait to eat dinner until my father gets home, my mouth has started watering in anticipation anyway. Pavlov's dog and all that. I guess my salivary glands automatically associate getting in the car after practice with eating. They aren't smart enough to know it's the middle of the day on a Saturday instead of a weekday evening.

"Good, I guess," I say. And I tell her how well things went with the free throw shooting at the end of practice, but also about how Coach Abrams doesn't want any showboating and I'm concerned he might mean playing like Bob Cousy.

"Who's Bob Cousy?"

I love my mom, today more than ever because of her sacrifice, but she sure doesn't know sports. I'm not sure if she's ever watched a basketball game that I haven't played in even though the Celtics have won eight out of the last nine NBA championships and nine of the last eleven.

"He was one of the greatest guards ever," I say. "He could score himself, but what he was really good at is setting up his teammates, sometimes with fancy passes and moves. He's the guy I try to play like."

"Oh," she says. "So that's bad."

"Ay-uh," I say, barely realizing I've lapsed into a saying I thought I'd left behind up in northern Maine.

"Well, I'm sure you'll win the coach over," she says brightly. "You always do."

That's Mom. When it comes to sports, she's convinced I could score on Bill Russell. She drives in silence for a while, although I can see that something is bothering her. Her face has clouded over and her two gloved hands on the steering wheel at the two o'clock and ten o'clock positions alternately squeeze and release every second or so. She takes a deep breath as if she's about to say something, and then stops. I might be bad in a poker game because I'm not good at covering up my emotions, but she'd be *horrible*.

"Mom, just say it."

She looks at me with alarm. "How did you know I—" She looks back to the road, then glances quickly back at me. "That's the second time today you've done that." She squeezes the steering wheel really hard. I'm sure if her gloves weren't on, I could see her knuckles turn white. "Do you have ESP or something?"

"What's ESP?"

"Extra, um…extrasensory perception. It's what they call it when people can read minds. Can you read minds?"

I laugh. "No."

"Then how did you do that? How did you know I needed to tell you something, but didn't know how to say it?"

"Because it was written all over your face."

"Really?"

"And you kept breathing deep and squeezing and releasing the steering wheel."

She relaxes her death grip on the steering wheel. "Huh."

I grin. "Mom, I can read you like a book."

"Okay, smarty-pants," she says, a bit more relaxed now, but not sharing my grin. "What am I thinking now?"

"You're afraid that I'm a freak and maybe I'm just covering up that I can read your mind anytime I want."

Her jaw drops. "How did you…I mean, I didn't think the word 'freak'—I'd never think that about you—but how on earth—"

"Mom, it's the only thing you could have possibly been thinking right then. Think about it!"

"I guess," she says with a shrug. She glances at me, then back at the road, then back at me, and back at the road once again. "Are you sure you can't read my mind?"

"I'm sure."

She bites her lower lip. "Okay, what am I thinking now?"

"That I'm a great kid and you're going to make me a banana split for lunch."

We both burst out laughing, and she reaches out and rumples my still-wet hair, at least as much as you can rumple a crew cut.

"Okay, wise guy," she says. Any hint of amusement leaves her face. "One more. What is it that I was thinking about before we got talking about you and ESP? What was the thing you somehow figured I need to talk to you about? Make it easy for me and just tell me."

I suddenly get the terrifying thought that my parents are going to get a divorce. That my father has decided to call my mom's bluff. Let her leave and take me away with her. After all, I'm only a pain in the neck. That way, he can spend all day at work and never have to come home at all.

But I can't even speak those words. Saying them out loud might somehow make that awful possibility come true. And if it does, it'll all be because of me.

Because I convinced Mom to stand up for me, and now she has to pay for it.

We both have to pay for it.

Even though there are times when I hate my father, and I even hoped a few months ago he would leave us and come here to Lynn and leave us back up in Maine with all my friends there, now I don't even want to think about our family getting split up. Even as messed up as it is, I want us to stay together.

And I sure don't want to be the reason we break apart.

But I can't say it.

"I don't know," I say instead.

Mom frowns. "I'm not sure I believe you. There's something going on inside that head of yours."

I swallow hard. Please, please, please. Let whatever she's going to say not involve the D word. My voice cracks as I say, "What do you need to tell me?"

She takes a deep breath, glances at me for a split second, and then tightens her grip on the steering wheel so it looks as if she might break it in half.

"That thing you figured out this morning," she says. "That I had to threaten your father that I would leave him." She takes another deep breath, her face suddenly pale. "I've never done that before and I don't ever plan to do it again.

"It was awful. You should have seen his face. He was crushed to hear those words out of my mouth. I might as well have told him I didn't love him anymore. He was devastated. It was only later that he got angry.

"These days, women have the right to vote, unlike a hundred years ago. And we're trying to get laws passed so we get paid as much as men do for the same work. But a lot of people say that God put the man as the head of the family, and the wife should submit to his authority. I always have up until now. Even when I didn't want to move here, I listened to him."

She turns the car onto our street, goes up the incline to our house, the sixth on the left, and pulls into the driveway. She shuts the car off, but we stay seated there.

"When I told him I'd leave him, I think it made him feel less of a man," she says. "He wasn't the person making all the important decisions. When he talked to you, he even said something about who was wearing the pants in the family."

Mom takes yet another deep breath.

"When I threatened to leave him, it was a blow to his…what they call the male ego. Do you know what that is?"

I think I might, but I'm not sure, so I shake my head.

"It's his belief in himself. His…oh, I don't know." She shakes her head, visibly frustrated. "What I'm trying to say is…" She looks me hard in the eyes. "You can't let him know that you know."

I finally see what she's been trying to get at.

"It's bad enough that I threatened him," Mom says. "I did the right thing. I'm almost certain of it. He's taken it very badly, but as long as he and I are the only ones who know about it, I think I can control the damage." She smiles at me wanly. "I can put Humpty Dumpty back together again, as you would say. There may be cracks for a while, but your father and I will get things straightened out. It may take time, but we'll be okay. I'm sure of it."

I nod, my heart in my throat.

"But if he knows that you know," Mom says, "that will make things much, much worse. His male ego could be shattered and then it really will be like Humpty Dumpty. We'll never put it back together again.

"So your father can't ever know that you figured this out. He will never, ever forgive me if that happens." Tears pool in her eyes. "Rabbit, promise me that you won't let this slip. Not now, not ever. To him, or to anyone."

"I promise, Mom," I say with a hoarse croak.

"I hate to put you in this position," she says. "I wish you'd never figured it out, or that I'd been smart enough to deny it when you asked. But that's the position we're in, you and me. We're a team. I'm counting on you."

I swallow hard and fall into my mom's embrace.

We're a team.

CHAPTER 11

On Monday morning, my heart leaps just a bit when I see Anna fifty feet down the hallway, her textbooks pinned against her chest, walking toward where I'm waiting at her locker. Her bluish-gray woolen coat is unbuttoned. Beneath it, she's wearing a pretty, peach-colored dress with white trim along the neck and hem. I've been here for a couple minutes thanks to my new teammate, my mom, agreeing to drop me off early so Anna and I would have a little more time to talk before homeroom. Anna is earlier than usual, too, so I wonder if she had the same idea and a similarly cooperative mother.

"So what happened with your parents?" she asks breathlessly. "I've been so worried. This was the longest weekend of my life. And did you make the team?"

"I made the team," I say. "As for my parents, there's good news and bad news. Mostly, I dodged a bullet. My father was going to force me to break up with you, and if I didn't, he'd make me quit the basketball team."

Her eyes widen. "You're kidding."

I shake my head grimly. "He was ready to go to war, and that's a war I would have fought. It would have gotten really ugly. Probably one of those wars that no one wins and everyone loses." I mention my comparison to Humpty Dumpty. "But my mom stood up for me. She—" I know I can't say exactly what my mom did. I've been sworn to secrecy and that's a vow I can't break. If I do, I could endanger my parents' marriage. But I want to do justice to what my mother did for me. "She somehow convinced my father to back down. She pushed really hard. He wasn't happy about it, but she finally won."

I tell Anna about how the rest of the two-week phone ban stands, but that when it's over I'll be able to take the phone in another room and we can have some privacy.

"Wow, that's great!" Anna says, but then she frowns. "You said there was bad news. Was that just about not being able to talk on the phone for the two weeks?"

I shake my head. I feel a little uncomfortable saying what comes next but plow ahead with it anyway.

"My father says we're too young to be going on actual dates," I say, cringing at having to say the words. "And on this point, I think my mom mostly agrees with him. It's like I'm still just a little kid. So for now, we need to stick to school and school events. And the phone."

"That's not so bad," Anna says. "I don't think my parents would let me go out on a date either."

"Really?"

"I've got an older brother and he's almost eighteen. He's a senior here. He can pretty much get away with murder, I think because he's a boy. My parents, especially my father, treat me different. I heard him say one time to his brother, my Uncle Johnny, that the first boy who comes to our house to pick me up for a date is going to get met by a shotgun. 'Meet my good friend, Mr. Remington,' he said, and they both laughed and called me a heartbreaker."

I blink, my brain going into overload trying to process everything Anna just said. I gulp. "A shotgun?"

Anna pokes at my arm in a you're-being-silly gesture. "He doesn't really have one. I mean, he does have a pistol in case someone breaks into the house or tries to hurt us. Two of them, actually. And he is tough. He's a former Marine. He even has a *Semper Fi* tattoo on his arm." Seeing the blank look on my face, she explains. "*Semper Fi* is the Marine motto. Always loyal. It just means he's really into 'God and Country' and that sort of thing. The Vietnam War protestors drive him absolutely crazy. He calls them cowards and says they should 'love it or leave it.'" She shakes her head. "But that's not the point. 'Meet Mr. Remington' is just the kind of thing fathers say about their daughters because they want to be protective. It's just a figure of speech. If you had a sister, I'm sure you'd have heard it, too, about her."

I try to imagine having a sister and my father saying something like that, and maybe that if I had a sister, he'd be hard on her instead of me. But my imagination fails me on this one. I can't see any of it. So I pick at one scab I've tried not to think about.

"So you haven't ever been out on an actual date?" I ask. "Not with…"

Anna blushes furiously. I don't have to say the name Jimmy Keenan. She knows who I mean. The two of them started going out just after the school year started and she seemed to look at him pretty dreamy-eyed when he was singing at the Halloween dance, just about a half hour before he lured me outside and, with two of his friends holding me down, attacked me with a baseball bat. After he got thrown out of school, her eyes were bloodshot and puffy for a few days, but since then neither one of us has said his name.

"No, I never went on a date with him," she says firmly. "Unless you count him taking me to the Halloween dance. That was it. We never really…it was just one of those things. We'd see each other at school and he'd call me a few times. I liked him and all that, or at least I thought I did, but I guess I didn't really know him. That's what upset me more than anything. I couldn't believe that he was really like that, that he had fooled me so badly. I'd thought he was a nice, charming guy. But underneath it all, he wasn't nice. He was…well…evil."

These are the words I wanted to hear and I should just leave them alone, but instinctively I ask, "Really?"

"Rabbit, I don't lie. Really and truly. It wasn't even what my mom calls puppy love."

"My mom says that, too," I say smiling. "I think there's a special language all moms have. It starts with 'clean your room,' and goes to 'because I'm your mother, that's why,' and also includes 'puppy love.'"

Anna smiles, but there's a tinge of sadness to it. "Don't ever think of Jimmy and me again. It was nothing." She brightens. "I never wrote him a letter, and he never wrote one to me."

And even though I know that Anna's letter only happened because of my father giving me the "phone-grounding," her words still make me smile.

"I loved your letter!" she says, her smile now fully radiant. "I wanted to say something about it right away, but I had to find out about your parents and the team first. I just had to know. But your letter was wonderful! I loved it!"

I'm sure that she's exaggerating about how good mine was, but I'll take it anyway. And there's no exaggeration in my response. "Yours was, too!" I want to add how I especially loved how she ended it: *Your girlfriend, Anna.* I'm even tempted to say how many times I reread those three magical words, and how I kept her letter in my pants pocket all weekend and it's in there now, too. How each time my hand brushed that pocket, I felt a glowing warmth all in my chest.

And how I am head over heels in love with her.

In love!

But I don't have the guts to say all that. If I did, she might look at me and say, "That's nice," but deep down inside think about what a sappy fool I am. Of course she'd think that. *I* think I'm a sappy fool. Why shouldn't Anna?

No, I don't have anything close to those guts.

But at least I have a letter for her tonight. And I was sure—I may be a dumb hick sometimes, but I'm not a total idiot—to match her "your girlfriend" ending with the comparable one of my own. It felt great to write, "Your boyfriend, Rabbit." Not quite as great as reading her ending, but pretty close.

I pull the letter out of the top book I'm holding and hand it to her. "This is for tonight."

She takes it with a look of pure delight. "Thanks!" But then a frown appears on her brow and she puts a hand to her mouth. She shakes her head in obvious dismay. "I didn't write you one this weekend."

The bottom falls out of my stomach. I force a smile to my face that must be the weakest one ever. "That's okay."

Anna bursts out laughing. "I didn't write you *one* this weekend. I wrote you *two*. One for each day."

My jaw drops and I start laughing, too. "You got me. You got me good."

"I should have said the second part faster, that I'd written *two* letters," she says. "You looked like you were going to cry."

"I wasn't going to cry," I say, maybe a little too defensively because, although that part is true—I'm not such a baby that I was actually going to cry—I had been so disappointed it felt as though I'd gotten punched in the stomach. "I just…"

"Okay, okay, maybe you weren't going to cry," Anna says. "You were just going to wet your pants."

We both laugh and then, as the bell rings, make a mad dash for homeroom.

*

Once again, a letter from Anna burns in my pocket all day, waiting to be read. Or more accurately, *two* letters! She is amazing.

L-O-V-E!

But what everyone else is talking about is the world's first heart transplant. It happened yesterday in South Africa when a doctor nobody ever heard of, Dr. Christiaan Barnard, took a heart from a young woman who'd been fatally injured in a car accident and put it into a man who was going to die without it.

Miss Minter assigns us all an essay in which we're to discuss the ethical and/or religious implications of heart transplants. We can either cover them all or just one in greater detail, but it needs to be at least four pages.

"No padding!" she says, reminding those of us in the class who use ridiculously wide margins on both sides and truckloads of adjectives and adverbs to turn two pages of content into the required four. I've used that trick a couple of times, but I don't think I'll need to this time. I haven't really thought about the topic that much—my mind has been elsewhere—but this paper should write itself.

That task becomes even easier when stuffy, white-haired Mrs. McPherson in History spends the entire period talking about the transplant, saying that history was made this weekend and we can get back to regular history topics tomorrow.

On the way from History to Math, Jeff Goodwin puts his humorous two cents in.

"I'd like it if that doctor could transplant a heart in Mr. Belanger," Jeff quips, referring to the bald, grim-faced assistant principal who is in charge of all disciplinary matters and sometimes seems to like his job a little too much. Those of us who are walking together—Cindy Murphy, Paul DiSimone, Anna, and me—give Jeff a mild appreciative chuckle that should tell him to quit while he's ahead. But lately, that hasn't been Jeff's style, and I fear he's about to ruin his modest punch line by explaining it, but fortunately he just tosses his net a little wider for another catch. "And if we could get a two-for-one special, I'd nominate Miss Sipowicz."

This sparks a string of nominations, including Anna's re-nomination of Mr. Belanger, prompting Jeff to ask me for mine.

"My father," I say.

Anna looks at me knowingly, while Jeff cries foul. "Parents don't count!"

But of course, they do.

*

On the ride home from practice, after answering the usual questions about school and basketball practice, I ask my mom about using pay phones. The cold weather has continued, but she's been running the heater while waiting for me so it's nice and "toasty" as she likes to say. I'm eating the egg salad sandwich she brought me, which tastes so good I don't mind how it smells up the car. It'd be different if Charlie or any of the other members of the basketball team were riding with us, or heaven forbid, Anna. Then, I'd be embarrassed at the strong smell, but it's just the two of us, so like they say, no harm, no foul.

"You know how Dad says I can't use the phone for another ten days?" I ask.

"Is it ten more? Is that it?"

"Definitely ten," I say with a little bitterness in my voice. "I'm counting."

She glances at me and nods. "I'm sure you are."

"Well, is that only from the house phone or any phone?"

"What do you mean?"

"What if, like, I called Anna from a pay phone?"

Mom's eyes widen. "Don't you dare. Not until the two weeks—the ten days—are up. Please, Rabbit. Don't even think about it."

"Even if there's no chance Dad finds out?"

"Rabbit!" she snaps. "I'm counting on you!"

"Okay."

"Don't even think about it," she says, her face ashen.

"Okay."

"Promise!"

"I promise."

"I'm counting on you."

Again, I say, "I promise."

Mom's breathing is ragged and she grips and ungrips the steering wheel fiercely. Neither of us says anything for a while. Finally, as we go past Fauci's Pizza on the left, I speak up.

"How about after the ten days are up? The five-minute limit at home each night is just because the message units on the phone bill get expensive, right? So calling from a pay phone should be okay, right?"

Mom groans. "Where are you planning on calling her from?"

"Anywhere," I say, but realize that isn't enough. I need to make her understand. "Like on Saturday after practice. I wanted to call Anna from one of the pay phones inside the school. She had to go all weekend not knowing whether Dad was really going to try to break us up. Not knowing whether I made the basketball team." And also not knowing about how much I liked her letter and not being able to tell me how much she liked mine. But I'm not saying anything about that. "I walked right past the pay phone even though I wanted to call her so bad."

"What if your father found out? Rabbit, I stuck my neck out for you. I stuck it all the way out. If you go and pull a stunt like that, you're going to get my neck chopped off. What were you thinking?"

"I thought of you," I say softly. "That's the only reason I didn't call Anna."

"What?"

"I thought of you. If you hadn't stuck up for me, I'd have called Anna and if Dad ever found out, he could do whatever he wanted. But I thought of you, and no matter how much I wanted to call her, I couldn't do it. Because you stuck up for me."

"Thank you!" Mom exhales loudly. "But please, please, please, for at least the next ten days, don't even think about it. We can talk about it after then. I don't know." She falls silent for a few seconds, then continues. "I suppose it would be all right, but your father might think you were being sneaky. Doing it behind our backs, you know? Trying to hide something. Finding a way around his rules. You know how he can be these days." She shakes her head. "Let's cross that bridge when we get to it, okay? Wait ten days, then we'll talk."

"Okay."

"You're giving me heart failure."

"Don't worry, Mom. I'll wait ten days. I promise. You can count on me."

She shakes her head, and her eyes look haunted. "Good Lord, what have I done?"

A few seconds pass before I say something. "Mom, you did the right thing." I'm not sure if what I'm going to say next will come out right. It might make me sound like a smart aleck and make her mad. But I say it anyway. "I know I'm sounding like a parent right now, but some day you'll look back on this and know you held this family together. We were at the breaking point, and you saved us. You'll feel proud of what you did. And I'll feel the same way. Someday, I'll bet even Dad will look back and thank you."

She gives me yet another shake of the head and rolls her eyes. "Listen to you."

"I mean it."

She takes a deep breath and turns onto our street. "How serious is this thing between you and Anna? You're too young to be getting serious with a girl."

I give a shrug of my shoulders and raise my eyebrows. This is one answer she really doesn't want to know.

CHAPTER 12

I live up to my promise with Mom. I don't cause a single problem. I stay away from pay phones, and at the table each night for dinner and in the morning for breakfast, I act respectful toward my father and, of course, to her, and I don't let on that I know why he backed down. Even though a part of me is angry—*really* angry—with him for how he was going to put the screws to me, I keep my big mouth shut. I don't challenge that "male ego" of his that Mom talked about. But I can't imagine that if I have kids I'll turn into a jerk just to show that I'm the boss, just because I have a male ego.

I suppose our time eating at the table has become a charade. We pretend that nothing is the matter even though there are brick walls between my father and mother and between him and me where before there were none. I see the frosty looks he gives Mom and have to bite my tongue to keep from saying, "Stop it! You were going to ruin everything! She saved this family!"

But the icy coldness seems to thaw just a little more each day, so maybe Mom is right and it'll all work out. I wonder, though, if that's just in my head. Maybe I'm just seeing what I want to see, kind of like that astronomer Percival Lowell we read about in science class a year ago back up in Maine. He looked into his telescope and was so sure he saw canals on Mars, he even mapped them out. He saw a whole network of canals, presumably built by Martians to get water from the polar icecaps to the dry, arid land nearer the equator. He saw it all because he *wanted* to see it, wanted there to be life on that planet.

But there were no canals. No water.

Years later, more powerful telescopes showed that, and according to Mr. Perrault, my old science teacher, the unmanned spacecraft that flew by Mars two years ago proved it for sure. It was all an optical illusion, a figment of Lowell's imagination.

Just like the slight thawing out of the deep freeze between my parents might be nothing more than a figment of my imagination. I want things to get better between them. I hate seeing my father's bitterness directed at my mom because I know it's *my* fault.

Well, it's really *his* fault. No one—to use one of Mom's favorite phrases when I make excuses for doing the wrong thing—put a gun to my father's head and forced him to act like he did, and act like he's doing now.

But still, it's only happening because Mom stood up for me. So I feel bad for her. I feel guilty. If I were the parent and he were the kid, I'd grab him by the shoulders, give him a little shake, and say, "Grow up!"

Instead, I bite my tongue, and let him do the talking. Which, since he's freezing her out, means mostly talking to me.

"How's the team look?" he says to me night after night as we eat dinner, which tonight is pot roast, potatoes and gravy, and peas. He asks the question because he can't think of much else for us to talk about, and if no one is talking, if I don't come up with something to say to Mom that I haven't already said on our drive home from school, then the only sound is the clinking of the silverware on the plates and the wall clock behind me.

Tick…tick…tick….

So I do my best to answer, but it's hard to say. I've never seen any other team down here play, so I don't know if we're amazing and are going to go undefeated, or if we'll struggle to win a single game. Compared to the teams I played on up in Maine, we're amazing. If Joe Thurman played up there, he'd be like Wilt Chamberlain and score a hundred points in a single game or average fifty points over the whole season.

"They're so tall and can jump so well," I say, which is close to what I said last night, but not a total repetition. "Almost everyone has a pretty good shot. It's like a different game down here."

Just like last night, my father once again says, "I'm sure you'll do great. You always do," adding a chuckle either for variety or because he's in a somewhat better mood.

But that better mood doesn't last long. "Don't forget my first game is on Friday," I remind him. "And then the next Tuesday and Friday. Three games before Christmas."

He looks stricken. Instinctively, he turns to Mom for support, then remembers he's in a Cold War with her and his face hardens into a glare as if she's been the one to give him the bad news. "Remind me again what time the games are."

"Freshmen games at four, JV at five-thirty, and varsity at seven. Almost always on Tuesdays and Fridays." It's all I can do to keep from rolling my eyes. He knows all this, or at least he ought to. I gave him and Mom all the details even before I made the team, and there's been a schedule posted on the refrigerator door ever since. But I don't roll my eyes or show even a hint of annoyance because I'm on my best behavior.

I practically deserve nomination for sainthood.

"Any chance you'll be playing for the varsity this year?" he asks.

My jaw drops, and I'm really, really tempted to throw my sainthood out the window.

"*Varsity?*" I ask. "Haven't you listened to what I've been telling you?" I realize, perhaps too late, that I've raised my voice in frustration, so I quickly dial it back. "Our starting varsity lineup includes a guy who's six feet, five inches tall at center. Our forwards are six-three and six-two. Our guards are just a shade under six feet tall and one of them is Joe Thurman, who is an amazing player. They all can jump and they all can shoot.

"I'm barely five feet tall. I'm not even *starting* for the freshmen team. I have no chance at all of playing on the varsity this year. Zero. There isn't a single freshman who has a *prayer* of playing on the varsity except for Charlie, and Coach Abrams hates him." I see my father about to interrupt on that point, but I keep plowing ahead so I can make my point without getting sidetracked. "And I won't play on JVs this year either. Last year's leading scorer and rebounder on the freshmen team, Rick Cassidy, got to play two games on JVs all year. And for all I know, he might have sat on the bench for most of those two.

"So if you're going to see me play this year, you should plan on watching the freshmen team." And to underline the point without being a jerk about it, I add in an even tone, "At four o'clock."

"Well," my father says. "We'll have to see how things develop. I have faith in you, Rabbit. I've seen you play, and I believe you'll be on the JVs in no time. I'm sure I'll be able to make a 5:30 JV game or two." Perhaps belatedly remembering his promise after the big Thanksgiving Day football game to make it a priority to see more of my games and put family first ahead of his job, he adds, "Well, more than that, of course. But let's shoot for some JV games, maybe after the holidays when you've had a chance to establish yourself."

He glares at Mom for a split second as if defying her to say something, almost begging her to even try to "wear the pants in the family." Then he looks back at me and softens his gaze. "I'm sure you'll do it."

I nod and swallow hard. "Sure." I want to say more, a lot more. Mostly that my father was obviously just one big phony when he made that promise to see more of my games. A phony or maybe even a liar, although I know that last part probably isn't fair.

But I'm on my best behavior. Sainthood and all that crap. Keep my big mouth shut. Don't do anything that might be interpreted as even the slightest challenge to his authority.

But I'm not cut out for sainthood. I *want* to run my mouth off and let him know just what I think.

I look to my mom. She gives me a warm smile of support that seems to say, *I know, I know.*

I take a bite of my pot roast. It doesn't taste half as good as a few minutes before.

Tick…tick…tick….
Tick…tick…tick….
Tick…tick…tick….

*

The remaining ten days of my phone-grounding pass. Anna and I can actually talk again outside of school. It feels like a miracle, as if Alexander Graham Bell just invented the telephone and we're the first two to try it. That first night, I duck into my father's home office after dinner using the new long phone cord, and close the door behind me. I could walk past the mostly empty bookshelves and get the chair from behind my father's desk over by the window and carry it over here to the door, but I don't bother. I sit on the floor, my back against the wall, and with a smile on my face and a quickening pulse, I dial Anna's number.

It's still the same old black rotary phone, just with a longer cord. My father didn't spring for one of the new touch tone types that have keypads to tap instead of putting your finger in one of the ten circular holes cut in the clear plastic wheel, rotating it around clockwise until it hits the metal bar, but I don't care. I'd use a tin can with a string stretched out to Anna's house where she had a similar tin can, if I had to.

"Can you believe it?" I ask. "I thought those two weeks would never end." I don't whisper, but I also don't speak loudly. My parents are still out there in the front room—I couldn't exactly kick them out of the house—and even though they've promised not to snoop anymore, at least not until I give them reason to, that doesn't stop them from hearing me through the rather thin walls if I'm being ridiculously loud.

"It's good to hear your voice, Rabbit," Anna says. "Over the phone, I mean."

"Yeah, you, too."

"So who's going to go first?" she asks.

We've agreed that we're only going to write letters once a week now that we can talk on the phone. We like the letters, but trying to come up with something new to write every day gets harder and harder. In fact, I may have gone too far last night in one of my attempts to say something different in the last of my daily letters to her. I hope she thinks it's funny. She has a great sense of humor, and I love to hear the sound of her laughter. But I suppose she could be offended. I'll find out soon enough. We swapped letters this morning and agreed—just this one time—to read those letters aloud to each other over the phone.

"Ladies before gentlemen," I say, then hold my breath.

A tearing sound comes over the phone as Anna rips open the envelope.

"What? Is this a trick?" she asks, clearly surprised. "There are three envelopes inside the one I just opened."

"Brilliant deduction, my dear Watson," I say. "And what's written on those envelopes?"

"There's a number on each of them. Numbers one, two, and three."

"Precisely, my dear Watson. Open the first one."

"Rabbit, I didn't do anything this fancy for you!"

"You came up with the letter idea first. And after our first weekend, you wrote me two letters and I only wrote you one. So maybe it's time for me to top you, just once."

"Yeah, but—"

"No buts. My turn this time."

"Okay," she says in a reluctant tone, but I can hear the smile in her voice. She rips open the letter and begins to read aloud.

Dear Anna,

The next two envelopes hold silly rhymes. One of them is really silly! I hope you don't think they're stupid, but I wanted to do something different. I hope you like them.

Your boyfriend,
Rabbit

"Okay, open number two," I say.

Anna giggles in anticipation, and opens the next one.

There once was a girl named Anna.
Who learned to play the "pianah."
She gave it up for the flute.
Then with one magical toot,
Turned her nose into a big green banana.

Anna howls with laughter, barely getting the last words out. "Banana! You think my nose is"—more uncontrolled laughter—"a big green banana?"

We both laugh so long and hard that my side begins to hurt. I guess she wasn't offended.

"There's not that much that rhymes with Anna," I manage to say through the merriment.

"I guess not," she says, still choking with laughter. "I mean…pianah? Really?"

And we laugh some more.

Finally, she asks seriously, "Do you think I have a big nose?"

"No, you have a beautiful nose! I just couldn't think of anything else that rhymed. And it just…it struck my funny bone and I thought…I thought you might like it in its own special, crazy way."

"I love it! *One magical toot!*" she says, and explodes again into laughter. "Rabbit, you are too much!"

I beam. I almost wonder if I should have quit while I was ahead, but I can't imagine Anna won't like her other poem.

"The next one is serious," I say. "If you can stop laughing, open the third envelope."

"Okay," she says, and tears it open.

I know this isn't Shakespeare,
Or Edgar Allen Poe.
But it's my way of saying,
You're special head to toe.

"Oh, Rabbit!" she says, breaking into tears. "You are amazing!"

My heart floods with an almost giddy happiness, with as pure a joy as I think I've ever known. *You are amazing!* Anna said those words about *me*.

In the days that follow, it feels as though she's painted a permanent smile on my heart, if not on my face. I'm walking on clouds. But soon, I'll need every bit of that joy in reserve to help me keep going.

*

In our first game, Charlie proves how utterly ridiculous it is that he's on the freshmen team instead of on the JVs, and maybe even the varsity. Jamaal, too, but especially Charlie. He's a man amongst boys. He and I aren't on the court much together—he's a starter, of course, while I'm not on the court much at all—but when we are, I just get the ball to Charlie. Even our dumbest players figure out that's the game plan. Pass the ball to him and get out of his way. He's unstoppable, whether it's driving to the net, hitting jump shots and free throws, or when he gets double- and triple-teamed, dishing the ball off to teammates who stop being spectators of the Charlie Watkins Show long enough to sink an uncontested layup or an easy shot themselves.

And when it isn't him doing it all by himself, he and Jamaal combine to be totally unstoppable. Jamaal makes his dazzling moves and fakes to leave his defender in the dust, and then either puts in a layup or, if another defender comes over, dishes off to the open man. And if our guy has failed to move to the basket—it's easy to get caught just watching Jamaal as if you're just a spectator—then Jamaal gets it to Charlie, who finishes it off.

"What'd I tell you?" Charlie says to me when he comes to the bench with 32 of our 63 points. There's still more than a quarter left to play, but we're ahead 63-41 so most of our starters have come out, either for a breather if Salem High closes the gap and they need to return or, far more likely, for good. I'm hoping for one more substitution so I can get back into the game.

"Abrams won't be able to ignore what you just did," I say.

"He will if he wants to." Charlie wipes the sweat dripping off his face with a dry, white towel. "And he wants to. He be like Stevie Wonder."

I can't disagree, but I need to say something to prop up my friend.

"Just keep knocking at the door," I say. "He'll have to let you in."

"Gonna have to break the damned thing down." Charlie looks wistfully at the scoreboard. "Bust it into bits. Tell the man it's a message from Harlem."

"Do it, man," I say. "Till it's nothing but splinters."

We pump fists and fall silent. I try to imagine what it's like to be judged based on the color of my skin—judged unfairly—and can't begin to put myself in his shoes. The closest I can come is how Coach Abrams refers to me as "the midget" instead of by name, and in both football and basket-ball, I had to prove myself a lot more than bigger players.

But that's fair. In football, almost any guy who's six feet tall and two hundred pounds will be better than one who's five nothin', hundred nothin' like me. I only survived because of my speed and moves. Same thing in basketball. A guy who is six feet, five inches tall, like Cedric Coleman on the varsity, will be able to contribute at least some rebounds unless he's so uncoordinated he trips over his own feet.

It makes sense to pre-judge me as inferior to bigger players until I prove myself because us little guys *are* on the whole inferior. So it's fair. But there's nothing fair about relegating Charlie to the freshmen team because he's black and he *plays black.*

What did Joe Thurman say about Coach Abrams? "He messes with your head. Tries to turn you white."

I can't imagine Abrams turning Charlie white. He may have forced him to shave his Afro, but only a fool would handcuff Charlie's abilities and make him and the rest of the team pass the ball fifteen times before taking a shot.

Same thing with Jamaal. His whole game is those flashy moves. His outside shot isn't very good—as soon as he improves there, he'll be unstoppable just like Charlie—but he fakes out every defender who tries to guard him. Take away those moves and he's nothing.

But I underestimate how much of a fool Abrams is. He doesn't show it right away, but when he does, he shows it for everyone to see.

CHAPTER 13

The following evening, I rush down the right aisle of the school auditorium toward the front row, my thick winter jacket folded over one arm, moving as fast as I can without actually breaking into a run. There are left and right aisles with rows of twenty seats in the middle and ten off to each side, and probably thirty or so rows, to total more than a thousand seats, but I want the best seat in the house.

Front row, center. So I can watch Anna and the rest of the band perform their Christmas concert. It'll actually be their second of four performances—they play the two Fridays and Saturdays before the holiday—but I missed last night's because of my game, and I'll miss next Friday's, too. So I'm not going to miss a minute of this one or next Saturday's, and I want to see them both as up close as possible.

It's half an hour before the performance starts, the doors have just opened, and most of my competition for the choice seats are who I assume are parents of the band members. I'm not wearing sneakers—I'm wearing black dress shoes to go with a blue shirt underneath a black sweater and matching pants—but if I can't beat a bunch of parents to the front, then my nickname needs to change from "Rabbit" to "Turtle."

I settle into the best seat in the house, the bull's-eye middle of the front row, and wait with eager anticipation as bustling parents sit down beside me on both sides. The heavyset woman on my right has put on *way* too much perfume—it feels like a cloud of it surrounds us—but even if it were *Parfume du Skunk* (and it's not *that* bad), I wouldn't move.

Anna told me over the phone earlier today that last night's performance went well, but she didn't want to give me the details.

"It'll be the same concert tonight," she said. "I don't want to ruin any surprises. Not that there are any actual surprises, of course. Just come tonight and see for yourself. You can tell me after the show what you think."

"Okay," I agreed.

"That is, as long as you like it," she said. "If we're terrible, don't say a word!"

We both laughed, but I could tell from the confidence in her laughter that she wasn't really worried about me not liking it. It was a lot like the time back when I first met her and I asked the dopiest of questions.

"Are you good?" I asked after she told me she played in the band. We were sitting in adjacent seats waiting for class to start.

"No, I'm horrible," she said, and laughed with an easy amusement you don't have if you really are bad, or close to it. So I'm guessing she's pretty good. Pretty soon, I find out just how good.

Five minutes after the starting time on the ticket, the band files into the auditorium, led by its conductor, the head of the music department, Mr. Wolfe, tall and thin with thick white hair, followed immediately by Anna and the rest of the flute section, then everyone else, about fifty band members in all.

Anna looks even more beautiful than usual, wearing a knee-length, Christmas-colored dress of green with a bright red belt and trim. A red ribbon is in her shoulder-length, blonde hair. My eyes lock on her as she takes the steps to the stage. Santa Claus himself could follow after her—heck, even Rudolph and the rest of the reindeer along with a few hundred elves—and I'm sure I wouldn't even notice.

I only have eyes for her.

I realize I'm clapping along with everyone else in the audience—I don't turn around to look, but it sounds like a big, enthusiastic crowd—and I have to remind myself to breathe. The band members take their seats on the stage, the dark maroon curtains drawn back to the sides, and my heart pounds and my palms feel damp just like before a game of my own.

I hope Anna isn't just good; I hope she's great. It occurs to me that this isn't like football or basketball games where fans from both teams are attending. No one is going to boo tonight, or hope for a misplayed note by the bad guys. There's only one team tonight, and everyone is rooting for it to achieve the musical equivalent of a big win. So am I, but I'm especially rooting for Anna to get the equivalent of a touchdown or a buzzer-beating shot. She spends so much time on her practicing, based on everything she's told me, so I hope that work gets rewarded.

Not that I'll be able to tell, I suppose. Either the whole band sounds good, or it doesn't, and I doubt if I'll pick out any sour or especially good notes by one flautist (a word I looked up before tonight's performance). Anna's notes will just fit in with everyone else's.

Even so, I'm rooting for her to hit the buzzer-beater.

The conductor, Mr. Wolfe, taps the score holder in front of him and raises his hands. A hush falls over the auditorium. He looks to his left at Anna's section of flutes and clarinets, the right section of trumpets, saxophones, French horns, and trombones, and the back middle section of drums and a tuba, its huge, tarnished brass bell dwarfing all the other instruments.

Anna sits closest to the audience, the four other flautists to her left, holding her silver-colored flute parallel to her shoulders and the mouthpiece to her soft lips. I think her position closest to us means she's the best player of that instrument, although she's never said that. Still, she looks like she must sound great. Maybe I'm biased—well, *of course* I'm biased—but the way she holds her instrument sure looks like she knows what she's doing.

The band launches into "Jingle Bells" and sounds pretty good. I particularly like the flute section, even though I don't think I've ever paid attention to a flute before in my life. Now all of a sudden that's all I can hear, and I'm convinced that section is the best in the whole band. And Anna, in particular, is especially terrific. I'm absolutely sure of it, would swear to it in any court of law, even though my poorly trained ear really can't distinguish one flute from another.

She's wonderful, that's all there is to it.

Fifteen minutes later, though, any possibility that I'm mistaken, deluded by my love for her, is blown to smithereens. Anna's greatness moves front and center for everyone to hear. After playing four more bouncy, cheerful tunes, the band switches "Silent Night." The first verse sounds soft and sweet—flawless, really—but then when the second verse starts, I almost fall off my chair.

Anna stands and plays solo.

It's the most beautiful thing I've ever heard. I've always thought "Silent Night" was one of the prettiest Christmas carols, but the notes from Anna's flute are so pure and perfect and gorgeous it takes my breath away. I sit there wide eyed, my jaw hanging in amazement, and I'm not the only one. You can hear a pin drop except for the sweet, high-pitched notes from that instrument. She decorates the melody, weaving in and around it, above and below it, at times unleashing an astonishing torrent of notes—how can she play that fast?—and then returning to the beauty of the melody itself.

Without realizing it, I've stopped breathing. Anna's performance is that stunning. I finally realize I'm holding my breath and draw in a gulp of air, but try to do so as quietly as I can. I don't want to miss a note or sully its beauty by even the tiniest amount.

When she finishes the solo and the rest of the band resumes playing for the third and final verse, I can't help but break into applause. I just start doing it as instinctively as my knee shoots out when the doctor taps it with his hammer. Fortunately, I'm not alone. It would be embarrassing to Anna and humiliating to me if I were the only one. But most of the audience briefly applauds the solo before falling silent to hear the rest of the song, and almost joins me in holding their breath during that final verse.

When the final, long note is sounded, the audience explodes in by far the loudest applause so far. The conductor points to Anna, who stands and curtseys, smiling broadly. I want to leap to my feet and shout out, "That's my girlfriend! Isn't she amazing?" But I keep control of myself. I may still be a bit of a country bumpkin, but I'm not *that* bad.

Still, a warm glow of pride floods over me as the almost deafening applause goes on and on. I am so happy for Anna. *So* happy. Euphoric, actually. Even though the concert is far from over, this wasn't the musical equivalent of a touchdown, it was the game-winning touchdown as time expires.

Wow.

I feverishly try to remember every note Anna played, although there were parts where there were so many of them, it's impossible. But I still try to memorize her solo as best I can so I can replay it in my mind, over and over, when the concert completes.

I get my breath back partway through the next song, "Frosty the Snowman," and to be truthful, the rest of the concert feels like an anticlimax. It really is good, including an excellent saxophone solo by some kid I recognize from the hallways, but nothing comes close to matching the perfection of Anna's solo.

*

After the concert ends, I wait in the locker-lined hallway outside the band room, along with what seems like a hundred or so parents and about half that many students, most of them arrayed in small circles. The smell of thick woolen coats fills the air. The band exited the auditorium to a standing ovation and its members are inside the band room packing up their instruments and perhaps hearing post-performance words from Mr. Wolfe. There's a constant buzz of conversation out here, most of it about how great the concert was and especially whatever son or daughter or friend that person came to see. So I suppose I'm no different than everyone else, but Anna really was the star of the show. Not even the saxophone soloist was even close.

A shriek of joy erupts as Colleen McArthur, a popular, dark-haired clarinetist, emerges from the auditorium's closed doors. Her best friend, Julie Frederickson, rushes to give her a hug, leaving what must be Colleen's smiling parents in her wake, slowly and silently approaching.

"You were great!" Julie says.

"Yes!" say Colleen's parents in unison.

The scene is repeated over and over, though most often without the shriek and sometimes without a hug, especially if it's just the parents, until I begin to wonder if Anna is ever going to show her face.

Before she does, a petite, blonde-haired woman, who based on resemblance has to be Anna's mother, approaches along with a broad-shouldered, grim-faced man, who I'm guessing is her father. The mother smiles; the presumed father, the former Marine whose hair is cut short in a crew cut like mine, eyes me skeptically.

"You must be Rabbit," she says, and when I acknowledge she's right, she introduces herself as Anna's mother and the frowning man beside her as her husband, Anna's father.

For only the briefest instant, I wonder how she identified me, but then I realize it's pretty obvious. The members of the basketball team are the only students in the entire school with crew cuts. We stand out like what my mom calls "a sore thumb." Everyone else tries to look as much like the Beatles as possible, with every guy's hair as long as his parents will allow, and if he needs glasses, wearing wire-rim frames like John Lennon's. I'm the only basketball player here, so I really do stick out and if there were any doubt, I'm sure Anna has described me as short. So her mother hardly had to be Sherlock Holmes to identify me.

She beams. "It's so nice to meet finally you. Anna can't stop talking about you. Rabbit this. Rabbit that."

I feel my face grow warm, but can't hold back my smile. *Anna—my girlfriend!—can't stop talking about me.* My smile broadens uncontrollably until I'm afraid I look like the biggest doofus ever, so I try my best to recover.

"She's…well…I talk a lot about her, too," I say. Quickly, I add, "That solo of hers was amazing!"

"Wasn't it?" her mother says, and clasps her hands together. "We certainly thought so. Didn't we, Bruce?"

He nods, but still seems to be giving me the evil eye, and I recall Anna saying how protective he was of her. I probably should keep my big mouth shut, but as soon as I consider a gamble to break the ice with him, the words are out.

"Is Mr. Remington here with you tonight?" I ask him.

He looks confused.

"Anna says that the first boy who takes her out on a date will have to meet your friend, Mr. Remington."

His jaw drops and his face briefly turns red, then he breaks into laughter along with his wife.

"That's an…um…a figure of speech," he says, finally.

"I know," I say, grinning, relieved that my risky gamble worked but admonishing myself not to take the next one. Take enough of them and eventually one will backfire. Badly. But I want Anna's parents to trust me. "I understand you want to protect your daughter. She's a wonderful girl, and I'm sure I'd feel the same way in your shoes. You have nothing to worry about me. I think she's special and will always treat her that way."

Her father blinks, looking as stunned as if I've just slapped him, and then nods. "We think she's special, too."

"Anna says you're the perfect gentleman," her mother says.

"You better stay that way," her father says grimly.

"I will. I promise."

I can almost sense he's about to say "you both are too young," when Anna saves us by stepping through the band room doors, holding her small black flute case by its handle. She looks radiant and beams even more when she sees me. I wish I could rush over and hug her like Julie Frederickson did to Colleen McArthur, and any number of other friends and parents did, but I've just gotten the "perfect gentleman" warning with the lingering reminder of Mr. Remington, so I just stand there and, not knowing what else to do, give a little wave.

It's got to be the dopiest gesture in the history of the universe—*a wave? Really?*—but Anna just smiles her warm smile at me, and behind her maroon-framed glasses her eyes tell me that everything is all right.

She likes me—maybe even *loves* me—in spite of my dopey lapses like the little wave.

After we all praise her effusively, she says to her parents, "I'm glad you got a chance to meet Rabbit."

"And I'm glad," I say, "I didn't meet Mr. Remington."

We laugh, all but Anna who briefly looks at us in confusion until she puts two and two together. Then she smiles, but gives me a look like I must be crazy.

*

I miss her concert the next Friday because we have a game against Revere, another blowout win in which Charlie and Jamaal play like men against boys, scoring at will, making it three-for-three in easy wins and also in dominating performances for both of them. Charlie has scored more than thirty points each game without even having to play the fourth quarter, while Jamaal fakes and spins his way through every defense like a hot knife through butter.

After the game, the Revere freshmen coach loudly complains to Coach O'Donnell, almost shouting, about them being on the freshmen team, humiliating his kids, instead of playing on the JVs where they belong. He calls us sandbaggers, gesturing angrily. Coach O'Donnell just shrugs his shoulders and lifts his hands, palms up, in a what-am-going-to-do gesture. It isn't his call, but it's got to be embarrassing to him. Everyone, including opposing coaches, can clearly see what Coach Abrams stubbornly refuses to admit.

The blowouts have given me more of an opportunity to play, since Coach O'Donnell can give me minutes Jamaal would get in closer games. And I've been taking advantage of that opportunity. In the second quarter, I see that the point guard I'm covering can't go to his left. If I play him straight up, he's unstoppable, always driving to his right.

So I don't play him straight up.

I overplay him to the side, actually lining up my right shoulder with his off shoulder instead of shoulder-to-shoulder, forcing him to his weak side. The first two times, he tries to fake left and still go right, but both times I ignore the fakes and he stumbles into me for offensive fouls. When he realizes that won't work and actually tries to go to his very weak side, I steal the ball twice in a row. At the other end, I work a succession of give-and-go's with Charlie, my bounce passes to him when he cuts to the basket resulting in easy layups. And when they protect against that, I hit three straight fifteen-foot jumpers.

Swish!

By the time I come out of the game, we've blown the game open. I get a huge cheer, and not just from my mom. Our cheerleaders are calling out my name. So are the fans. Coach O'Donnell claps me on the back and so do all the players on the bench.

I'm coming around as the backup point guard to Jamaal.

So as I settle into my front row, center seat to hear Anna play in the final concert of the holiday season, I'm feeling pretty good about everything. I'm never going to be the star on basketball teams down here. The competition is just too strong. And I'm certainly not going to get elevated to the JV team this year, no matter what my parents think. But I'm making a contribution and having fun. Playing backup point guard to Jamaal, our own version of Earl the Pearl, isn't too bad.

Plus, Christmas is in two days and next week is school vacation. Although I won't get to see Anna during the days, she's said she's going to come see our games on Wednesday and Thursday, days she'd normally have band practice. But what I'm really excited about is that we got both our parents, well, really our moms, to reluctantly agree to us exchanging small gifts. It has to be little because we're not supposed to be serious. We're too young for that…blah blah blah. I tune out that part of the agreement because I've heard it so many times already.

The important thing, the really surprising thing, is that we can get each other anything at all. I'll be going over to Anna's house late Christmas afternoon, after all of both families' celebrations, and we'll exchange our gifts. Which is really, really great! I wonder if my father was even paying attention when Mom mentioned it to him. But she obviously did, and caught him at the right time. When things are bad between my father and me, there doesn't seem to be a good time. But we've called off our Mutually Assured Destruction, and over the past week things have really calmed down. We're okay with each other right now, as okay as I guess we're going to get, and Mom found that right time.

She also brought me to the stores earlier today to buy something for Anna. I found something I hope she likes. I really, really hope she likes it, although I'm a bit nervous I'll be bringing it back to the store for a refund and have to get something else. I hope not. I really, really hope she likes it.

But for now, I'm just going to sit here, my winter jacket in my lap, the auditorium comfortably warm, with heavily perfumed mothers of band members on both sides of me, and enjoy the concert.

It turns out to be the exact same concert as a week ago, except for one thing. Anna told me it would all be the same, so I didn't really have to come if I didn't want to, but the smile in her eyes as she said those words, standing beside her locker days ago looking so pretty, told me she really wanted me to be there. And of course, I don't want to be anywhere else. If not for our Friday night games, I would have been here for all four performances.

But one thing is different. At least, I think so.

I've played and replayed Anna's flute solo over and over in my head this past week, trying as best I can to remember how she played *around* the melody of "Silent Night," maintaining its pristine beauty—you can almost imagine snowflakes falling softly through the air—while soaring over and above it, then plummeting below it and finally rejoining it at just the right moment. But as she plays her solo now, standing there in her green dress with a red belt and a red ribbon in her shoulder-length blonde hair, I swear it's different.

Not better or worse. Still wonderful. Amazing. But different.

I wouldn't notice the difference—and maybe it is all in my head; I'm pulling a Percival Lowell—but I tried so hard to memorize what she did a week ago, and I'm *sure* this is different.

Magnificent. Astonishingly beautiful. But *different*.

I can't wait to ask her after the performance, but mostly I hope her solo never ends. She is amazing.

*

"This may be a really dumb question," I say after Anna emerges from the band room, all smiles, and joins her parents and me where we're standing along the rows of green lockers, surrounded by the noisy family and friends of other band members. We've already complimented her on the concert and especially her amazing solo, and she's blushed a little and thanked us. But now I risk looking foolish because I have to know. "Was your solo different this time? It was amazing! Both times! But I'd swear it was different. Or am I crazy?"

"You noticed!" she says, beaming the most beautiful smile ever. "You were really paying attention."

"Of course," I say, intoxicated by her smile and relieved that I'm not nuts. "The roof could have caved in and I wouldn't have noticed it during that solo unless it hit me over the head and knocked me out cold."

Her father frowns and I remind myself to tone it down. We're not supposed to be serious. We're too young. Blah blah blah blah. Mr. Remington.

So I quickly add, "Your solo was great the other night. Why change it? And how did you come up with another version?"

"It's called improvisation," Anna says. "Jazz musicians do it all the time. They make it up as they go along. There's a famous saxophone player, a legend named Charlie Parker, who never played the exact same solo once. Never repeated himself. Always a little something different."

"That sounds impossible," I say, unable to comprehend such a thing.

"I can't do that," Anna says. "At least not now. I planned most of the solo, but I did give myself a little section where I made it up. The string of arpeggios where the words are 'holy infant, so tender and mild.'"

She looks at me expectantly. I gulp. "What's an arpeggio?"

"Oops, my mistake," she says, barely suppressing a laugh, her free hand going to her mouth. "Sorry. It's a musical term for when the notes of a chord are sounded one right after another instead of all at once."

I nod, having no idea what she's talking about. But I refuse to ask, "What's a chord?" and let them know the true depths of my ignorance. So I just keep nodding, which probably makes me look like an idiot anyway.

"It isn't important," Anna says, surely recognizing my discomfort. "It's just a term that describes what I did in the little part that I made up on the fly."

"It sounds awfully difficult," I say, anxious to get the conversation away from what I know and back to what she did. "Aren't you afraid you'll… you'll hit a dead end? A musical dead end and you'll just be stuck?"

Anna smiles. "It is kind of a tight wire act without a safety net, but that's what makes it fun. I guess it's like taking the final shot in a basketball game with your team down by a point. You're a hero if it goes in. A goat if it doesn't."

I nod even though I'm not sure the two things are comparable at all. Improvisation sounds a whole lot tougher and riskier than taking a fifteen-footer.

"That's really impressive you noticed the difference," Anna's mother says, and I realize Anna and I have accidentally been excluding her parents from our conversation. I make a mental note to watch out for that in the future as her mother continues. "We've been to all her concerts, so we know all about this. But most people wouldn't notice. Especially someone who isn't musically…um, someone…" Her face turns red.

"Someone who's a musical imbecile," I say with a shrug and a grin. "Someone who doesn't know an arpeggio from an aardvark." I could also add that I don't know a chord from a cockroach, but figure I may have gone too far as it is.

"I didn't mean to be insulting," her mother hastily adds.

"You weren't," I assure her. "I know next to nothing about music. Although I certainly plan to learn now."

"So how did you notice the difference between the solos?" Anna's father asks, his head cocked a little to the side, a frown on his face reminding me of Mr. Remington.

"I tried to memorize last week's version," I explain. "As much of it as I could remember. I've been replaying it in my head all this week."

"You have?" Anna says, delighted, radiant.

"You have?" her father says, scowling. Not delighted at all. Most certainly not radiant.

Inwardly, I groan. I can hear the words that scowl says. *You're too serious. You're too young.* Blah, blah, blah.

Mr. Remington.

CHAPTER 14

On Christmas Day, at exactly four o'clock in the afternoon, I ring the doorbell at Anna's house. Her father answers, wearing the same Mr. Remington scowl and frown from two days ago, but he lets me in. We shake hands and wish each other Merry Christmas. He leads me through a small foyer that opens onto a front room that smells of pine needles and freshly baked chocolate chip cookies. A brightly decorated Christmas tree sprinkled with tinsel and blinking lights is tucked into the corner on our immediate right. There's only one remaining wrapped gift beneath it, something smaller than a paperback book. I wonder if it's for me. Beside the tree along the right wall is a brown leather couch and matching reclining chair. A color TV—a *color* TV!—and stereo system run along the left wall, windows above them looking out on snow flurries blowing through the air.

All day, I waited for this moment. We had a nice family Christmas, and as relieved as I am that my father and I are basically getting along—peace on Earth, good will toward men—I'm even happier that he and my mom seem to be back on track. They exchanged not only gifts, but a quick kiss, too. A rarity in front of me.

Seeing that was maybe even better than the gifts I opened, much as I liked them, and the stuffed turkey we ate, much as I devoured a drumstick, bread stuffing and potato stuffing both covered with gravy, and butternut squash. The drumstick meat was so tender, it literally fell off the bone. Delicious. But all of it faded into the background compared to going over to Anna's and giving her her present.

I'm wearing dark blue pants, a light blue dress shirt, and a dark blue sweater that was one of the presents I opened early this morning. I've got a big shopping bag with crumpled up newspapers to conceal the shape of my gift for Anna. As soon as she sees it, it'll be obvious what it is, so I've got it buried in the middle of the newspapers.

"Hello, Mrs. Levesque. Merry Christmas," I say to Anna's mother when she appears at the opening between the front room and dining room. She's wearing a bright green dress with red trim. Very Christmassy. "You look very nice."

She smiles broadly, thanks me, returns the compliment, and wishes me a Merry Christmas, too, a much cheerier greeting than the Mr. Remington look her husband gave me when I wished him the same. She walks to the TV and shuts it off. "I'll go get Anna."

Anna appears in an instant, as if she's been just waiting for me. She looks even more beautiful than usual, again wearing Christmas colors, but this time a red dress with a white belt and green trim, and a green ribbon in her hair.

I want to tell her how beautiful she looks, but not with Daddy Remington peering over my shoulder. So I just say, "Merry Christmas, Anna." And in as neutral, cautious a voice as I can manage, I add, "You look very nice."

I want to hug her, and can tell she wants to hug me, too, but she knows the rules even better than I do, so, like her mother, she returns my compliment and wishes me a Merry Christmas before motioning me to the sofa. Her mother offers us chocolate chip cookies and after we politely decline, both parents make a big show of disappearing into an adjoining room. Her brother has gone over to a friend's house so we're sort of alone.

"I'm glad you could come over," Anna says.

"Me too."

"Just be very careful," she says in a whisper. She glances over her shoulder. "My father wasn't crazy about this, and it won't take much to set him off."

"Okay," I say in the softest whisper. "Just stay away from the mistletoe."

She blushes, then smiles nervously. "Don't even say that word."

I put my thumb and forefinger to my mouth, and pretend to zipper it shut.

"Okay," she says. "Who goes first?"

"Ladies before gentlemen."

"Oh! That isn't fair."

"We'll take turns," I say. "Next time I'll go first."

"Okay."

I reach into the bag nestled against my leg and take hold of her present. But I don't pull it out yet. "I don't know if you'll like this. You might already have it." I look into her expectant eyes. "You have to promise to tell me if you don't like it or if you already have it. Then I'll take it back and get you something else."

"I promise," she says. "Just hurry up!"

We both smile.

I pull her gift out of the bag, and her eyes widen. It's wrapped in light blue decorative wrapping, but the shape is so obviously a record album—twelve-by-twelve inches and very thin—that there's no mystery about that.

"Oh, Rabbit." Anna tears off the wrapping, looks at the album, and breaks into a huge smile. "Jean-Pierre Rampal! My favorite!"

Rampal is the greatest flute player—flautist!—in the world, pretty much the only really famous soloist. At least, that's what the short, squat, bald man behind the counter at the record store said, and there were several Rampal albums there so it made sense.

"Do you have this one?" I ask, and point to the title *Rampal Plays Mozart.*

"No," she says, joyfully. "I have two of his other solo albums, but not that one, so it's perfect! Thank you! You are the sweetest!"

She glances over her shoulder, and I can tell she wants to hug me. But she doesn't dare, and it's a good thing because her father pokes his head around the corner and says, "I forgot something." He trundles into the adjoining dining room, grabs something off the table, and disappears with a wave.

Anna rolls her eyes. "I should have known he'd do something like that."

"No harm, no foul."

"What?"

"It's a basketball term," I explain. "It means the ref doesn't need to whistle a foul if the defender really didn't affect things. No harm. No foul."

Anna nods, then begins to look distressed.

"What's the matter?" I ask.

"This is much nicer than what I got you. It was supposed to be little, so I just did something tiny that I thought you might like."

"That's great! Where is it?"

"But it didn't cost me hardly anything. You spent more than you should have. I don't think my parents will object, because they know it's the perfect gift for me. But…you'll have to promise just like I did that if you don't like what I got you, you'll tell me so I can get you something nice, too."

"I'm sure I'll love it."

"Promise!"

"I promise!"

"Swear to God, and hope to die?"

"I swear!"

Anna takes a deep breath, slides off her seat, and reaches underneath the Christmas tree for that one remaining unopened gift. Smaller than a paperback book and thinner. She holds it uncertainly out to me.

"I don't know if you'll even be able to use it," she says. "But I couldn't ask without giving it away."

"If it's from you, I'm sure I'll love it."

I put my hand out, but she still hesitates. "You'll love it even if it's a five-day-old hamburger?"

"Yummy," I say with a smile, and rub my stomach.

She thrusts the package into my hands and I tear the paper away. It's…

I'm not sure what it is. It's a plastic case of some kind with some contraption inside.

"I love it," I say, worried. "But…what is it?"

Anna's shoulders slump. "I knew it!" She exhales loudly and looks about to cry. "It's a cassette recording. But if you don't know what it is, then I'm sure you don't have a cassette player."

I shake my head. "I don't. But maybe we—my parents—can get one. I'm sure they can." I point to the plastic case. "So what's on the cassette?"

"It's stupid!"

"Tell me!"

"Promise you won't laugh."

"I promise."

"All this week, you talked about how much you liked my solo. You couldn't keep quiet about it. And you said how much you hated missing two of the concerts. You even tried to memorize my first solo and replay it in your head!" She looks at me sheepishly. "I hope you don't think it was egotistical, but the band recorded the concerts, and I copied my solos— actually all of "Silent Night," not just the solo—from each night onto this tape so you could listen to them."

My jaw drops. I can't think of what to say. This is amazing.

"But you don't have a cassette player," Anna says.

"I'll get one!"

"I'll get you something else," Anna says, still looking troubled. "Something nice like the record you bought me."

"No! No! No!" I say. "I love it! I just want to…how can I…" I shake my head. "Can we listen to it now? On your cassette player?"

"Of course. But are you sure—"

"I'm sure!"

When I first stepped in Anna's house and saw she had a color TV, I thought I'd want to watch it for hours. A *color* TV! But there might as well be no TV in the room at all. We listen to that cassette over and over, the tape hissing and static covering up some of the softer parts, but it's still wonderful. It's the best present I've ever gotten.

*

Coach Abrams blows his whistle with what seems like an exceptionally shrill ferocity to start practice. It looks like he's in a foul mood, his jaw set and anger in his eyes. The freshmen team won its two games after Christmas, both blowouts thanks to Charlie and Jamaal outclassing the opposition. That was great not only because it brought our record to a perfect 5-0, but also because I got to play more and Anna was watching in the stands. Unfortunately, however, the varsity lost both games, falling to a 2-3 record.

Today is Saturday, our last practice before the new year starts, and it seems like the perfect time to elevate our two freshmen superstars to the JVs. Usher in 1968 with those lineup changes. Maybe make it a short stay for Charlie and move him up from JVs after a couple games to help the varsity. It isn't hard to see that he's getting little satisfaction scoring thirty or forty points against overmatched competition, nor is it forcing him to take his game to the next level. It's like taking candy from babies.

So when we gather around Abrams in a semicircle underneath the hoop closest to the locker room, down on one knee so at six-two, he towers over all of us, I wonder if we'll hear that overdue announcement. The smell of sweat is in the air, although nothing like it'll certainly be like in another half hour or so. The gym is a bit on the cool side, perhaps because of the rest of the school being shut down for the holiday vacation.

"We have a problem here and I'm going to nip it in the bud," Abrams says, his jaw set and his penetrating gaze moving slowly from left to right, locking in on each player before moving on to the next. He breathes in deeply, making his broad shoulders even wider.

I feel my eyes widen. This isn't what I expected. Beside me, on my left, Charlie stiffens. This can't be about the freshmen team. It has to be about the struggles of the varsity, but it's never comfortable to hear harshly delivered words about any of your teammates, even the ones of the varsity when you're just a freshman. And it sure feels like we're going to hear some harshly delivered words.

Turns out, I'm wrong about everything else, but right about that.

Coach O'Donnell, our coach, and JV Coach Silveri stand behind Abrams, whistles dangling on black cords about their necks, wearing gray LEHS Bulldogs warm-up suits, just like him. Coach O'Donnell looks embarrassed and uncomfortable, looking down at the ground and shifting the weight on his feet. As if he just got taken to the woodshed, as the phrase goes.

"The problem we have here started on the freshmen team," Abrams says, his brow furrowed. "My focus is on the varsity, as you all know, so for a while I let it be. I knew Coach O'Donnell would address it eventually. But these last two games I've begun to see signs of it on the varsity. I believe it's why we lost both games.

"The cancer has spread. It's time to cut it out right now while there's still time. Still time to save the varsity season. Time before this cancer that started with the freshmen destroys us all."

He glares at each player on the freshmen team in succession, a silence that probably only lasts ten seconds or so, but it feels like ten years. His face becomes a shade brighter crimson. I gulp. What can he possibly be talking about? We're 5-0 and haven't had a close game yet.

We're a cancer? We're the reason his varsity team just lost two games and is now under .500?

"If you're going to play basketball for the Lynn English High School Bulldogs," he says, "you will play for the team, not yourself."

The urge to look at my teammates is almost overwhelming. But Abrams' visible anger is so raw and intense, I don't dare look away. Then he says words that make my jaw drop and my heart sink.

"You *will* play fundamental basketball, Bulldog basketball," he says. "You will *not* freelance and turn our carefully constructed game plans into nothing but a series of one-on-one moves designed to show off your athletic abilities at the expense of the team. Playground basketball is for the playground. If that's how you want to play, take off your jersey now. Just leave. We don't need you, and I won't have you."

And if anyone can't figure out who he's talking about, who's the root of this cancer, Abrams stares directly at Charlie, practically challenging him to take that jersey off. Then he glares at Jamaal, who's on Charlie's left.

Jamaal looks down, but Charlie looks like a volcano about to erupt. His eyes, wide with disbelief at first, narrow in anger. His lips purse, his jaw sets. Then his fists clench and unclench.

But he says nothing. He holds his head high and just stares back at Abrams.

I can't believe it. Everything Charlie said that day back when the teams were posted on the wall and we learned he'd been relegated along with Jamaal to the freshmen team has just come true.

"When a guy like Abrams says 'fundamental basketball,'" Charlie said back then, "he's talking about *white* basketball. Pass the ball around a lot. Don't do anything flashy. And when he says 'playground basketball' he's referring to *black* basketball, but like it's a bad thing. Abrams don't like me because I play too black"

When Charlie said it, I had my doubts. Not because he was one to make stuff up, because he certainly wasn't, but because it just sounded so outrageous, so hard for me to believe. Why would a coach be like that?

But Charlie was right. He hit the bull's-eye dead center. Abrams isn't an overt racist like George Wallace, the former Alabama Governor who just four years ago tried to block the first black students from entering his all-white University of Alabama, and who is now running for President.

Abrams isn't like that. He doesn't use the N-word, or tell the black players they need to sit at an end of the bench all to themselves or drink from a separate water bubbler like still happens in Alabama. But his kind of prejudice is maybe even more dangerous than Wallace's because for someone like me, it's easy to miss it at first. And for some people, it's easy to pretend it doesn't exist. I'll bet half the white guys on the team, maybe even more, are thinking right now that Abrams is right and Charlie is a cancer. And Charlie is somehow, inexplicably to blame for the varsity teams two losses this week.

After all, who *doesn't* believe in "fundamental basketball?" Isn't that the sport's equivalent of freedom and democracy, things that no one would argue against? Or as my mom would say, "It's as American as apple pie."

Of course, fundamental basketball is a good thing. It's just that Abrams has corrupted that term to mean something else, something that says that being white is good and being black is somehow inferior.

And Charlie is his target.

Either that or he's the dumbest basketball coach ever. Anyone who has watched our games would know that the way Charlie has played isn't selfish or designed to show off. Not at all. It's to give us the best chance of winning. Since when isn't your best option to take the highest percentage shot you can take? Charlie hasn't scored over thirty points every game by accident. He just can beat one-on-one any opponent who tries to guard him. And it isn't coincidence that we get a lot of easy baskets after Jamaal fakes out his man with flashy moves that leaves someone wide open.

And to say that any of that has somehow affected the varsity is ridiculous. I've watched every single game they've played—the freshmen play first, then the JVs, then the varsity—and they aren't playing any differently now than the beginning of the season. Joe Thurman hasn't suddenly changed into a one-on-one player. The varsity point guard, Alan McLeod, isn't making flashy moves like Jamaal. He couldn't if he tried.

Abrams is, quite simply, making Charlie the scapegoat. A kid on the freshmen team is why the varsity has a losing record. It's ludicrous and disgusting.

And if there's even a hint of doubt as to whether Abrams is either evil in at least a subtle way, or just drop-dead stupid, he removes it with what he does next.

"Yeah, you, Watkins," Abrams says, focusing on Charlie presumably because Charlie won't look submissively down like Jamaal has. Charlie glares right back as Abrams continues. "I'm talking about you. You and your friend, Jamaal. I've been watching the display you two put on. Playground ball like that might impress a lot of people, but not me. Your type doesn't fool me. You might have fooled a couple of seniors who should know better." He flings a hand in Thurman's direction. "But you don't fool me. You're going to play fundamental basketball or you're not going to play at all. It's my way or the highway."

A deathly silence falls over the gymnasium and it feels like it lasts forever. Players shift their weight from one foot to another. They tear their eyes away from Charlie and look at each other, eyes wide with surprise. Or maybe it's more than surprise. Absolute shock.

I remind myself to breathe.

"You hear me?" Abrams says.

"Yes, sir," Jamaal says softly, still looking down, but Abrams doesn't even seem to care about him anymore. Abrams' eyes are trying to burn holes in Charlie's.

Charlie grits his teeth and gives a curt nod.

"I can't hear you," Abrams says, and at that moment I'm convinced he must be the most despicable person on earth. Not only has he made Charlie the scapegoat, he has to make sure Charlie's humiliation is complete.

"Yeah," Charlie says in a barely audible, raspy voice. He breathes in and exhales loudly.

"I can't hear you!" Abrams shouts.

Charlie's eyes fix on Abrams, and the silence becomes deafening. Silence except for Charlie's labored breathing. I can imagine he's trying to decide whether to go after Abrams—and who could blame him?—or meekly submit like a whipped dog.

Finally, through gritted teeth, he says, "Yes, sir."

"Okay, then," Abrams says, his face brightening. He blows his whistle and turns away, as if he's done nothing more than slap and kill an annoying mosquito, and though its blood is on his hands, it's time to move on to something important. "Three lines!"

CHAPTER 15

We ring in the new year, 1968, with our first loss. Facing Lynn Classical, our crosstown archrival, the freshmen team plays Coach Abrams' style of basketball. Charlie plays as if he's in handcuffs, passing the ball around robotically like everyone else instead of taking his overmatched defender to the basket for an easy shot or layup. Easy shots are forbidden if they're achieved by one-on-one moves instead of "fundamental basketball." It's the most ridiculous thing I've ever seen, followed not far behind by Jamaal hamstrung by not being allowed to make his flashy, spinning moves.

It's like Wilt Chamberlain, who one time scored 100 points in a single NBA game and averaged more than fifty points and twenty-five rebounds a game for an entire season, not being allowed to use his seven-foot-one, 275-pound size and strength advantage to score at will. Like telling Bill Russell he can't block shots or grab rebounds. Like telling Bob Cousy he can't dribble the ball or make a behind-the-back pass to a wide open man.

Just stupid. Stupid, stupid, stupid. Or maybe equal parts stupid and evil.

I sink a few shots, including three bank shots off the backboard from the right side, and set up a few more, but who cares? We lose by three points. To our top rival. After blowing out every other team.

I want to scream, watching it all unfold. But my frustration is microscopic to what I see on Charlie and Jamaal's faces. They aren't just frustrated. They're *angry.*

So angry they can't even speak. As we walk, defeated, into the locker room, Charlie just stares straight ahead, and through a clenched jaw says, "Don't say a thing." Not even me with my big mouth is dumb enough to ignore that request.

There wasn't a single player on that court who could stop Charlie or Jamaal. Only one person could.

Abrams.

And he did.

*

The next day at practice, Coach Abrams decides to make his point again, even if the first time resulted in the freshmen losing a game, and to an archrival, they should have easily beaten. Even though his varsity squad lost again, despite his surgical removal of the supposed cancer.

Or maybe what happens is *because* the varsity lost again.

First, though, he's summoned his older brother, Delvin, the other half of the supposedly legendary "Amazing Abrams Boys" who made Lynn English great at basketball back in the Dark Ages, twenty years or so ago, right after World War II. Teachers still speak about them in reverential tones. At first I swallowed it all hook, line, and sinker, but when Abrams began to show his true colors, I got to thinking. That was a completely different era. No blacks in the NBA; mostly set shots, taken without any jumping at all, hardly any jump shots; no twenty-four-second clock; no athleticism at all. There was no need to have an NCAA rule against dunking because the mostly white players couldn't dunk. Bob Cousy hadn't yet come along and added behind-the-back passes and dribbling, no-look passes, and other fancy, but effective, play to a guard's repertoire.

Abrams has just been trying to force us back into his era, the Dark Ages of basketball.

Now, so does his brother. He's wearing an LEHS gray warm-up suit like all the coaches, although the gray in his suit hasn't faded as much as the other coaches'. He also has no whistle dangling from his neck on a black cord like the others. But other than that, he's a dead ringer for his brother. About six-two or six-three, broad shoulders, and a crew cut, though even more of his black hair has turned gray.

He's every bit as stupid.

"Boys, there's a reason Lynn English High School was so successful when my brother and I were playing here," he begins, and he's off. Blah, blah, blah. Same old tired sermon, different preacher. Same old *stupid* sermon. Play like it's still the late 1940s. Same old *white* sermon. Fundamental basketball is good; playground basketball is bad.

Blah, blah, blah.

When Delvin Abrams finally finishes, Coach Abrams nods and thanks him. Then, to further prove his point about how he has to root out the cancerous play of the freshmen team, Coach Abrams announces that we're going to scrimmage, his virtuous varsity against us evil freshmen. The two Abrams brothers grin in smug superiority, sure of the outcome. Of course, that's like matching up Muhammad Ali, 236 pounds of pure muscle, against a 120-pound lightweight. Seniors against freshmen. We don't even get to add any of the JVs. Not a fair fight at all. All of us but Charlie, and perhaps Jamaal, will look foolish out there.

Which is just what Abrams wants.

"Go right ahead and play your playground ball," he says, looking right at Charlie, then at Jamaal. He draws in a deep breath so his six-two, broad-shouldered frame fills out to its fullest. Then he exhales slowly. "Don't let me stop you from doing a thing. Play like the Harlem Globetrotters if you want. We'll see how effective that is against fundamental basketball."

Abrams just wants to humiliate Charlie and Jamaal. But the rest of us freshmen are going to get the worst of it. I feel my palms getting sweaty just thinking about it. My mouth tastes as dry as cotton. I'm getting better at dealing with taller, athletic kids my own age, but I'll have no chance against seniors. I'm still not an inch over five feet tall, and there will be seniors towering over me, six-feet, five inches tall. Even the shortest member of the varsity is almost a full foot taller than I am.

But it turns out that those worries are all for nothing. I never get into the scrimmage. The fireworks explode with me still on the sideline.

It starts predictably. The varsity easily wins the opening tip and scores. Then, because Abrams wants to rob us freshmen of all our dignity, he orders a full-court press. As if that were needed to make his point. Sure enough, Joe Thurman picks off an inbound pass and lays in another easy two points. The farce is barely seconds old, and already it's 4-0.

But then Jamaal takes the inbound pass and when the full-course pressure closes in, he fakes and spins, leaving behind two defenders, then dribbles behind his back to speed past another. He's at half court and all that's left between him and the basket is the team's superstar, Joe Thurman.

Jamaal bears down on Thurman, dribbling with his right hand, and appears to give the senior an opening to steal the ball. Thurman goes for it, and—

Jamaal does "The Pearl!" Without actually palming the ball, he continues the dribble with his right hand, cupping it while spinning *three hundred and sixty degrees*, leaving Thurman behind looking foolish, wondering where the ball went.

The Pearl! Jamaal did The Pearl!

I let out an involuntary whoop—"*Whoa!*"—and I'm not alone. All around me, players gasp. Jaws drop. Eyes pop out.

"Did he just do what I think he did?" Tim Peterson, next to me, whispers as Jamaal lays it in.

I just nod in amazement. *He did The Pearl!*

As Jamaal runs back up court, he turns to Abrams and smiles.

Abrams blows so hard on his whistle, I halfway expect its shrill racket to shatter the windows. His face has turned beet red and looks about ready to explode. Beside him, his brother looks every bit as furious.

"You think you're funny, don't you?" Coach Abrams yells at Jamaal.

Jamaal just smiles back. He isn't looking down at the floor like he did at that other practice when Abrams singled out him and Charlie. Perhaps he did that because down South where he lived until this year, he was expected to do that. I don't know.

But he isn't looking down now. He just did "The Pearl!"

"Keep it up," Abrams says. "Maybe you'll play for the Harlem Globetrotters someday. Like the rest of your kind."

That knocks the smile off Jamaal's face. The joy, the jubilation, is gone.

Abrams turns to his varsity. He points to Jamaal. "If that showboating punk scores so much as a single point after this, you're all benched for the first quarter on Friday! You're not the Washington Generals playing Meadowlark Lemon and the Harlem Globetrotters! You're the Lynn English High School Bulldogs!"

The seniors pass the ball around on the next play, sure to follow Abrams' style, before Thurman puts in a short jumper.

Again, the seniors pressure the ball, and again, Jamaal fakes and spins his way past all of them until he and Charlie are coming up on Thurman, two-on-one, Charlie on the left and Jamaal on the right. Mindful that Jamaal must not be allowed to score, while also making sure not to get embarrassed by "The Pearl" again, Thurman squares up on Jamaal, who passes behind the back to Charlie for an easy layup.

The whistle shrieks again. "Get over here!" Abrams yells, a pulsing vein now visible on his forehead. Thurman looks around, confused, then points to his own chest. Abrams nods. "Yes, you! You can't even stop a couple goddamned freshmen! What's wrong with you? What kind of captain are you?" Thurman goes to the sideline, replaced by Scottie Joyce, a pretty good shooter, not quite six feet tall, who'd start if Joe Thurman weren't so good.

The varsity misses its shot, clanging it hard off the back of the rim. The rebound bounces high out to Charlie, who takes off like a greyhound down the left side. He crosses over the midcourt line with four defenders trying to catch up and only Scottie Joyce between him and the basket.

Charlie fakes to the middle, and Scottie Joyce bites so hard on the fake, he staggers when Charlie goes left. Charlie streaks by and lays it in.

The shrill whistle blasts. Coach Abrams races onto the floor.

"Can't anybody stop those two? It's goddamned nigger basketball!"

Abrams' eyes widen. He opens his mouth to speak…then closes it.

A deathly silence fills the gymnasium, covering it like a shroud.

"I didn't say that," Abrams says, his face suddenly flushed. "I meant Negro basketball. Playground style. Undisciplined."

"You said it," Charlie says, his voice hard and filled with seething anger. He points a finger at Abrams, twenty feet away. "And you meant it. All of it."

Charlie turns, sweat streaming down his face, and walks toward the locker room, the squeak of his sneakers the only sound to be heard.

"Where are you going?" Abrams demands.

"I can't play for you," Charlie says over his shoulder. "I can't and I won't."

Jamaal races to Charlie's side. "Neither can I."

"If you two walk through that door," Abrams says, pointing at it, his hand shaking either in anger or fear. "You're not coming back. Not this year. Not ever. Not for as long as I'm the coach here."

Charlie turns to face Abrams. "I wouldn't play for you if you're the last coach on Earth."

He and Jamaal head for the locker room, and as they do, Ray Thompson, a muscular power forward and the only black player on the JVs, races over to join them.

"Me, too," he says, and then is joined by Tim Peterson.

Willie Jenkins, a starting forward on the varsity now that he's over the knee injury he suffered in the Thanksgiving Day football game, steps forward, and after him, J.P. Clayton, the first guy off the varsity bench. They walk slowly, deliberately, toward the others, their heads held high.

Of the seven blacks on the team, only Joe Thurman remains. He looks uncomfortably at the six, a pained look on his face, then at Luis Ramirez.

Thurman shifts his weight from one foot to another. He's the one with the most to lose, a possible college scholarship next year. He looks away, then bows his head and stares at his feet.

"Let 'em go," Delvin Abrams says with a dismissive wave of the hand, his chest thrown out proudly. "You're better off without the whole lot of 'em. The cancer is removing itself!"

I finally awake from my stunned slumber—my total, wide-mouthed astonishment at everything that has happened—and, not sure if I'm totally out of place, I belatedly make my own stand.

"Me, too," I say and race over to join my six black teammates.

I hear a snicker, and see out of the corner of my eye that it's come from Rick Cassidy. He's probably right. Me leaving the team in support of Charlie and Jamaal and all the other black players is kind of a joke. I'm just a backup on the freshmen team. Maybe it's all I'll ever be.

I'm not important at all. But the principle sure is. There's right and wrong, and Charlie, Jamaal, and my black teammates are indisputably on the side of being right, just as Coach Abrams and George Wallace and all the others like them are indisputably wrong.

"Midget! What the hell are you doing?" Abrams demands. "Since when are you black?"

Maybe this isn't my fight. The look on Jamaal's face seems to ask what I'm doing here. But I think it's everyone's fight. Just like those three Civil Rights workers the Klan murdered down in Mississippi four years ago: James Chaney, Andrew Goodman, and Michael Schwerner. I've read a lot about them. Chaney was black, but the other two were white. Their deaths made a difference because it was everyone's fight.

And I can see in Charlie's eyes that he agrees. Jamaal, perhaps getting over his initial surprise, seems to grudgingly accept me being there.

"I don't have to be black, to know they're right." I say to Abrams. "I stand with them."

We walk through the doors to the locker room.

And off the team.

CHAPTER 16

It doesn't really hit me, what I've done, until I get out to Mom's car where she waits. And I suppose the real impact doesn't register until a day later when I see my name in Lynn's newspaper, the *Daily Evening Item*. But my mom's reaction is the first one I get outside of the team, and it hits me like a bucket of ice cold water.

"You did what?" she says, her voice raising higher in pitch with each word. She looks at me with a disbelieving stare as if I've just sprouted horns on the sides of my head.

She sits there frozen, her hands on the steering wheel still waiting to shift the transmission into drive, and says it again. "You did what? Tell me you're joking."

"I'm not joking. Why would you say that?"

"But..." She shakes her head, mystified. "Sports is all you ever think about. It's all you ever do. Football and basketball and baseball mean everything to you."

"They're important. But not everything. Not anymore."

"I don't know what's happened to you." Then, as if a light has gone off in her head, she says, "It's the girl, isn't it?"

Now it's my turn to be incredulous. "Mom! What does Anna have to do with this? She doesn't even know yet."

"But...you've changed."

"Before, it used to be that my thinking only about sports was a bad thing."

"But...well..." Again, she shakes her head, though this time in obvious frustration. "Don't twist my words around." She looks at me more closely, as if her eyes can bore inside my skull and read my mind. "Charlie seemed so nice. But he's a troublemaker, isn't he?"

"*Mom!*"

I get more of the same when my father gets home. He's barely inside the door and doesn't even have his black winter coat off when Mom says, "Rabbit, tell your father what you've done."

I'm sitting at the dining room table doing my homework, as ordered by my mom, instead of at the desk up in my bedroom, apparently so she can keep an eye on me. Is she worried that if she doesn't, I might climb out my bedroom window and join the Black Panthers, if that's even possible, or go down to Mississippi and be killed by Klan like Goodman and Schwerner? Or is it that she doesn't understand me anymore, so she wants to study me like a biologist examining a rare bug? Or does she want me here so we'll have this discussion with my father without even a second's delay?

Who knows? Sometimes, it's hard to understand how a parent thinks. And when I asked her why, she crossly said, "Because I said so!"

So with the rich cheese smells of the evening's dinner, fettuccini alfredo, floating through the air, I put down my pencil, and wait for my father to shrug out of his coat and hang it up in the closet.

When I tell him, he explodes. My father, who has practically gone into cardiac arrest at the thought of leaving work a little early to see my game, putting in only sixty-seven hours on the job that week instead of his usual seventy, is suddenly a huge basketball fan.

"I knew you should never have become friends with that…that Negro!" he says, so angry he can't remember Charlie's name even though I've just used it. Or perhaps he doesn't want to remember it.

"Yes, look at what's happened," I say, feeling more than a little angry myself. "I stood up for what's right."

"You defied the coach's authority!" my father bellows, his face flushed red with fury. "Just like you defy *mine*! Sassing back like you always do. Like just now."

Daggers shoot out of his eyes. I don't care. I can take it.

But then he directs them toward my mom. His implication is clear. This is her fault.

*

The shouting match ends, and an icy silence descends over us as we eat dinner. It's like we've gone from inside a fiery volcano, its molten hot lava spewing everywhere, to the Arctic chill of an igloo at the North Pole. The fettuccini alfredo Mom made might just as well be cardboard. I can barely taste it.

After I wash and put away the dishes, I tiptoe into my father's office, carrying the black rotary phone. I gently shut the door behind me and slide down the near wall to the floor. Sitting cross-legged, I call Anna.

Nothing has been said about my use of the phone tonight—after the explosion, hardly anything was said at all—but I suspect if my father thought about it, he might have revoked the privilege. So stealth is my friend.

Anna is as astonished as my parents when I tell her I've quit the team.

"You did what?" she asks, and for a heart-stopping moment, I think she's mad at me, too.

But I haven't had a chance to explain why, and when I do, her words do more than warm my heart.

"What a brave thing to do," she says. "What a sacrifice. You're giving up something that's really important to you, just so you can stand up for others. Rabbit, I'm proud of you."

Emotions flood over me. My throat tightens and I can barely swallow, can barely breathe.

Rabbit, I'm proud of you.

I wish I could reach out over the phone line and hug Anna. Hold her tight. And tell her that I love her.

*

Anna gives me that hug the next morning before Home Room. She sees me approaching her locker, my thick winter jacket unzipped but still on, races to greet me, and throws her arms around me, almost knocking my English and History books to the floor, which is A-OK with me.

Then she says again those magical words: *Rabbit, I'm proud of you.*

I almost get all blubbery. I really needed to hear those words last night, and then today all over again. My father isn't just mad at me; he's furious. In his eyes, I'm a totally rotten kid now, no different than the long-haired hippies in Haight-Ashbury trying to tear down society, according to him, or the college students protesting the Vietnam War. Or maybe even worse in his eyes, I'm like one of those scary men and women, mostly black but some white, marching for Civil Rights with Dr. Martin Luther King. That sounds like a good thing to me, but it sure doesn't to him.

Mom doesn't think I'm rotten, but she sure is disappointed. She loves to watch me play, and now I've robbed her of that. She supports Dr. King and his fight for Civil Rights—though she's learned not to argue with my father about it—and she supports Charlie, but she doesn't understand why I had to sacrifice my basketball season, and presumably my entire high school basketball career, to stand with him.

"Couldn't you have done something short of quitting?" she asked on the way to school this morning. "Support your friend, but just not throw away a sport that means so much to you?"

So I guess she understands a bit, even though I seem to have become a mystery to her, but she's just so disappointed.

"Your games are the most exciting things in my life," she said.

So when Anna says she's proud of me, it's just what I need to hear.

And from just the right person.

*

News spreads fast, and soon I'm getting strange looks from friends like Jeff Goodwin and Paul DiSimone, not to mention my teachers, and outright dirty looks from others. Before math class starts, Mr. Robinson stares at me as if I'm some kind of alien from outer space, and my science teacher, Mr. Tempkin, looks down his nose at me as if I'm a steaming mound of garbage on a hot, summer day. As I go from one class to another, someone behind me in the crowded, dusty hallway calls out, "Quitter!" and someone else says, "Yeah!"

I'll bet a month ago these same people were slapping me on the back and calling me a hero for my performance in the Thanksgiving Day football game. From fame to infamy, I guess. I'm sure none of them really care that a benchwarmer on the freshmen team, even one that had hopes of getting into the lineup, has quit. But the others, the six black players, have left gaping holes in all three teams, including the varsity. I want to whirl around and defend myself, but beside me Anna squeezes my hand and softly says, "Don't let them get to you. You did the right thing."

So I hold my tongue, but it isn't easy. I tune out the catcalls as best I can. I ignore lanky, dark-haired, and eternally smug Rick Cassidy when, walking past me in the other direction, he laughs and waves goodbye.

But I can't ignore what I see at my locker when I stop there before lunch. Anna sees it first, tightens her grip on my hand, and gasps. "Oh, my!"

Etched into the green paint of the locker, presumably scraped by some sharp object, are two words in ragged letters with the ugliest of messages.

NIGGER LOVER!

I freeze. I can't speak. I can't move. I can't breathe.

I can't take my eyes off those words.

*

I'm summoned to see Coach Abrams after school in his office just outside the gym. It's Friday, and the team is playing a home game against Saugus. The varsity won't be taking the court for several more hours, but it still must be a busy time for him. I gave the equipment manager, my uniform. What else could he want?

I step inside the small, musty eight-by-ten office. There's just a desk that he's sitting behind, a chair in front of it, and a messily erased chalkboard on the wall. Chalk dust and the smell of stale sweat fills the air. Abrams points me to the chair, and I sit down.

"I'll make this brief and get right to the point," he says. "I'm offering you a chance to get back onto the team. You can even suit up for tonight's game."

I feel a catch in my throat, a longing to get out there. I love playing basketball, and this will be the first game I miss. And I will *miss* it. Not being on the team leaves a hole in my life. And if I don't come back now, I'll never be allowed back. That's what Abrams said, and I believe it.

It's now or never. The longing to play is so intense, I can taste it, both bitter and sweet at the same time.

"I'm not happy about you taking off with those Negroes," Abrams says, "but I'll take you back. You'll accept that you were wrong to walk out on the team, apologize, and promise not to undermine my authority ever again. I'm the coach and what I say, goes."

I can't help wondering if Charlie, Jamaal, and all the others are getting the same offer. I'll feel foolish—humiliated!—if they all come back to the team and I'm the lone protestor who refuses. The white kid who didn't come back. I'll feel that hole in my life that basketball has always filled, and I'll feel it until the day I graduate. Maybe until the day I die. All for nothing. I'll always wonder what it would have been like if I'd come back.

"With that fancy pants Negro gone, you'll be starting point guard on the freshmen team," Abrams says, obviously referring to Jamaal, who either isn't getting the same offer or has already declined it. Abrams continues, "You're a midget. But you've got a good basketball head on your shoulders, you're fast as a lightning bug, and I like the way your free throw shooting challenges some of the seniors. So although I'd normally be inclined to just say good riddance to you and all the rest of them, I'm going to make this exception."

"You're not making the same offer to the black players?" I ask. "Why not?"

Abrams jaw hardens. "No, I'm not. And that's my business, not yours. But I'll tell you anyway. The whole lot of them are troublemakers.

Troublemakers who just like to look flashy for the girls. Showoffs. They play playground ball. Not like you. I can work with you.

"I heard you got friendly with the Watkins kid because you played together on the football team. So maybe you just fell under his influence, tried to be a good friend, and made a mistake. A mistake that's going to cost you your basketball career. This is your chance to come back and maybe become a basketball star, just like you were on the football field."

"Thank you for the offer," I say, almost instinctively adding the word "sir" as I would to most coaches in a show of respect. But Abrams doesn't deserve my respect. He doesn't deserve to be called sir. He deserves only my contempt. "But unless the other players get the same offer and come back, neither am I."

Abrams' eyes narrow and his face flushes. "If you walk out this door, you'll never, ever play for me. You'll never again wear the Lynn English High School jersey. Think about it."

"I have. And that's my decision."

Abrams shakes his head. "It looks bad, a nice, clean-cut kid like you associating with that crowd."

"Looks bad for you, or for me?"

Abrams stares at me, his jaw set, for a long time. "Why are you throwing your basketball career away for those...those *pieces of trash*?"

I stand.

"Charlie Watkins is not a piece of trash. Jamaal Bryant is not a piece of trash. None of them are pieces of trash." I point at Abrams. "You are the piece of trash."

I guess I burned that bridge down to the ground.

*

Mom has a fried egg sandwich waiting for me when I climb in the car. I could take the bus home now that I'm off the team, but she still picks me up. I had a problem back at the start of school year with one of the tough guys on the bus, so she insists on driving me.

I unwrap the wax paper and bite into the sandwich. It tastes great even though I'm not as ravenous as I used to be after practices. It's almost two hours earlier now and I haven't burned through a bazillion calories running up and down the court. I feel restless, filled with nervous energy, antsy to do something physical.

Mom's first two questions have always been, "How was school?" and "How did practice go?" but now there's only the first one. I admit to her that some kids razzed me about being a quitter, which makes her frown. I'm tempted to leave it at that, but reluctantly I tell her about the awful message scratched onto my locker.

Her eyes widen. "You're kidding." Her grip tightens so hard on the steering wheel, I'm sure beneath her gloves her knuckles have turned white. "That's awful!"

Then I tell her about my talk with Coach Abrams, and for a brief moment her eyes light up. Her whole face brightens with an expectant smile. I feel badly that I've described the meeting in such a way that she's gotten her hopes up—*He might return to the basketball team! Yay!*—because then she looks so deflated when I say that I'm not turning my back on my friends and on the principle involved.

I don't add that I called Abrams a piece of trash. She's already disappointed enough, her shoulders slumped beneath her winter coat and her face grim. She doesn't need to know that, too.

"I can't say I'm not disappointed," she says, sadness in her eyes where seconds before there was such joy. "I love to watch you play. You're so exciting to watch, and not just because you're my son."

I think it's almost entirely because I'm her son, at least on the basketball court, because I'm boring compared to guys like Charlie and Jamaal. But I let it go and take the compliment.

"But I should have known that you'd stick to your guns," she says. "You're as stubborn as—"

I know she was about to say that I'm as stubborn as my father. And she knows that I know. But she also knows that comparisons these days to my father are most definitely not welcome. She might as well compare me to the Celtics' arch-villain, Wilt Chamberlain, who finally beat them last year, or maybe even George Wallace. So she recovers quite nicely.

"—as stubborn as a mule," she says, and gives me a wink.

"Good one," I say, and we both smile.

Then her face grows serious. "Loyalty to your friends, especially to the point of great sacrifice, is an honorable thing, something that shows great character." She pauses, appearing to choose her next words carefully. "So is sacrificing for your principles, even if it breaks your heart."

I can't help but think of her sticking up for me with my dad, and the sacrifice that involved. To use one of her pet phrases, my mom doesn't just talk the talk; she's walked the walk.

CHAPTER 17

The phone is ringing as Mom and I walk through the front door. We both make a dash for it, so of course I beat her to it, even with three textbooks in the crook of my arm, but she tells me in no uncertain terms to give it to her.

"Rabbit!" She holds out her hand, eyebrows raised.

I hand the receiver over.

She listens for a bit, still wearing her beige winter coat, and then frowns. "Why do you want to speak to him?"

My ears perk up at that even though I'm putting my books onto the dining room table. "Who is it?" I mouth silently.

But she shakes her head and makes a stopping gesture with her hand.

"I'm not sure that's such a good idea," she says, and now my curiosity is about to explode. Who wants to talk to me and why might it be a bad idea?

Finally, she says, "Hold on," and holds the receiver against her the stomach.

"It's a reporter from the *Daily Evening Item*," she says. "He wants to talk to you about you quitting the team."

The words hit me like a brick. The newspaper wants to talk to me? I stand there, dumbly. To me? About quitting the team? The paper is popular throughout Lynn and the surrounding cities and towns. We get it delivered to our front porch each evening by a paperboy who tosses it from his bike, and it's on all the newsstands. I read its sports pages every day, and kept the copy from the day after Thanksgiving because it talked about my touchdowns in the game against Classical. Well, it didn't just describe the touchdowns. The headline read, "Freshman Labelle Rallies English in Comeback Thriller." So my mom went and bought another five copies at the Shop Kwik half a mile down the road. I couldn't believe seeing my name in the paper—in the headline!—then, and I can't believe a reporter wants to talk to me now. Although I suppose this explains why Abrams tried to get me back on the team. He can't just call it a black insurrection when I'm part of it. I'm making him look bad.

"Rabbit?" Mom asks, eyebrows raised, still holding the receiver against her stomach to muffle her words. "Do you want to talk to him? It might be best to wait and see what your father thinks."

That's enough to spur me out of my state of disbelief. I step forward, hand extended, and nod.

The man, Lou Tomisetti, introduces himself. "I remember writing about you in happier times, in the Thanksgiving Day game article."

"Yes, thank you," I say, which I suppose is a dumb response, but it's all I can come up with.

"I don't know if you've seen today's paper yet, but there's an article about you and the six black boys quitting the team," he says.

"No," I say. "We get it delivered, but it hasn't arrived yet. It's usually here when I get home, but that's later because I've been at practice." I feel like I'm rambling, so I stop and wait for the reporter to speak next.

"That was a straight news piece, as you'll see," he says. "But I wanted to talk to you about a column I'm going to write on the subject."

A column?

"Okay."

The questions begin, and we talk for about ten minutes. He thanks me, says that the column will be in Monday's paper, and hangs up.

Even though she heard every word I spoke, Mom asks excitedly for a play by play. When I'm done, she asks, "Do you think he's on your side?"

"I…" I shrug, the question catching me off guard just like a number of Mr. Tomisetti's questions did. "I don't know. I guess so. He didn't say anything bad about me."

Turns out, Tomisetti saved that for his column.

*

My father's jaw clenches as he reads the newspaper article. Not Tomisetti's column, which won't be out until Monday, but today's news story. He's just stepped in the door, still has his winter coat on, and looks to be getting angrier with every word he reads.

The article, only six short paragraphs, makes me angry, too. It says that the seven of us quit in protest of the "alleged use of a racial epithet, which Abrams denies using." It even quotes him saying that he used the term "Negro" and the rest of us just misheard the word.

Alleged use? Abrams denies it? How can that be? We all know what we heard. An entire gymnasium full of basketball players heard what he said. And even after he backtracked and did say "Negro basketball," he then equated it with undisciplined basketball.

Why didn't Tomisetti mention Abrams' denials to me? He asked me what happened and I told him, unaware there was any question about what the truth was. Why did he ask me about all kinds of things about the team and about Charlie and myself, but didn't get a quote from me about whether there is *any* chance the seven of us misheard what Abrams said?

Abrams is a liar. I'd have said that if given the chance.

Reading that article and especially that quote two hours ago made me want to crumple the paper and then burn it. I'm still furious. I tried doing my homework, but just read the same words over and over, not comprehending them, unable to get Abrams off my mind.

When I see my father's visible anger build as he reads the story, it makes me feel good that we're finally on the same page. We're a team again, like back in the old days. I'm not quite ready to rush up and hug him, but it feels good to have him on my side.

Finally.

But it turns out, I'm wrong. He's angry for an entirely different reason. He isn't on my side at all.

"Look at what you've done!" he says, shaking the newspaper angrily at me when he finishes reading the article.

My jaw drops. It feels as though the floor has opened up under me, and I'm plummeting down, down, down.

"Your coach probably didn't even say anything," my father says, waving the paper.

"He did! And that's exactly how he treats the black players."

"Maybe you misheard him."

"There was no misunderstanding what he said at all! Not a chance. He's lying!"

I feel sick to the pit of my stomach. My own father believes Abrams. *My own father!*

"You could be wrong!"

"No, I'm not! I'm not hard of hearing. All seven of us are not hard of hearing. And the rest of the team heard it, too. There was no mistaking it. After he said it, the whole gym turned like a tomb. Nobody could believe he used that word. He even said, 'I didn't say that.' Why would someone say, 'I didn't say that' if they didn't say it?"

"You should have given him the benefit of the doubt. He's your coach!"

"He said it, whether you want to believe me or not. It's pretty sad that you won't believe your own son. When have I ever lied to you?"

That stops him for only the briefest of moments. "When you and that girl came up with the story about stealing a car and avoiding the police!"

"That wasn't a lie!"

And we're off.

*

On Monday, it's even worse. Much, much worse. It's almost indescribable.

I pounce on the *Daily Evening Item* as soon as I hear it thud on our front porch, more than half an hour after I first poked my head around the dark brown curtains and looked out the front picture window, hoping to see it there. Every few minutes, I'd check to see if it had arrived. Then, disappointed, I'd go back to the sofa with my homework arrayed on the coffee table in front of it, and pretend to study while my mind remained stuck on Tomisetti's column.

What is he going to say about Charlie and me and the others? Is he going to question the credibility of Abrams' denial, even a little? Which words of mine has he used, and did he use them in our defense or did he use them against us?

I bring the paper inside, and Mom races into the front room to read over my shoulder as we both stand beside the coffee table and its now-forgotten homework. She leans close, smelling of talcum powder, as I open to the Sports section. There is Tomisetti's column running down the left edge of the section's first page.

What he says defies the imagination. The column portrays me, and by extension all seven of us, as something just short of Communist, bomb-throwing radicals, intent on destruction of the country and the moral fabric of society.

After giving a distorted wrap-up of the events, taking Abram's lies as gospel truth, he pounces on me like a tiger on raw meat. Mom gasps. I'm torn between a sense of mind-boggling disbelief and a fiery, red-hot fury that burns with greater and greater intensity with every sentence.

Labelle whines about the reaction of his classmates. "A lot of kids call us quitters," he says. Well, isn't that what he is? He quit the team. Doesn't that make him a quitter?

Deal with the consequences of your actions, young man!

I'd actually opine that "quitter" is about the nicest word I'd use to describe Labelle and his rebellious friends. What they've done represents in a microcosm everything that's wrong in our present day society. Our society is falling apart at the seams because of spoiled brats like these seven rebels without a cause. They all need a good spanking, if you ask this humble writer. Or they needed a lot more of them when they were growing up.

They walked out on their teammates, decimating the Lynn English High School basketball team, with no thought to its effect on presumed "friends" like senior guard Joe Thurman, who may need the Bulldogs to advance in the state tournament to make his case for a college scholarship next year. How do the seven rebels live with themselves after abandoning this fine young man, who lest the point be lost, is black and did not walk off the court? He is a credit to his race. The others, especially Labelle of whom more should be expected, are a disgrace.

Even more importantly—and tragically as it represents the fraying fabric of our society—the seven rebels flagrantly defied authority, the authority of a coach who is a legend at the school, having led the Bulldogs as a player, along with his brother, Delvin, and with some modest contributions from this writer, to the highest finishes in the state tournament in the school's history.

Let it be noted that Coach Abrams steadfastly denies using the racial epithet. As a close personal friend of his for going on twenty years now, I can attest to his unquestioned integrity. I believe him. I believe Coach Abrams used the word "Negro" and not that epithet, and these spoiled babies, who don't like getting hollered at because they've been pampered their entire lives, heard what they wanted to hear. They heard what would give them a way out of their commitment to the team. They heard what would allow them to lash out at their legendary coach in an unprecedented action.

Are these seven rebels any different than those who burn our cities during lawless riots, supposedly in support of "Civil Rights?" Are they any different than college students, privileged to attend the greatest schools of learning on the planet, instead protesting the Vietnam War because they are unwilling to fight to defend the country that has given them so much? Are they any different than the hippies in Haight-Ashbury, tripping out on LSD, dropping out of society with no intent to get an honest job, and espousing the Godless immorality of free love?

Make no mistake, our society is at a crossroads. And the subversive course these seven rebels have taken is the same as those who are trying to lead our great country and society down the path of destruction. History teaches us that even the great Roman Empire could not withstand the deterioration of its moral fabric. The Roman Empire fell because it became rotten to the core. We as a country and a society face the very same threat, and we see Exhibit A in our midst.

Make no mistake. These rebels, as evidenced by their reprehensible actions, are rotten to the core.

Speechless, I turn to my mom. Her face is ashen, eyes wide with disbelief. Tears pool in her eyes. Her lip trembles.

"How could he—" Mom shakes her head. "How could he say those awful things about you? None of that is true! You're a wonderful kid. A terrific young man!"

I can't even speak.

"What did you say to him?" she asks.

My mind is so scrambled I can't even remember a word. It takes what feels like minutes, even though it might have only been ten or fifteen seconds, for me to recall that she was standing there listening to my every word.

"You were right there. You heard every word I said," I remind her. "How did anything I said provoke that attack?"

She shakes her head, eyes wide, as if in shock. "I don't understand it."

We stand there in stunned, silent disbelief until Mom groans. "What is your father going to say?"

*

Turns out, a lot. He's late, even for him, so he mouths a quick apology as soon as he steps inside the door, but quickly forgets it.

"Look at this!" he shouts, still wearing his black winter coat. He unbuttoned it before starting to read the column, but got no further, his eyes widening and jaw clenching with every word. The three of us are standing in the middle of the front room, Mom behind me, her hands resting on my shoulders, her grip tight even as her hands tremble. My father shakes the paper angrily. "It's a disgrace!"

I'm not sure if he means the column, which I agree is a disgrace, or me. I'm pretty sure, though, he means me, and he clears that up, leaving no question at all, with his next words.

"You are an embarrassment to this family! Do you have any idea how humiliating this is to me?"

So I get dragged publicly through the mud in a newspaper everyone in this region reads, get smeared with every possible unfair comparison and label, and this is about *him*?

"My bosses are going to read this!" he yells, moving so close his beet-red face is just inches away from my own, his breath smelling of coffee. "My co-workers. My subordinates. All of them! They're going to read this and think this sort of rebellion against authority is the kind of thing I stand for. I raised a rebel—just like it says, a rebel without a cause—so what does that say about me? I must also have no respect for authority. This could ruin my career. Do you realize that? Do you have any idea what you've done?"

I feel like lashing out with words about exactly how I feel about his stupid career, and how if he gets demoted and has to crawl back to Maine with his tail between his legs like a whipped dog, it would be A-OK with me. Just so long as Anna comes along, too, of course. But as dumb as I can be sometimes, I'm not that dumb. My father's fury is volcanic right now, every word filled with fury and venom, and though I suppose it's raging so far out of control that tossing gasoline on that fire won't make a bit of difference, I somehow hold my tongue.

Then, he really gets savage. He stabs his glasses, which have slid down slightly, back to the bridge of his nose so fiercely I wonder if he'll have a bruise. Behind the glasses, his eyes bulge.

"You know what? I agree with him, with this guy!" He shakes the paper again, without moving his head an inch away from my face. "I don't know what's happened to you. You used to be a good, respectful kid, but now you are rotten to the core!"

"Andre," my mom says from behind me, her voice shaking, "you don't mean—"

"Shut up!" He glares over my head at Mom. She recoils from his anger, pulling me back with her, her grip so tight on my shoulders her long fingernails dig into my skin.

"Dad!" I yell back, horrified at the venom I see in his eyes.

"*You, be quiet!*" he shouts, glaring at me now, and though his fury rages, I'm glad to see it focused on me instead of Mom. "I ought to beat this out of you."

Mom gasps. "*Andre—*"

He shakes the paper at me one more time. "I ought to give you the whipping you deserve. The one this man talks about. Make up for all the ones I've missed."

He straightens up long enough to pull back his coat and the suit jacket beneath it to unbuckle his belt. He yanks it out, angrily pulling it free when it snags on one of the loops. He doubles up the leather strap in his hands even as my mother sobs, and says, "No, Andre!"

But before he turns me around, bends me over, and uses the strap on me over and over, he says the words that hurt me far worse.

"Remember that argument we had a month or two ago?" he asks, his teeth bared like a wild animal. "You told me you hated me. Well you know what? *I hate you!*"

*

I don't know why that bothers me so much. I suppose what's good for the goose is good for the gander, as my mom so often says. Whatever a gander is. It's all racing through my head as I lie on my bed, my homework still untouched on my desk. Mom popped in briefly, her eyes red and puffy from crying, and said that my father really didn't mean that.

But he did. And she and I both know it. She couldn't say much more after that.

I suppose I shouldn't care that he hates me. In fact, I try to convince myself I don't. It doesn't matter. He's a jerk, and I hated him a month or two ago back when we were fighting. And now that he's said he hates me, I'm certainly hating him back.

Hating with a passion.

So why do I feel so bad that he hates me?

Goose, gander?

I suppose if I'm going to dish it out, I have to take it. And a couple months ago, I dished it out first, even though I thought we'd bounced back from that. This time, he dished it out. And isn't it different for a parent?

Things sure were easier six months ago when we lived back up in Maine, and we weren't fighting all the time.

But at least down here, I've got Anna.

CHAPTER 18

Even from a distance, I can tell something is wrong. Horribly, horribly wrong. I've been waiting for Anna beside her locker, the smell of the pine-scented disinfectant strong off the shining, clean floors. When she sees me, she breaks into a run, as best she can with three books in her right arm, wearing dark blue dress shoes that match her dress but certainly aren't made for running. Her open winter coat flaps about her as she dodges other students in the hallway.

I race toward her and can see she's crying.

Actually, not just crying. Sobbing.

She crashes into me, and in another place and time I would joke about her hitting me like a linebacker. But there's nothing funny going on here. She throws her free arm around my neck and holds me close. Her body shakes with her sobbing.

"What's wrong?" I ask. When we talked last night on the phone, before my father came home because he was so late, everything was fine. Or at least as fine as it could be in light of the hatchet job the *Daily Evening Item* did on me. Anna was horrified at what the reporter had done to me. Had said over and over how unfair it was, for anyone really, but especially for me. But the two of us were fine. Anna was fine.

"Oh, Rabbit!" she says, the words choked and barely recognizable.

She squeezes me tight for just one more instant, then pulls away. She shakes her head. Tries to wipe away the tears streaming down her pretty face.

I reach out and gently try to help brush away the tears. Someone walking past mutters the word, "Quitter!" but I barely even hear him. I don't even look to see who it is. My eyes, and all my attention, are only on Anna.

"What's wrong?" I ask again, a sick feeling in my gut.

She says nothing until we get to her locker, I think because she can barely speak. She's swallowing hard, trying to get control of her emotions. She opens the locker, hangs her coat up, and exchanges two of her books for one that's already in there. She slams the locker shut.

Finally, she turns to me. Her lower lip trembles, and then the tears begin again, pouring down her face like Niagara Falls. I'm almost ready to burst into tears myself, and I don't even know why.

"What's wrong?" I ask for the third time. I feel an overwhelming sense of dread like nothing I've ever felt before.

"They're making me break up with you!" she says, the words exploding from her before the wracking sobs come again. She falls into me again, and wraps her arm around me.

I stand there, frozen. I feel her damp tears on my shoulder, but at the same time, I can't feel anything. "Who?" I ask, and realize as soon as the word is out what a stupid question it is. Obviously, her parents. Who else? But I was just so stunned, the word popped out.

"My father, actually," Anna says, and pulls away. "My mother kind of liked you, or at least she used to. But my father..."

Anna shakes her head, and a fresh set of tears roll down her cheeks. I brush them away as best I can, even as my heart sinks deeper and deeper. *This can't be happening. It can't be happening!*

"I think he always wanted an excuse to break us up," she says. "He doesn't want me going out with *any* boy, not just you. Even if we're not really going out on dates, you know?"

I nod.

"But he exploded when he saw the newspaper," Anna says, her face covered in pain. "Just *exploded*. Didn't give my mom a chance to say a thing, whether she agreed with him or not. He said—no, he didn't just say, he *shouted*, and at just about the top of his lungs—that you're exactly what's wrong with America today. No respect for authority. Spoiled brats. The breakdown of our country's moral fabric.

"It was awful! He took everything that horrid column said about you and swallowed it hook, line, and sinker. All those terrible lies. He hollered them right at me.

"He said I was too young to be interested in boys anyway, but that no matter how old I am, I'm not *ever* going out with *you*! No subversive rabble-rouser—those were his exact words, subversive rabble-rouser—is *ever* going to date his daughter. Not now. Not when I'm eighteen. Not when

I'm a hundred! He'll lock me away in a convent before a filthy degenerate like you ever puts your dirty paws on me!"

The homeroom bell rings. We take one last desperate look at each other. Anna gives me a quick hug and sprints for homeroom. I follow right behind for only half the way.

Then I stop running, and slow down to a crawl.

Like I really care whether I'm on time or not for stupid homeroom.

*

I walk with Anna toward her first-period English class, even though my class is in the opposite direction.

"I can't do this," Anna says.

I open my mouth to respond, but can't think of what to say. Whenever I used to read about someone, like a character in a novel, having a broken heart, I'd roll my eyes.

Good grief, get over it! I would think. *Quit being a baby!*

But now I'm on the other side of that window. My heart *is* breaking. I'm not being a baby about it. I feel like I'm dying inside. Like my heart is just being torn out of my chest. I know that sounds like I'm being a baby, like I'm being…what's the right word?…like I'm being melodramatic about it.

But I'm not.

I love the best girl in the world. And she's being taken away from me. Why? Because I tried to do the right thing? Maybe it would feel just as awful if it were for some other reason. Maybe it would feel even worse if it were because she liked someone else better than me, like if she dumped me for a psycho like Jimmy Keenan.

But I can't imagine anything worse than this.

"Can't you just…" My throat closes up on me. I can't speak. Or swallow. Or anything.

"I want us to keep going out," Anna says, her voice shaking. "I…I like you too much. I like you a lot. You're so sweet and nice." She smiles weakly. "And handsome." She gulps, the smile gone. "But I'm not a fighter like you are."

The words hit me like a brick square between the eyes. "What's that supposed to mean?"

Anna shakes her head in frustration. "What I mean is…" She takes a deep breath, then exhales loudly. "What I mean is, you holler at your father when you fight. I've never hollered at my father in my life. Not once. He'd *kill* me. I told you he's a former Marine. Tough as nails. Not even my brother can sass him back. Rabbit, sometimes you talk about *defying* your father. I can't defy mine. I can't even imagine it!"

I feel like a drowning man sinking beneath angry, dark waves. "So just go out with me here at school," I suggest, grabbing on to the only life preserver for us that I can find. "We can go back to writing letters. We'll still have that. It won't be that bad."

"I'm not good at lying to my parents," she says, and I wonder if that means she thinks that I am. Then I realize what I'm trying to persuade her to do. Lie to her parents. Write letters to me and hide them, along with the ones I write to her. Defy her parents' order that we break up.

I guess I'm every bit the subversive her scary Marine father thinks I am.

But I can't just let Anna go. "What if—"

"Besides," she says. "My older brother is a senior here. He'll see us in the hallways and rat me out. He's always calling me a Goody Two-Shoes. Nothing would make him happier than getting me in trouble."

I have no answer for that.

We've reached Anna's class so if I'm going to avoid being late for my own class, I'll need to make a mad dash for it. My homeroom teacher, Miss Matthews, was preoccupied so I didn't get in trouble for being a few seconds late for that. But if I keep it up, it's only a matter of time before I get sent to the principal's office.

Not that I really care anymore about that stuff. After all, I'm a delinquent subversive, right? That's what Tomisetti said, and I can see in the way some teachers look at me that they believe it. Anna's father believes it. I'm everything that's wrong about America. I'm going to ruin the country, bring it crashing down just like happened to the ancient Roman Empire.

So what difference does it make if I'm late for class? What difference does it make if I get sent to the principal's office? I'm just a bad kid in the process of destroying the United States of America.

I'm rotten to the core.

Rotten and alone, now that I've lost Anna.

"I gotta go," I say. I turn on a dime and run.

Rotten and alone.

*

One period later, still feeling like a truck has run over me, I walk with a leaden heart to history class. On my way, I spot Charlie walking the other way with Jamaal. I make a quick U-turn and sidle up next to them,

Charlie on my right and Jamaal to my far right. In the few days since we left the team, I've given a nod of recognition to them when I've seen them in the hallways but never stopped to talk.

"How you doing, man?" I say to Charlie, then glance to Jamaal. "You, too."

Charlie shrugs. "Been better."

Ain't that the truth, I think. But they don't want to hear about my problems. Jamaal doesn't look at me. He just nods.

We walk in silence for a few seconds as all around us conversations buzz, locker doors open and slam, and behind us someone erupts in laughter. The air feels stale and heavy, although perhaps that's all in my head because the three of us are in such a glum mood.

"It ain't fair," I finally say, because I can't think of anything else. I realize this is why I haven't stopped to talk before. There's nothing much to say. Nothing we can do. We're powerless. Rebels without a cause.

Charlie nods, but says nothing. Distant, as if he's mad. But of course he's mad.

"Where's your girlfriend?" Charlie finally asks.

"We broke up," I say, trying unsuccessfully to keep my voice steady. It shakes with emotion.

Charlie raises an eyebrow in momentary surprise, but then the sullen curtain descends again. Eyes distant. Jaw set. I can almost feel his seething anger.

"Her father forced her to break up with me," I say, not sure if they want to hear about my problems, but the bitter words just spill out. "I'm everything that's wrong about America. No respect for authority. Tearing down the moral fabric of our society. Just like the guy in the newspaper said."

Charlie says nothing. He looks even more angry, if that's possible.

"Why'd that guy call you and not me?" Jamaal says, a razor-sharp edge in his Southern-accented voice.

I'm stunned. "He didn't call you? I thought he called everyone."

"Nah, just you and Charlie," Jamaal says. "None of the rest of us was worth his time. We didn't matter. 'Cause we just *Negroes*."

My heart sinks.

"He hardly talked to me at all," Charlie says. "How long he talk to you?"

"Maybe ten minutes," I say.

Charlie swears softly and shakes his head. "'Cause you the only one that matters."

"White boy," Jamaal says, in case I haven't gotten the point.

I'm so shocked, I stop dead in my tracks, jaw agape. Charlie and Jamaal don't look back. They just keep walking.

I run to catch back up to them.

"But…that isn't right," I say.

Charlie looks at me like I'm so dumb he can't believe it.

"Welcome to the real world," he says.

"*Our* world," Jamaal says, in case once again I'm too stupid to get it. "You catch that phrase in the paper where the man calls us a disgrace?"

"What phrase?" I ask.

"Figures," Jamaal says, and gives Charlie a dirty look. "Thought you said the midget white boy be different. He ain't different. He just like 'em all."

"What phrase?" I ask again, panic rising in my throat. "There were a lot of them. That reporter said just about everything possible to humiliate all of us."

Jamaal shakes his head. "Reporter say, 'The others, *especially Labelle of whom more should be expected*, are a disgrace.'" Jamaal says the words about me as if something foul is in his mouth. Now he glares at me. "Tell me, white boy. Why should more be expected of you? 'Cause you white? Us *Negroes* expected to be a disgrace? The only surprise be you?"

I can't even speak. Then, unbelievably, it gets worse.

"Didn't notice that, did you?" he says. "Maybe 'cause that's what you think."

I shake my head, but words fail me.

"That's why he was *never* my friend," Jamaal says to Charlie. "I have white teammates. I have white classmates. But I ain't got no white *friends*." Jamaal turns to me. "Get lost, white boy."

*

Does *everyone* hate me?

It almost feels that way. Well, Anna doesn't *hate* me, but I've lost her. And my mother doesn't hate me, but it sure seems like I've become a mystery to her. She doesn't know what to think about me. Turns out Jamaal was never my friend even though I thought he was. Even guys like Jeff Goodwin and Paul DiSimone, with whom I spend so many classes and have shared lots of laughs, have distanced themselves as if it's all my fault the basketball season is ruined.

Or maybe they feel like I'm "a traitor to the white race," as Rick Cassidy said with a sneer after cornering me in the hallway the other day. I expect him to be a jerk, but not Jeff and Paul, who I had thought were okay guys. If that's what it is, I don't want them as friends.

Good riddance to bad rubbish, as my mom would say.

But mostly I'm like a ship barely afloat in the ocean in the middle of a storm, its rudder broken, bobbing up and down as each angry wave crashes over the bow. I'm just hoping to avoid going under.

Thoughts like these crash through my head all through History until I resolve to stop feeling bad for myself—*poor baby*, a part of me mockingly sneers even while the other part wants to cry—and do something about it. The instant the bell sounds, I bolt out of my chair and out the room, past a startled Anna and stuffy, white-haired Mrs. McPherson, and race back down the hallway where I left Charlie and Jamaal.

"Hey," I say when I catch up to them. At first, they're surprised to see me, then their faces harden.

"What do you want?" Jamaal asks.

"I can't leave it this way," I say. "If you both are going to hate me because that reporter singled me out so he could humiliate me a little more than both of you, then maybe there's nothing I can do. That'll really bother me—I'll *hate* it!—because you're both great guys, and I value your friendship.

"Jamaal, I hope what you said wasn't true, because I've considered you my friend ever since I got to know you. And Charlie, I *know* you've been my friend, as good a friend as I've got. So I'm not going to take losing our friendship lying down. I'm going to fight for it. For both of you, but especially you, Charlie. We've been through a lot together."

Charlie looks away. The hardness in his face softens.

"That reporter was a jerk," I say. "A jerk and a bigot. There's no excuse for him not talking to all of us. He wasn't even on a deadline. That wasn't a late-breaking news story; it was a column. He had all the time in the world to make his calls. He was just lazy. He had decided what he was going to write before he even talked to us." I look to Jamaal. "Sorry. Before he talked to Charlie and me.

"I apologize for not noticing that phrase. It is awful, and I should have noticed. But I was just so humiliated by everything he was saying about us, and yeah, by him singling out me. I was in shock. I've never seen anything like it. There's never been anything bad about me in the papers before. Just me scoring a touchdown, or back up in Maine, leading the league in batting average and stuff like that. Seems like everyone down here reads the *Item*. Must be tens of thousands or maybe even hundreds of thousands. And Tomisetti, the reporter, was trying to make me seem like the Devil himself."

It looks like I've convinced Charlie, but not Jamaal. And I suspect Jamaal, who apparently was never my friend, hard as it is for me to accept that, is the one who convinced Charlie how awful I am—how *white* I am—in the first place. Jamaal came here to Lynn from down South. Maybe not Mississippi where they killed Chaney, Goodman, and Schwerner just because they were trying to get black people registered to vote, but North Carolina and, before that, Georgia.

And although it's clear that we've got plenty of bigotry up here, it seems like it's more flagrant, almost flaunted, down there. They've even got the Ku Klux Klan burning crosses and killing people. So maybe Jamaal just expects most white people to be evil. Or at least not friendly. He's been given reason to feel that way. So it was natural to lump me in with all the white people who openly treated him with contempt.

I have to think that Charlie only listened to him because he's so upset about what happened. Or at least I sure hope so. I hope he wouldn't naturally jump to this conclusion.

A bolt of inspiration hits.

"I was humiliated, but also I can be really dumb sometimes," I say.

"Oh, stop," Jamaal says. "You taking accelerated courses. You on the college track. You ain't dumb. Who you trying to fool?"

"I may be book smart, but sometimes I'm everything-else stupid," I say. "Charlie, remember you introducing me to Jessie Stackhouse?"

Charlie begins to chuckle.

"We were on the football team together," I say, "and Charlie was telling me what a great hockey player Jessie was."

"I don't know nothing about hockey," Jamaal says. "But I heard he's good."

"Well, Charlie started telling me about Jessie scoring hat tricks," I say, and now Charlie's hand is covering his mouth and his shoulders are shaking with laughter. "And I thought a hat trick must be when a player puts the puck under his hat, sneaks in unobserved, and scores a goal!"

Charlie explodes in laughter.

"Oh, come on!" Jamaal says. "Nobody that stupid."

"Yes he is!" Charlie says, and now we're all laughing, even Jamaal. "Yes he is!"

*

None of us laugh after school, though, when we see lanky, dark-haired Rick Cassidy coming the other way, making a beeline for the gym as we head to the front door and our rides home. The basketball team plays

Gloucester today in an away game, and from the look of sadness and longing in the eyes of Charlie and Jamaal, they're as sick about it as I am.

Cassidy gives us an extra kick where it hurts, smirking and calling out as he passes, "Going anywhere, girls?"

"Jerk!" I mutter, loud enough for Cassidy to hear.

He laughs, clearly pleased that he got under my skin. Not the smartest thing I've ever said. We say nothing more until he's well out of hearing range.

"I miss it. Miss it a lot," Charlie says, a distant look in his eyes. "Some of us played at the Y yesterday. Pickup starts there at 4:30. Join us, if you want. But it ain't the same." He shakes his head. "Anybody any good be somewhere else, practicing on a team. Like we should be. We should be getting on that bus to Gloucester, not going home."

"Yeah," I say, and feel a vast emptiness inside.

There's a huge hole in my heart that Anna used to fill. I've avoided her since she told me this morning that she can't defy her parents and keep going out with me. Not that I can blame her. She's sweet and nice. Not a rebel without a cause. Not rotten to the core. Maybe I really am that bad and she's better off without me. But that doesn't make me feel any better about it. So I've avoided her, not knowing what to say, not knowing if there's *anything* I can say.

But on top of that, there's also that other huge hole that basketball, or at least playing some sport, has always filled. I've always been throwing or catching a ball, or shooting one. Racing up and down a field or a court. I remember one day just half a year ago, back up in Maine, when I had a cross-country race in the morning, a Babe Ruth baseball game in the afternoon, and a summer league basketball game that night. My mom thought I was doing too much, but I thought it was the best day ever.

Now, I've got nothing.

I'll have to see if she can get me to some of those 4:30 pickup games at the Y. That's an awful time for her, mostly picking me up when it's over, but maybe she can do it a couple days a week. It may be a poor imitation of the real thing, but at least I'll be playing a little. It's not like I can go to a playground in freezing weather with a foot of snow covering the court. It's the Y or nothing at all. It makes me sick to see a jerk like Rick Cassidy getting ready to go to a game I should be going to, and rubbing my nose in the fact that I can't.

"Every day," Charlie says, "my body wants to be down in that gymnasium. Sweat pouring off of me. Sinking shots. Grabbing rebounds. Hearing the squeak of my sneakers on the floor. Even doing some of that crazy coach's drills. Instead..." He shrugs again, then shakes his head. "My mom says she's going to petition the school committee to let me attend Classical next year. No way I can play for Abrams, and it's too important to just give up 'cause I could get a college scholarship."

"Of course you could!" I don't know anything about basketball scholarships. I just know how great a player Charlie is. I belatedly turn to Jamaal, with whom I seem to have patched things up, at least a little, though apparently not enough to be his friend. "You, too."

"She says she'll threaten to sue," Charlie says, then snorts derisively. "As if we have money for a lawyer." He shakes his head. "But if I don't get a scholarship, then no way I can go to college. And if I don't go to college, you know what that means."

"What?" I ask. The possibility of not going to college is so far from my mind, I haven't considered it.

"What happens to all black boys who can't afford college," Jamaal says bitterly, his eyes narrowed. "Unlike you rich white boys."

It hits me just before Charlie spells it out, and icicles shoot up my spine and into the back of my neck and brain.

"Vietnam," Charlie says. "Unless the war is over by then. And it don't look like it's ever gonna be over. They just sending more and more of us over there to fight that war."

My father's words, blithely spoken a few months ago, hit me like a stone fist between the eyes. *The ones who aren't smart enough to get into college or can't afford it…well, those are the ones who are most expendable. The lower classes have always done most of the fighting. Always have and always will. It's the way of the world.*

I feel sick to my stomach. I had never considered that Abrams' impact could extend this far.

As if to underline the point—as if underlining it is even necessary—Charlie says, "Some of us come back in wheelchairs. Some of us in body bags. Some not at all."

A mental image forms of Charlie and Jamaal in body bags. Lifeless. Their parents grieving. Me, safely tucked away at some university. And Abrams smugly looking on and saying, "They're just niggers."

"We've got to get Abrams fired!" I hear myself blurt out, and I'm as astonished to hear the words as Charlie and Jamaal.

"*What?*" Charlie says. He and Jamaal stop walking and stare at me like I'm a lunatic. Students stream around us on both sides, giving us odd looks that I barely notice.

"They ain't gonna do that," Jamaal says. "Man, you really are stupid, you think that."

"He and that damned brother of his are legends here," Charlie says. "Fired? You crazy if you think that's happening."

My mind races. The spark flares into a flame, then it's a bonfire, then an entire forest is burning to the ground.

"Listen!" I say, thinking of recent scenes from the evening news. "That reporter compared us to those protesting for Civil Rights, like the ones who march with Dr. King, and to college students protesting the Vietnam War. As if those are bad things. What if we give them a dose of that medicine? What if we protest what Abrams has done to you guys? Call for his firing." The words spew out of me with no filter. "Don't take this lying down! Let's stand up to prejudice. Let's stand up to Abrams. He deserves to be fired!"

"Who you think you are," Jamaal asks. "Martin Luther King?"

"I'm…I'm a nobody," I say, shaking my head and shrugging. "I'm not even good at basketball. Not compared to you guys, at least. You guys have a chance to be great. You have a chance to earn college scholarships. But Abrams and his prejudice are denying you that right! And that could result in you going to Vietnam, and not coming back alive! Don't let that happen! Don't let Abrams win!"

"You crazy," Jamaal says, shaking his head. "Crazy-ass white boy."

Charlie stares at me. "Are you serious?"

"Yes!" I say. "Why give up without a fight? Why should you have to petition the school committee to escape his…his evil, when *he's* the one who did something wrong? Ever since he stuck you on the freshmen team, where you don't belong, he's been treating you like…like that awful name he called you. Then what does he do when you're slaughtering the competition? Does he move you up to the team you belong on? No, he tells you you're playing too playground! Which even he *admitted* is just a code word for black! Or in his case, that awful word that begins with the letter N. And if you're going to play for him, you've got to stop playing…black!"

No one says a thing for a long time. I wonder if I've said too much, or said the wrong thing. More students stream around us, buzzing in their conversations. One even mutters, "Quitters!" as he passes by, but none of us even looks to see who said it.

"You really are serious," Charlie finally says.

"Dead serious," I say. "As dead as you could be if you go to Vietnam instead of college."

"He is crazy, no doubt about that," Charlie says to Jamaal. "But he's right."

CHAPTER 19

My mother is horrified. She almost drives off the road.

"*Whaaaat?*" she shrieks. "You're going to do *what*?"

I guess that went over well.

I suppose I should have told her before she shifted from park into drive and pulled out of the pick-up area in front of the high school. If I thought she'd almost wreck the car, I would have. Instead, I ate my sticky-sweet fluffernutter, washing it down with milk, then wiped my hands off with a napkin.

Only then, with the heater blasting warm air as she drove past the fire station and funeral home on our right, did I drop the bomb.

"It's the right thing to do," I explain.

"Your father will kill us!"

She's got a point. Not literally, of course, but considering how he blew up over the newspaper article and column, this could be like Mount Vesuvius erupting and destroying the ancient city of Pompeii. I can't even imagine his reaction.

Not that I care. A cynical side of me recalls that "the Negroes" was one of his concerns when he moved us here from the boonies in northern Maine where we never saw any of them. Little did he realize what flavor of "Negro problem" could arise, namely his son taking a very public, possibly controversial—and who am I kidding, I *know* this is going to be controversial—stand supporting them.

Recently in English, we learned the word *schadenfreude*, a word from the German that refers to enjoying the misery of others. I guess I'm feeling *schadenfreude* over the discomfort my father's prejudice is about to cause him.

Good! He deserves it.

But the warmth of that guilty pleasure doesn't last long. It turns into an icy chill in the pit of my stomach as soon as I think of how his discomfort will translate to anger directed at Mom and me. It could get ugly. In fact, it almost certainly will. But we've still got to do it.

"College scholarships for Charlie and Jamaal and maybe others are at stake," I say. "I can't let Dad's prejudice stop me from standing up for them. Standing up for what's right. Standing up for all the black players that will be coming after them in future years."

"But Rabbit…" she says, fear visible in her eyes. She's gripping the steering wheel so hard it looks like she might snap it in two.

"This is a matter of right and wrong," I say, hating how I've made her feel, but unable to back down. "Charlie and Jamaal, and all the black players on that team, are in the right. Coach Abrams is—"

"What about that star player on the varsity? The black kid who beat you at free throws?"

"Not every time," I say with a smile, even as I wistfully think back to how much fun those free throw competitions were against the team's star, and how much I miss them.

"You know what I mean," Mom says with more than a hint of exasperation. "He didn't quit."

"I'm sure he wishes he could," I say, thinking about the one time I saw Joe Thurman in the hallway, and he quickly turned away, looking "guilty as sin" as Mom would say. "But he's a senior. If he quits now, he's throwing away his chance at a college scholarship. That's too big a sacrifice, especially after all he's put up with dealing with Coach Abrams till now."

"If he could put up with Coach Abrams, why can't your friends?"

"Mom! Abrams stuck them on the freshmen team only because they're black and they play black. Now, he's said they play nigger basketball." She flinches at the word, just like I inwardly flinched saying it. "What are they supposed to do?"

"Don't holler!"

I belatedly realize how loud I've cranked up the volume. "Sorry."

Mom shakes her head. "Oh, Rabbit. What am I going to do with you?"

*

Charlie and Jamaal talk to the other black players who quit, but only Tim Peterson agrees to join us. The others make what sound like weak excuses, so it'll just be us four freshmen. Mom, who has sworn me to secrecy as far as my father is concerned so she can "tell him at the right time," has volunteered to create the placards we're going to carry. For someone who was horrified at the idea, she sure has stepped up with her support.

I think she wishes she could march with Dr. King for Civil Rights and protest the Vietnam War along with all the college students who are doing it. She gets a wistful look in her eye and in the tone of her voice when she talks about those protests.

"I'm just a white housewife," she said once while we were watching the news together, waiting for my father to get home from work. The news story was about Dr. King's next march. "What am I supposed to do? Leave you and your father and march on Washington?"

And when in my blithe ignorance I asked why not, she just shook her head. "Besides," she said, "have you seen what the police do? They turn attack dogs on the protestors, even the women and children."

So maybe for her this is the next best thing. She can do what's right without facing attack dogs in Alabama or getting murdered like Goodman and Schwerner in Mississippi.

For me, it's a long, nervous wait until Friday.

*

The day before the big protest, on Thursday morning before home-room, I approach my locker to see Anna waiting.

Anna. Waiting for me. Smiling!

My heart leaps into my throat, my hands feel suddenly clammy, and my mouth goes dry. I gulp hard.

"Hi," I say.

She looks beautiful, wearing her peach-colored dress with white trim. She always looks beautiful. Her smile melts my heart.

"Hi, Rabbit," she says shyly. She holds two textbooks to her chest. Her cheeks flush, and I feel my own grow warm. It's only been two days since she tearfully told me that her parents were forbidding her to have any-thing to do with me, but it's felt like two years. Hardest of all have been the classes I've shared with her. I've had to force myself not to look at her, and make sure I wasn't walking anywhere close to her. Otherwise, I'd just feel so sad. Yesterday morning, I found myself starting to walk to her locker, on autopilot, I guess you could say, although that may just have been where I wanted to go, where I wished I could go.

"How are you doing?" I ask, my voice cracking. I cringe at how pathetic I sound.

"I've been pretty sad since we…you know…"

"I know."

"I'm not going to stop liking you. I can't," she says, the eyes behind her glasses briefly blazing. "I just can't." But then that fire dims. She holds a hand out to the side, palm up, in a what-am-I-going-to-do gesture. "But I can't defy my parents." She gives me a weak smile. "At least not openly."

I'm riding an emotional roller coaster with Anna's every word. She can't stop liking me. Up, way up. But then she can't defy her parents. A sickening downward plunge. Can't defy her parents *openly*. Back up again?

"What do you mean?" I ask cautiously.

"I want to still be your girlfriend."

"Yes!" I say, a broad, probably stupid-looking smile filling my face. "Yes!"

"Wait!" she says. "Let me finish."

"Yes, yes, yes, yes, yes," I say. I don't care the conditions. I'll climb Mount Everest for this girl. I'll crawl from here to California. Whatever she says.

She laughs, and the old twinkle is back in her eyes. "Let me finish."

"Okay," I say, "but yes, yes, yes, yes, yes."

"Stop it!" she says, but can't stop laughing. Those eyes can't stop twinkling. But then she does get serious. "We have to at least pretend to have broken up."

My heart sinks. My shoulders slump. No, no, no, no, no.

"No letters. They might get found," she says. "We can read the old ones each night. At least I can. I've kept them all. Have you?"

"Of course!"

"So we'll have that. But no phone calls. We can walk with each other to class. There's no law against that. We share a lot of classes. We'll look like classmates, nothing more. Just friends. No more holding hands. No hugs. Nothing my brother can see and tattle to my parents about. So it'll look like we've broken up. And on a certain level, we will have. So I won't be lying to my parents."

I nod grimly. This is better than nothing, I suppose, but not by much. No phone calls, no letters, no holding hands. What can we do?

"It can be better than you think," she says.

I raise my eyebrows, not believing there's much that can make this farce of a relationship bearable.

"We have our imaginations," she says, and now her eyes blaze with a red-hot intensity. "So when we walk down the hall together, we can imagine holding hands. We can imagine me giving you a hug, not just a few times, but before *every* class. And we can pick some time every night when we'll both *imagine* a ten-minute conversation with each other instead of a five-minute real one. What do you think?"

Pretend phone calls? Imagined hugs and holding hands? It doesn't sound very good, but then I look at her beaming face and my grim outlook crumbles brick by brick. It sure is better than nothing.

"When did you come up with this?" I ask.

"While trying to keep from crying the last two nights. I had to do something."

"It's brilliant!" I say, overstating it by a little. Probably by a lot. But it's given us a chance.

"It may get frustrating," Anna says. "In fact, I'm sure it will at times. We may decide that all that imagining is just driving us crazy. Then we'll have to come up with something else. What do you think?"

"Yes, yes, yes, yes, yes," I say. "Although I think I'm repeating myself."

She laughs. "Some repetition is good."

So I say yes all over again.

Anna looks furtively up and down the hall, and appears to decide that the coast is clear. "Just to give us one last memory to use for our imagination, here's one for the road." She puts her books on the ground and wraps her arms around my neck in the most wonderful hug ever. I drink in the lilac smell of her perfume, the strawberry smell of her hair, and the softness of the skin of her neck against mine. My arms hold her tight. I don't want to let her go.

It's bittersweet, because I know I might never get another hug like this one again. Or at least not for a very long time. But it's mostly sweet because I already thought I might never get another hug from her, ever, so this one feels like an unexpected gift.

And I know for sure I'll get a bazillion more of these in my imagination.

*

It takes some getting used to, but imagining we're holding hands as we walk from one class to the next isn't that bad. I just think about her soft hand in mine, our fingers intertwined, and it's pretty good. At first, though, I stop talking without realizing it just so I can think about us holding hands.

"Rabbit," Anna says, a bemused look on her face. "Imagining we're holding hands misses the point if we can't talk at the same time."

I realize what I've been doing, and feel like the punch line in the worst of the dumb-jock jokes. A guy who can't chew gum and walk at the same time.

I feel my face flush. "Sorry."

Anna laughs. "Don't apologize. Just relax."

I nod. We keep walking and I say something about the homework assignment we've just been given, all while thinking about her hand in mine.

"What did I just do?" she asks.

I blink. "I don't know."

"Think about it," she says. "Imagine what I just did with my hand."

"You..." My mind is blank for a moment, but then it comes to me. "You squeezed my hand with yours."

Anna smiles broadly. "You're a natural."

We come to our classroom and pause outside the door. I imagine a hug, and without actually smelling it, my mind remembers lilacs and strawberries. The hair on the back of my neck stands up as I remember the touch of her wrapping her arms around me.

I can get used to this. Oh, yeah, I can really, really get used to this.

We repeat our imaginings before each shared class, then walk to our seats with big smiles on our faces. Our friends look at us curiously, as if we're a little bit crazy, and I guess we are.

We're the happiest sort-of-broken-up couple in history.

CHAPTER 20

There's no smiling on Friday. The four of us—Charlie, Jamaal, Tim, and me—leave through the school's front doors and step outside, our faces grim and determined, masking an inner nervousness that I'm sure all of us feel.

I know I do.

We've kept this as much of a secret as possible. Other than the seven of us players and whichever parents we felt would be supportive, we've told no one.

"No one else," Charlie said. "I don't want no surprises. No cops waiting for us or nothing like that."

"And no girlfriends," Jamaal said, looking pointedly at me. He and Charlie looked oddly at me earlier in the hallways as I walked with Anna, laughing and, in our minds, holding hands. I'm sure we didn't look much like a couple that had broken up, and even though they didn't ask, they had to know.

So I didn't tell Anna. I kept my promise and didn't totally spill the beans, but I didn't want to totally keep her in the dark either. It doesn't feel natural, or right, to hide things from her. So I was vague, and just said that the group of us former teammates weren't going to accept our plight and the maligning of our character by jerks like Tomisetti. We were going to fight back.

She'd frowned, looking concerned, and said, "Like…letters to the editor, or something like that?"

That was actually a good idea, something I'd mention to the guys. Either one from everyone who was willing to participate, or a single collective letter signed by us all. But our primary response would be more active than that.

"Not exactly," I said. I ran my thumb and index finger across my lips in a zipping-shut gesture, then forced a smile.

"Rabbit, are you going to get in trouble?" she asked.

"Trouble seems to be my middle name."

Now, I wonder how much trouble we could be getting ourselves into. It's not like we're going to break any laws. We're going to march along Goodridge Street, so we aren't even going to be on any school property, but I can't help but be nervous. On TV, I've seen police, especially down south, beat protestors with billy clubs and unleash attack dogs on them. I can't imagine that happening to us. We aren't threatening an entire society built on subjugating black people like when Dr. Martin Luther King leads protests, but according to people like Tomisetti, we're a threat to society in our own way. My overactive imagination sees us all getting our skulls caved in by angry police.

So my heart is in my throat as I point the way to my mother's light blue Ford Fairlane out on Goodridge Street, just outside the entrance to the semicircle driveway that curves toward the school's front doors and then back out to the street. We walk past classmates happily boarding the three yellow buses about fifty feet away, idling in the part of the semicircle closest to the front doors and the ancient-style columns that stretch three stories high to the concrete marquee above that reads ENGLISH HIGH SCHOOL in big block letters. Our classmates are ready for the weekend, laughing and talking, feeling not a care in the world.

A stark contrast to us.

We've caught a bit of a break. The temperatures are above freezing, in the mid-thirties, with almost no wind at all. Cold, but it could be a lot worse. We plan to be here for hours, and an arctic wind or low temperatures would quickly freeze us to the bone.

Mom pops out of her car, and has the trunk open before we get there. She's reaching in for the first placard when Tim Peterson—six-one and all long arms and legs, so uncoordinated I expect him to drop his sign at least once—speaks up.

"Guys," he says, shaking his head. He gulps. "I can't do this."

He bolts for the school buses, almost tripping over his own feet, before anyone can say a word.

The rest of us look at each other and let out a collective sigh.

"Anyone else want to leave?" Charlie asks. "No hard feelings."

Jamaal and I shake our heads. Mom looks sadly on.

"I'd call him a coward," Charlie says, "if I didn't have half a mind to do it myself."

"This is important," I say. "For both of you. For all the black players, now and in the future."

"That don't make it easy, but we're gonna do this," Charlie says. "And we're gonna do it before those buses leave. I want everyone leaving now to see us, especially anyone who's called us a quitter or worse these last couple days. Mrs. L., I'll take one of those."

The placards are made of white poster board about a foot and a half wide and almost twice as high, attached to a four-foot-long, sturdy wooden post. Charlie hefts the wooden post with both hands, nods, and reads the message neatly printed in large, black, block letters.

ABRAMS MUST GO

SAY NO TO BIGOTRY

As she hands placards to Jamaal and me, a familiar car pulls up behind us: a rusted-out, old Rambler, shaped like a gray box. Charlie's mother steps out. She's a strong-looking woman with a kind face and a huge Afro.

"Ma," Charlie says. "I got to do this."

"Yes, you do," she says with a proud smile. "And so do I."

She reaches out her hand for a sign. Mom gives her one and looks at me with a conspiratorial smile. Then she grabs one for herself and slams the trunk.

"You didn't think," Mom says, "we were going to leave you here all alone, did you?"

*

Jamaal's mother arrives fifteen minutes later, a thin, wiry woman with the blackest of skin and streaks of gray through her close-cropped hair. And after her, Tim Peterson's mother, a big woman both tall and wide, who looks both disappointed and relieved when we tell her that Tim bolted for the bus. She offers a quick apology, and leaves.

We begin marching back and forth, spreading out single file, along the cleanly shoveled Goodridge Street sidewalk, from one tip of the semicircle to the other, a bit more than the length of a football field. Charlie is about fifty feet in front of me, and I'm about fifty feet in front of Jamaal. Tightly packed homes line the opposite side of the street, almost all of them two- and three-family houses, interrupted only by side streets that stretch off to Western Avenue in the distance and Mandee's Pizza on one corner. On our side, the normally grassy, tree-lined area between the street and the semicircle driveway is covered by half a foot of thinly crusted snow. It's split in half by a shoveled walkway fifteen feet wide, a white flagpole at its center, halfway between Goodridge Street and the school entrance. The trees along the sidewalk and walkway, spaced at irregular intervals that average out to about fifty feet or so, are barren of leaves, their tangled, snow-coated limbs towering over us. The school itself, gray concrete and three stories high, extends the length of three football fields.

We chant, "Abrams must go! Say no to bigotry!" It feels awkward. Who are we chanting to? Parents picking up their kids? Women inside their homes on the other side of the street trying to watch soap operas? It feels silly. The freshmen game is still over an hour away, and those are always poorly attended. The larger audience won't start arriving until close to seven o'clock when the varsity game starts.

But protestors on TV chant, so we chant. We shrug, give each other embarrassed grins, and chant the words written on our signs in bold black letters.

"Abrams must go! Say no to bigotry!"

The yellow buses pull out of the drive, turn left and pass us on the way to Chestnut Street, belching their exhaust. Now we have someone to chant to, so we chant and shake our placards for emphasis. It isn't a receptive audience. The same classmates who would have likely cheered our exploits on the court call out insults and stretch their arms out the windows to give us the finger.

"Quitters!"

"Better off without you!"

And then, sadly, "Go back to Africa!" followed by, "Go back to Roxbury!" referring to Boston's black, mostly impoverished neighborhood.

That feels like a sucker punch to the gut, but Charlie and Jamaal appear to shrug it off fast enough. We go back to marching and chanting to a nonexistent audience, unless, that is, pigeons strutting on the sidewalk and cooing from the porches of the three-deckers across the street count as an audience.

It gets boring pretty fast. Cold and boring. Mom, seeming to think of everything, brought not only my black wool hat and gloves but enough extras for an army. At first, the three of us all declined them. We're tough. But within minutes we're pulling them on over cold ears and fingers, wishing we had something to heat up our toes as well.

We scratch our scalps because the wool hats are itchy, but we put them right back on. It's cold and uncomfortable. But more than anything else, it's boring. We walk back and forth, up a bit more than the length of a football field and then back, holding our placards, at first shaking them for emphasis but soon tiring of that. We chant. The placard, light as it is even with its sturdy wooden post, gets heavy fast. We switch it from one hand to the other, occasionally saved from splinters by the thick gloves we're wearing. Then up and back some more. Chanting, though with decreasing frequency and plummeting enthusiasm.

Boring.

We stay spaced about fifty feet apart from each other so fans arriving for the freshman game have to walk close to at least one of us and see our signs and hear our chants, no matter whether they're entering at one of the two ends of the semicircle or heading down the walkway that cuts through the middle. We aren't setting up a picket line, and asking them not to cross. We just want them to see us and hear us. We want them to think about what we're saying.

We want Abrams fired.

Some fans, mostly parents and more often than not mothers, duck their heads down and ignore us, walking briskly to escape our presence as quickly as possible. Others look on us with disdain, some of them uttering the predictable insults. One father, a six-foot-tall hulk of a man who looks like he lives in a gym's weight room, snatches the placard out of my hands and snaps the wooden post over his knee.

"What you gonna do about that, you little puke?" he says. When I say nothing, he shoves me sprawling into the snow. "I say no *to you!*"

As the others quickly come rushing to my side, the brute brushes his bare hands off and heads down the walkway to the school entrance. When he passes the flagpole, he cuffs it with his bare hand, either to get out more of his aggression or, suspecting I'm watching, let's me know that's what he'd like to do to me.

Flustered and humiliated, my face feeling quite warm and my heart thumping loudly inside my chest, I borrow the keys to Mom's car. I angrily fling the pieces of the ruined placard in the trunk and take out another. I tell myself to forget the incident. This isn't going to stop me. But there sure are times I wish I was Wilt Chamberlain's size, seven-one and 275 pounds. Let the jerks of the world try to push me around then!

"You okay, man?" Charlie asks, when I get back from the car.

"Ready to take on Muhammad Ali," I say.

Charlie shakes his head and laughs. "Jamaal's right about one thing. You are one crazy-ass white boy."

Who am I to disagree?

*

Charlie suggests that the three of us switch from walking single file, spread widely apart, to all three of us walking abreast. It just isn't that important, he says, that every fan walk within twenty feet of one of us. He may just be trying to protect me from the next guy who's twice my size and doesn't like what I'm saying, but even though I'm not worried about that, I don't argue. It's boring walking alone, chanting the same thing over.

So we change it up and walk three abreast while behind us, our mothers doing their own thing, sometimes staying single file, sometimes the three of them walking together just like us. The placards make it crowded and we occasionally bump shoulders, and we still smell the same dirty exhaust from the passing cars, but the conversation certainly livens things up.

We talk about the Celtics and whether they'll get back to winning the NBA championship every year again like before. Wilt finally broke our streak of eight straight titles last year. We're convinced Bill Russell won't let him do that again. Jamaal talks about Earl the Pearl, and how he's certain to win NBA Rookie of the Year. Then we talk about the upcoming second Super Bowl on Sunday between the Green Bay Packers and the Oakland Raiders, which we all agree the Packers will easily win. The first Super Bowl last year was a joke, not super at all, and this one will be, too.

We walk up and back, up and back.

We talk about TV shows. We debate *Bonanza* with Ben Cartwright and his boys on the Ponderosa versus *Gunsmoke* and Marshall Dillon. We choose who each other's character is on *Gilligan's Island*. Charlie and Jamaal decide that I'm the professor. Charlie and I decide that Jamaal is Gilligan. And Jamaal and I decide that Charlie is Mary Ann. That one provokes howls of outrage from him and howls of laughter from Jamaal and me.

We talk about music. I like the Beatles, of course, like everyone else, while they're fans of the Temptations, James Brown, Marvin Gaye, and the Supremes. I guess we listen to different radio stations. I'd never even heard the word "Motown" before.

Up and back.

Finally, I ask Jamaal a question that's been bugging me for what feels like forever. I've been afraid of the answer, but I can't hold back any longer. So with him in the middle and me on the outside, closest to the street, I blurt it out.

"So am I your friend or not?"

"What?" has asks. He looks at me in surprise. He heard me, and he knows exactly what I'm referring to, but is just stalling. I'm sure of it.

"A while back you said you had no white friends, and I was just like all the others," I say. "I could be your teammate or your classmate, but I could never be your friend."

He takes a while to respond. "That's just how it is where I come from. I didn't have no white friends and didn't want any. And ain't nobody white wanted to be my friend, that's for sure."

"This ain't Carolina," I say. "Or Georgia or none of the places you lived before that. And I ain't like all those others who didn't want to be your friend."

"Why is it a big deal to you?" he asks.

That stops me. I'm not sure why, but it is.

"I guess..." I fumble for the words. "I guess I can't understand why skin color should make a difference. Why is it I can't be your friend just because I'm white? Why can't you be my friend just because you're black?"

"You think it's just that easy?" Jamaal asks.

"I *told* you he be like that," Charlie says.

"I'm like what?" I ask, befuddled.

Charlie chuckles. "Sometimes, man, you are just so naïve. You think everything should be just…the way it *ought* to be. You don't understand our world. Especially where Jamaal comes from."

I guess I don't. "So help me understand."

"How many years you got?" Jamaal says.

"To explain why I can't be your friend? I'm okay as a teammate, but not as a friend?"

"Actually, you suck as a teammate," Jamaal says.

I blink, stung at the words. I know I'm awful compared to him and Charlie, but—

They break into wild, uproarious laughter.

"I'm not *that* bad," I say.

They laugh even harder. Charlie waves me off, letting me know I've got it wrong. He finally manages to choke out the words, "*Sooo* naïve!"

Jamaal makes a big show of picking up a small rock nestled against the snow beside the sidewalk. He brushes the snow off.

"Hockey puck!" he pronounces. He props his placard up against his hip, pulls his black woolen hat off, sets the rock on top of his head, and slips the hat back on.

He tiptoes ahead in exaggerated fashion, like a cartoon character trying to be sneaky, looks both ways, and slips the rock out from beneath his hat. He puts it down on the ground and swings at it with the wooden post of his sign.

"Hat trick!" he cries, throwing his arms up in the air in jubilation. He jumps up and down. "Hat trick!"

He and Charlie howl with laughter, and I have to join in, even if it's at my own expense. When I'm dumb, I'm really, really dumb. Funny-dumb, even. And Jamaal's comic routine makes it even funnier.

But I still don't get it.

"Of *course* you don't suck as a teammate," Charlie says when we finally all stop laughing. "Only you would be gullible enough to stand here and think it." He gets serious. "There's only the three of us here. The others..." He shrugs. "They couldn't be bothered, or didn't have the guts. Only Jamaal and I are here standing up for ourselves, for our race. And only *you* are standing up for someone else. That isn't a good teammate. That's a *great* teammate!"

I'm overwhelmed with emotion. I'm getting choked up, but I manage, "Thanks, man."

"And that isn't just a good friend," Charlie says. "It's a *great* friend. You are one loyal SOB."

I'm so moved I'm unable to speak. I just nod, and gulp hard.

"I guess that leaves me no choice," Jamaal says. "A friend of Charlie's… is a friend of mine." He rolls his eyes and grins. "Even if you is white."

"And dumb," Charlie adds.

*

Around 4:30, not yet halftime of the freshmen game, the sun sets, and soon we're enveloped by darkness. It's broken only by the soft yellow glow of streetlights high above the other side of the street. That, and the light pouring through the three-feet-high-by-eight-feet-wide window at Mandce's Pizza.

Even though our signs are big block letters on white poster board, they're now impossible to read from more than ten feet away. The moms fish flashlights out of their cars, and we all shine them on our signs, but that feels ridiculous.

What are we doing here? This is stupid. We're chanting slogans no one hears and carrying signs no one can read.

Whose stupid idea was this?

Oh, yeah, it was mine.

What a moron.

I look longingly over at Mandee's Pizza, its oval neon OPEN sign brightly lit and beckoning. A slice of cheese or maybe pepperoni would taste really good right now. Heck, I could go for the whole pie. My stomach growls, but I say nothing, not wanting to seem distracted even though I am.

I wonder aloud if we shouldn't have started later, closer to seven, the starting time for the varsity when a lot more spectators will be arriving, instead of now, while the freshmen are still playing, which just seems like a waste of time. Attendance is always spotty for the freshmen and JV games. Mostly family and a few friends. We're freezing our butts off for nothing.

But Mom gives me a knowing look and advises patience.

"Don't you think we've made our point?" I finally ask, cold and hungry and bored out of my skull, and more than a little embarrassed at how few people have seen our protest. It feels as if we've made no impact at all. No one cares. "Should we pack up and call it a day?"

"No!" Mom says. "You can't quit now. Trust me."

When I remain visibly unconvinced, she offers to get us a pizza over at Mandee's, and that hits the bull's-eye.

"Yeah!" we reply in unison, and suddenly the most popular person in Lynn, if not the whole planet, she walks over and places the order.

Somehow, I don't think Dr. King has to bribe his followers with pizza to get them to keep marching, but it doesn't look like any of us feel guilty over our suddenly rejuvenated morale. We're grinning and slapping each other's gloved hands.

Mandee's Pizza. Yeah!

When Mom emerges fifteen minutes later, we descend on that white pizza box like a pack of starving wolves. I attack my first slice—deliciously gooey cheese, spicy pepperoni, and a thin, chewy crust—so fast I burn the roof of my mouth. But I don't care. I don't slow down. I've been getting hungrier every time I've glanced over at Mandee's, so I'm starving.

We're relieved—actually euphoric—that the mothers all decline a slice, so the three of us dive in for seconds. It's every bit as good the second time around. But then I realize there are two slices left, and there are three of us wolves. I decide to be gallant and tell Charlie and Jamaal to finish it off.

"Thanks!" Charlie says.

"Yeah," Jamaal says, then grins. "How very white of you."

I'm not quite sure how to take that, but he's agreed to make me his first white friend, so I don't press the issue. Mom crumples the empty pizza box and heads back into Mandee's to toss it out. We get back into our routine, up and back, then up and back some more.

But the pizza-induced morale boost doesn't last for long. I'm about to question again whether we're wasting our time when a pudgy, balding, ruddy-faced man in his forties approaches from a car he's parked up the street. He introduces himself as Luke Hennessey, a columnist with the *Boston Globe.*

Our jaws drop. The *Boston Globe!* I've seen his picture atop his column in the Metro section. I've never stopped to read it, just flipped past it to the Sports section, but Hennessey seems pretty famous, at least for a newspaper guy.

He seems disappointed, though, that there's just the three of us players and our mothers. It seems he expected more. And we're carrying placards that are only visible by the wobbling beams from our flashlights.

We're minor league, he seems to be thinking, and who can blame him. That's what we are. As protestors go, we aren't varsity or JV or even freshmen quality. We're kindergarten. But he takes a thin black notebook out of his back pocket and pulls us aside one by one to talk to us beneath the nearest streetlight. Remembering how Charlie and Jamaal were offended at how Tomisetti zeroed in on me—even though it wound up making me feel like his pincushion—I prepare to insist that Mr. Hennessey talk to them first, but he does this anyway.

When he gets to me, he asks curiously, "Son, why are you involved in this?"

I try to explain that it's a matter of conscience and it's a stand we all have to take, black or white. But I fumble for the right words. This is the *Boston Globe!* Every other sentence includes a "you know" and at least two or three um's and ah's. I'm afraid I sound like a fool, an inarticulate moron.

But what I really fear is that this reporter will do like Tomisetti did over the phone, nod and seem friendly while talking to us, then savage us afterward in print. What's the phrase, *once bitten, twice shy*? That's how I feel. Shy as all heck. Shy and nervous. But Mr. Hennessey seems sincere, and asks all the right questions.

He's about to leave, tucking his notebook in his back pants pocket and looking around one last time to make sure he's gotten everything he needs, when Jamaal's father arrives in a black Ford. He joins us and we all gather around him and the reporter. Not quite six feet tall with a thin, angular face, he's dressed in a dark suit with a white shirt and tie. He gives off a sense of proud dignity as he speaks softly but firmly in a way that reminds me of Martin Luther King, only with a more pronounced Southern accent.

"What we are seeing here," Mr. Bryant says, pronouncing the last word, *he-uh*, "is a microcosm of the struggle this country is facing. People with closed minds and evil in their hearts can try to keep the black man down, but we shall overcome. Men like Coach Abrams can denigrate the character of these fine young men, and try to break their spirit with the most damning of epithets, but we shall overcome. Men like Coach Abrams will find themselves on the wrong end of history just as surely as George Wallace, Bull Connor, and the Ku Klux Klan. We shall overcome."

I'm mesmerized by the words, the rhythm of his speech, and the power and authority behind his message.

Wow! I wish I had a father like that.

But my mom soon proves yet again there's no better mother, and not just because of the pizza. After the *Globe* reporter leaves, a white van with Channel 4, WBZ-TV, inscribed in big black letters pulls up. A cameraman and a reporter emerge.

A TV camera?

I look at my mom in total shock—*Channel 4!*—and she gives me a knowing look and broad smile. I put two and two together. She must have contacted both the *Globe* and Channel 4—and probably any number of other media outlets that ignored her—as soon as she realized the rest of us, the rawest of rookies at this sort of thing, hadn't considered it.

The reporter introduces himself as John Ahern as the unnamed cameraman sets up his gear on a tripod, a bundles of cables running back to the truck. They're both white and about the age of my parents and average-sized, although the dark-haired Ahern is wearing a suit and tie while the cameraman has on jeans, a brown winter jacket, and a dark blue Red Sox baseball cap propped up at a steep angle covering most of his curly red hair.

Charlie, Jamaal, and I look at each other with wide, nervous smiles. We never in our wildest dreams expected this. Never even dreamed of it, actually. So now we're excited as all heck, but we're also scared stiff that if Mr. Ahern asks to talk to us, we're going to say something stupid and look like fools. My heart is jackhammering. My mouth is dry.

"How's my hair look?" Charlie whispers.

"You ain't got none," Jamaal says, and we all crack up.

Soon, we're bathed in the TV camera lights. There's no problem reading the message on our placards now. No need for flashlights. We hold the placards beside our heads as we gather behind Mr. Ahern, who is looking into the hooded camera and speaking into his microphone. He describes what has led to the protest in clear language without fumbling for a single word. Not even an "um" or an "ah". Very professional. He must have written his script, at least in his head, and memorized it on the way here. I wonder how much mental rehearsal it took to be so smooth. Compared to him, I'm sure I'll sound totally incoherent if I'm asked to speak. So I start some mental rehearsal of my own.

When it comes our time, each of us sounds pretty good, the others all gathered around, keeping the message on the placards visible to the camera. Even I do okay. But no one comes close to Mr. Bryant. Our version of Dr. Martin Luther King repeats his short, riveting speech, and I'm spellbound yet again.

CHAPTER 21

On our drive home from the protest and its stunning coverage by the *Boston Globe* and Channel 4, I'm filled with love and admiration for my mom.

"You set that up?" I ask.

"What's the key to any protest?" she says, shrugging as if it was no big deal, but at the same time beaming with undisguised pride. "It's getting your message to the most people. You can either get it only to the people attending the game—a small number and possibly not very sympathetic to your cause—or you can get it to all the readers of a newspaper and viewers of a TV station.

"It was a long shot. I called all the Boston TV stations and every newspaper within a hundred miles." She smiles. "Well, except for the *Item* and Tomisetti." We laugh at that, and she continues. "Originally, I thought there was a pretty good chance no one would show up. Even after I talked to them all, I thought that still was pretty likely. But the Civil Rights movement is big news, and the local papers and TV stations can't cover Alabama or Georgia or Mississippi. So I thought we had a chance. Not a good one, but a chance.

"Luke Hennessey was our best shot, at least among the major papers. He writes a lot of gritty, neighborhood-based columns, and he didn't totally dismiss the idea when I called him. I was *so* happy when he arrived. Even if Channel 4 never showed up, getting Hennessey was a major victory."

"Wow, you really did your homework," I say.

Mom smiles. "We got lucky. I *never* thought we'd get a TV station. It was a pipe dream, really. A million-to-one shot. But Channel 4 seems to be doing more of this type of on-site reporting, so it didn't hurt to try. Maybe they had to be in the area anyway for something else. I don't know. But it worked." She shakes her head in amazement. "I never imagined we'd get both the *Globe* and Channel 4. I still can't believe it!"

Hours later, we see ourselves on the Channel 4 eleven o'clock news, clustered around Mr. Ahern, the reporter, who holds the microphone to Jamaal's dad as he speaks so eloquently. A red banner at the bottom of the screen says in white letters: RACIAL CONFLICT IN LYNN.

It would be a moment of great rejoicing for Mom and me except for one thing.

My father.

Ashen-faced and in shock, he watches in horror from the tan lounge chair while Mom and I sit on the edge of our seats on the sofa. Before he got home, Mom admitted that there really hadn't been "the right moment" to tell him earlier, and she'd figured that there was a good chance the protest would get no publicity at all, so why provoke an unnecessary fight?

Well, Channel 4 News has changed all that.

I await my father's explosion. All color has drained from his face. His lips purse together tighter and tighter. He grips the arms of his chair so hard it looks like he might snap them off.

He says nothing.

When the segment ends, he wordlessly stands, looking leadenly straight ahead, and leaves the room.

*

The next day, Saturday, I wake up early, just a few minutes after six, and tiptoe downstairs through the dark to wait for the paperboy. It's all I've been able to think about, especially after last night's segment on Channel 4, which I replayed in my head over and over, unable to sleep.

I'm like a little kid on Christmas morning. I just can't wait. Last night was an amazing present to open, a gift I never could have imagined just a few days ago when Tomisetti was savaging all of us. Now, I wait for the other gift, not knowing for sure that there's even a second present under the tree. Mr. Hennessey may have decided we weren't worth writing about, or he may have postponed it because another topic for his column is even more pressing.

Or it may not be a gift at all.

Hennessey may attack all of us just like Tomisetti did, and my high expectations are just a piece of cheese in a mousetrap, and it's going to snap down on me as soon as I take the first bite. Heck, I've done more than take the first bite. I've wolfed the whole thing down. Today's *Globe* will decide whether the trap has snapped down on me or not.

I know I'll be waiting awhile. On Saturdays, we're lucky to get the paper by seven. If I had a cassette player, I'd listen to Anna's concert until it arrived, but I'm still saving up for that. Mom says as long as I keep quiet about it, she'll go halves with me, so it shouldn't take much longer. Until then, though, the sound of her flute remains trapped in my desk drawer.

So I've brought with me a book called *The Fire Next Time*, by James Baldwin, a famous black writer. But I'm hoping I'm not reading it for too long this morning. What I really want to read, what I'm *dying* to read, is Mr. Hennessey's column. In fact, I'm so eager to read it, I probably won't even be able to concentrate on the Baldwin book, reading the same words over and over. But if I'm not doing anything, it'll feel like five lifetimes before the paperboy gets here.

I check the front porch just in case the paper has miraculously arrived early, but there's no *Boston Globe* on the red bricks or on the dark brown mat with the word *Welcome* in cursive and facing outward. In fact, I see that snow has fallen overnight and continues to fall. There are a couple inches on the walkway and some has blown onto the roof-covered porch.

Great. Now the paperboy will never get here.

I turn on the outside light, as if this welcoming gesture will hurry him along. I'd shovel the walkway, too, if I didn't think that would wake up my parents. Heck, I'm almost ready to run the mile or so to Shop Kwik, snow in my face and inches of it on the ground, freezing my toes, to buy a copy so I can read it *now*.

This instant.

I can't wait. Come on!

I make myself a bowl of Cheerios. I sit down at the dining room table in my accustomed chair, facing the kitchen, the clock on the wall behind me, and with the front door down the hall to my right. I open the Baldwin book, prepared to hide it beneath my leg as if it's a dirty book if I hear my father approaching.

My parents remain upstairs, but I have trouble concentrating on the book as the clock behind me ticks off the seconds.

Tick…tick…tick….

Tick…tick…tick….

I'm tempted to peek on the front porch every few minutes just in case I missed hearing the paperboy arrive, and even give in a couple times, but the red bricks and welcome mat stare back at me, barren except for the patches of snow. It's just my luck that on the one day I most want to see the *Globe* early, it's snowing. Who knows when it'll get here.

Tick…tick…tick….
Tick…tick…tick….
Finally, at 7:47, I hear a *thunk* on the porch. I race outside, still trying to be as quiet as possible, and in the darkness just before dawn, I retrieve the paper. I scan the pages, my heart hammering, as I walk back to the dining room table.

Then I spot it.

There, on the front page of the second section of the paper—what's called the Metro section, a part of the paper I normally skip to get right to the Sports—is Luke Hennessey's column. It runs down the entire left edge of the page, from the top all the way down to the bottom. An artist's drawing of his smiling face, so realistic it's almost like a photograph, sits to the right of his name in small letters, and then below that in much larger letters, the headline: OFFENSIVE FOUL DEALT TO LYNN HOOPSTERS.

I read with growing amazement and…and *jubilation*. As much as Tomisetti's piece in the *Item* was a vicious attack, this column amounts to a full-blown advertisement for our cause.

If we're honest with ourselves, we must admit that a Northern brand of racism permeates our workplaces, our churches, our schools, and yes, even our sports teams. To contend otherwise is foolish. The latest exhibit can be found on the Lynn English High School basketball team.

•••

Charlie Watkins was compiling Wilt Chamberlain-like numbers on a freshmen team, averaging almost thirty-five points a game while rarely needing to play the fourth quarter. One rival coach says, "any fool can see he doesn't belong there," but was he elevated to the junior varsity? No, instead he was told (allegedly, but the witnesses are numerous) that he and another black star, Jamaal Bryant, play nigger basketball.

•••

Coach Ralph Abrams, who declined our request for an interview, has clashed with black athletes in the past, one of whom says, "He tries to make us as white as he is." Another gave a far more damning claim. "He told me privately, in his office, that if I was going to play for him, I had to get the nigger out of me."

Seven young men showed courage in the face of this evil, leaving the team rather than subject themselves to this bigotry. Three of them were protesting along with several of their parents early last evening.

And then Hennessey finishes his column with the magnificent words of Mr. Bryant, our version of Dr. King.

It's glorious.

*

I keep rereading it over and over, the thrill building each time, not fading even the slightest with every repetition. It's so wonderful it makes my head spin. I'm so engrossed that I don't hear my parents approaching from the hallway behind me until they're only a few steps away.

"Andre," Mom says. She's wearing her belted white bathrobe and white slippers, trailing my father by a few steps, half running to catch up. "Let me make you some breakfast."

When I look at my father, my blood runs cold. He's already dressed in his dark blue suit, white shirt, and striped tie, ready to head into work. There's nothing unusual about that even though it is Saturday. What chills me is his stony face, drained of all color, and the distant, ice-cold look in his eyes. Arctic. He stares straight ahead, appearing to see nothing. Walking robotically, he ducks into his office and emerges with his tan leather briefcase.

I realize the Baldwin book is visible on the table off to the left of the newspaper, which is still open to Mr. Hennessey's column. A double-header of doom. I quickly flip the paper to the next section, the Sports section, covering the book, but he sees nothing.

He heads for the front door.

"Andre, let me make you breakfast," Mom says. "At least some coffee."

But he keeps walking. Robotically. As if he can't hear her any more than he saw me as he passed. He opens the front door.

"Andre! Your coat!" Mom says.

But he keeps going.

Alarmed, Mom races to the closet, grabs his long black winter coat, and races outside after him into the snow, holding the neck of her bathrobe close, cold air and some flakes of snow gusting in the front door as she leaves.

Soon, she's stepping back inside, empty-handed, the coat somehow delivered, but almost as ashen-faced as my father was. Snow is sprinkled in her hair. Clumps of it are on her slippers, but she seems not to notice. Her eyes look haunted. Her shoulders slump.

As I run to console her, her hand goes to her mouth and she begins to sob.

*

Sometime later, Mom reads Hennessey's column with me—I have no problem rereading it yet again—but she can't share the euphoria I felt before my father's appearance.

I've lost much of that joy, too. Everything feels different now.

She forces a weak smile. "That's wonderful, Rabbit."

But I can tell she can't feel it. As distressed as I was to see my father's stunned, cold reaction last night, and its even more arctic appearance this morning, it had to hit Mom ten times as hard. A hundred. That haunted look of hers makes me want to cry myself.

"Let me make breakfast," I offer.

"You don't need to," Mom says, distant and empty. She adds, as if on reflex but with no feeling, "I'll make you something. What would you like?"

"No, I'm making breakfast," I insist. "French toast."

I beat the eggs, add the milk, and dip the bread in just like I'm supposed to. But what I produce has got to be the worst French toast ever. It tastes milky and is so soggy the bread is practically falling apart.

"It's not that bad," Mom says, sitting across from me at the table, after I point out my French toast's shortcomings. "Thank you for trying."

"What did I do wrong?" I ask.

"You put in too much milk and you soaked the bread for too long," she says. "But they weren't that bad. It's the thought that counts."

"Mom, they were terrible."

"Well," she says, and a hint of a smile actually breaks through the clouds. "If you insist." Her smile becomes more than just a hint. Its warmth is weak, but I can still feel it. She says, "Rabbit, you're right. They were terrible."

"Worst ever," I say.

She nods, gently laughing now. "Worst ever."

And even though this isn't true, I say, "I did it on purpose, so you'll never ask me to cook again."

She swats my hand and bursts out in full, exuberant laughter. It rolls off her, releasing the tension in his shoulders, in wave after wave. "You rascal," she says, and shakes her head.

Suddenly, as if a master switch has been clicked, the laughter slackens, then gives way to tears that stream down her face, followed by wracking sobs. I rush to her side of the table and, still standing, put my arms around her shaking shoulders. She buries her head in my chest.

"I'm sorry, Mom," I say, and I realize that I'm crying, too. "This is all my fault."

"Don't you say that!"

"But it is!" I insist.

She pulls back and holds me at arm's length. She swipes away the tears off her face, and locks eyes with mine.

"Now you listen to me, young man," she says. "You stood up for what was right, and for your friends. This isn't like times when you've sassed your father and you've even sassed me. Those times, you were wrong, at least about the sassing. But not this time. You did nothing wrong."

She points to the newspaper and Luke Hennessey's column. "Just like he said. You young men showed courage and integrity. Maybe you the most because you have nothing personally to gain from making this stand. You'd be the starting point guard on the freshmen team if you were willing to turn your back on your friends. You've sacrificed to do the right thing."

I nod glumly.

"It isn't always easy to do that," she says.

I nod again, but still feel empty inside.

And then she says the best thing of all. "Rabbit, I am so proud of you!"

Those magical words wash over me. *I am so proud of you!* They heal that aching emptiness inside.

She's proud of me. It's the most perfect thing she could have said.

"Thanks, Mom," I say. The tears flow and there's nothing I can do to stop them. They stream down my face, warm and salty when they reach my lips, and I lick them away. I say it again, choked and strangled with emotion, but the one word still clear.

"Thanks."

CHAPTER 22

At the next protest before Tuesday's game against Swampscott, the pile of racial dynamite we've been standing on explodes.

The school has been abuzz about the protest. It's all anyone can talk about. Everyone has an opinion, and our supporters are certainly in the minority. Jeff Goodwin and Paul DiSimone, my two best friends—at least the ones with whom I share most of my classes—have turned their backs on me. Sometimes I've caught them even joining in with the jeering in the hallways, which hurts because we shared so many laughs before. I guess they weren't the friends I thought they were.

I wish now I'd made more of an effort to reach out to the kids in some of my classes who aren't white: especially Janice Downing and Mike Mitchell, who are black, and Angela Santos and Wayne Sanchez, who are Spanish. I've always been nice to them, and they were the same to me, but I never did anything more than that. We just said hi to each other. I naturally gravitated to Jeff and Paul—perhaps because there were no black or Spanish kids up in Maine—and I guess Janice and Mike and Angela and Wayne did the same with each other. It feels wrong to suddenly want to be best buddies with them now that it's convenient for me, now that my closest white friends have tossed me aside. Why wasn't I trying harder to include them before? Just laziness, I guess, or inertia.

Anna is sticking by my side, but even she said, shaking her head, "Ooooh, Rabbit. If you thought my father hated you before, you can't imagine what he's saying about you now. He's thinks you're pretty much the Devil. He said the only way you would ever be allowed to go out with me is over his cold, dead body."

"That can be arranged," I said grimly.

"That isn't funny."

"I know. Sorry."

I can't go from one class to another without hearing some catcall, whether it's the easily ignored "quitter" or that truly awful, hateful phrase that was scratched onto my locker ten days ago. What is wrong with people? Is the basketball team that important to all of them?

Or is it that the same racial hatreds and prejudices that are out in the open down south exist here in Lynn, Massachusetts, part of the supposedly more enlightened North, but their evil lurks below the surface, like a hidden alligator in a swamp, all but invisible until it attacks and snaps its powerful jaws shut on its prey?

I don't know.

All I know is that I've gone from being the hero after the Thanksgiving Day football game, everyone slapping me on my back and giving me nothing but smiles, to what feels like Public Enemy Number One.

It's also gotten physical, though not too bad. Not yet, at least.

On Monday, as I was walking with Anna, so pretty in her yellow dress, to history class, in my imagination holding her soft hand in mine, fingers interlaced, even as we actually stayed at least a foot apart, Rick Cassidy snuck up from behind and knocked my books to the ground. As I whirled around to face him, a buddy of his put a leg out behind me. Cassidy then gave me a hard shove, toppling me over the extended leg and sending me sprawling to the floor.

"Stop that!" Anna said to Cassidy, rushing to my side. "Leave him alone!"

I scrambled to my feet, my books still strewn on the dark gray tiled floor, wondering if punches were about to fly, dreading that possibility. It wouldn't be a fair fight. Cassidy is so much bigger than I am, and he had all his buddies with him and I had none, only Anna, but he just sneered and called me that awful phrase from my locker door, painted over since it first appeared, but not forgotten. He leaned close. His breath smelled as if he hadn't brushed his teeth in a week.

"I wonder who scratched that into your locker," he said, and laughed.

So it was him. I should have known.

This morning, it was back, scratched again onto my locker door. Three times for emphasis.

NIGGER LOVER.

NIGGER LOVER.

NIGGER LOVER.

But not even that prepares me for what happens on Tuesday night.

*

Our small group of just seven protestors on Friday night—Charlie, Jamaal, and me, our mothers, and Mr. Bryant—has exploded to over fifty. My mom won't be buying pizza tonight. If she does, she'll go broke. The other four players who quit the basketball team have joined us—seniors Willie Jenkins and J.P. Clayton, along with Ray Thompson and Tim Peterson—as have two men and a woman from the NAACP, and a large portion of the black Lynn English High School student body. It's a small minority of the school's overall population of more than 1600 students, but they're filling the Goodridge Street sidewalk.

The temperature is hovering around freezing and will drop after the sun sets, so everyone is bundled in their winter coats and jackets over dress clothes, except for the three adult men who are braving the elements in just their dark suits. Most are wearing hats and gloves, and a few scarves are on display. Fortunately, there's no wind, but I'm sure that within an hour my toes will be freezing inside my otherwise comfortable, almost sneaker-like shoes.

I recognize Janice Downing, a shy, black classmate. I've never heard her say a single word except when called on, even though we share English, math, and history classes. I go to where she stands on the cleanly shoveled sidewalk beneath the tangled, snow-coated limbs of a tree thirty feet tall. She looks at me shyly and smiles, then her brown eyes look away. I thank her for coming.

"No," she says softly, meeting my eyes for only an instant. "Thank you."

We've also been joined by Mike Thompson, another black classmate with whom I share several classes, and Wayne Sanchez, whose family is from Mexico. I thank them both and make a mental note that these are worthy friends, not Jeff Goodwin and Paul DiSimone. There's also a smattering of whites, some of whose allegiance I doubt based on their buffoonery and constant craning of their necks to search out the TV cameras so they can get in the background.

Which are here in full force. Camera crews from all three Boston TV stations, channels 4, 5, and 7, are filming. Not live, of course, but getting material they'll edit back at the studio just like Channel 4 did a few nights ago. Same for the two radio stations. Plus seven reporters from newspapers, including Luke Hennessey again from the *Globe*, Tomisetti from the *Item*, and reporters from the *Herald Traveler*, the *Record American*, the *Salem Evening News*, and several smaller papers.

It's a zoo. The stretch of sidewalk spanning the two entrances to the semicircle drive, a bit longer than a football field, teems with activity and excitement. It's so crowded the pigeons have left to perch on the porches on the three-decker houses across the street. We don't have anything close to enough placards to go around, so people are sharing them, swapping them back and forth, or just joining in the chants empty-handed, a few of the adults and girls linking hands in solidarity.

"*Say no to bigotry. Abrams has to go!*"

"*Say no to bigotry. Abrams has to go!*"

"*Say no to bigotry. Abrams has to go!*"

It boggles my mind. I can't believe the tiny spark that has become a fierce, all-consuming fire. Our group exudes enthusiasm and belief in the rightness of our cause. Not even the jeers and the worst of racial epithets thrown our way from the yellow buses by own classmates—along with three or four rocks that miss their marks—can dampen our mood.

As Mr. Bryant and Dr. King would say, we shall overcome!

The reporters weave in and out along the sidewalk, presumably trying to get as many perspectives as possible: former players, parents, classmates, and of course, the NAACP. The TV crews try to achieve the same thing, but bring their interview subjects to their stationary positions in front of their hooded cameras in white casings, mounted on tripods, cables trailing out to their station's van, its identification in bold letters on the sides. Channel 4—John Ahern with his red-headed cameraman, once again wearing his blue Red Sox cap—is centered where the sidewalk meets the walkway the leads into the school. Channel 5 is more than forty yards away near the entrance to the semicircle drive closest to Chestnut Street. Channel 7 is an equal distance from the middle, at the opposite end.

Absolutely amazing.

I notice Mom corner Tomisetti. He's easily identifiable from the tiny one-inch-by-one inch, black-and-white photograph atop his column in the *Item*. He's short and squat, in his fifties, with what I've come to think of as a feral, weasel-like face. A cigarette dangles from the corner of his mouth.

"How *dare* you say that about my son?" she says, stabbing him in the chest with her finger. I grin. He'll no doubt twist everything he sees and hears into his own warped perspective, but Mom isn't just going to give him a piece of her mind. She's going to dump the entire thing right over his head. Clobber him with it. This is as much of a mismatch as the not-so-super Super Bowl was on Sunday, which of course the Green Bay Packers easily won.

Go, Mom.

I talk to Channel 5 and then to Channel 7, many in the crowd gathering around to hear what I say, or perhaps just get their faces on the TV. Probably the latter, but I feel more comfortable each time I repeat the same words I've spoken before. We all have a responsibility to stand up. There's no question Abrams used that despicable word, no matter how he tries to cover it up. No, he didn't just have an "unfortunate slip of the tongue." He's a bigot through and through who will cost my black friends potential college scholarships.

I'm about to confront Tomisetti myself, finishing off a tag team play with my mom, when two police cars pull up, blue lights flashing. They come to a halt right in front of the center of our group, near the walkway, blocking off the near lane of Goodridge Street.

Reporters hustle over, as does almost all of our group. TV cameras point toward the cruisers, and I hear John Ahern, suddenly positioned so all the action forms a background behind him, says into his microphone, "We have a new development. Two police cars have arrived."

Four officers emerge, all white men. One is taller than all the others, another shorter and a bit pudgy, the other two of ordinary size. They wear dark blue caps that match their uniforms, and beneath the caps all have their hair cut short in crew cuts. The short, pudgy one, who is about forty or so, and has a pockmarked face, takes the lead. His name badge identifies him as Officer Flanagan.

"I'm going to have to ask all of you to leave," he says loudly, and all chants and conversation stop. "You've made your point, now it's time to disperse."

Mr. Bryant—Jamaal's father—steps up, head held high, again dressed smartly in a black suit, white shirt, and dark tie. He's flanked by the three NAACP representatives and the mothers, all decked in their Sunday finest. I realize they've formed a wall in front of the rest of us.

"With all due respect," Mr. Bryant says, "we must decline."

The adults nod in unison, and a few say, "That's right!" I belatedly nod, too, and I notice a few of the others also join in.

Officer Flanagan's face hardens and turns a bit more crimson. "That's not a request. It's a command from an officer of the law. Now move along. No loitering."

All the side conversations and media interviews have come to a halt. The silence has become deafening.

"Again, with all due respect," Mr. Bryant says, holding his head high, "we must decline." The last word, spoken loud and clear in his Southern drawl, emphasizes the first syllable and then draws out the second. *Dee-cliiine.* "We are peacefully assembled. We are marching solely along this sidewalk, which is public property. Our Constitutionally guaranteed right to peacefully assemble allows us to gather here and make known our grievance."

I nod, barely able to breathe, and croak out, "That's right!" like some of the adults, like I've seen people in Dr. King's crowds so often do.

"You don't have a permit!" Officer Flanagan snaps.

"Is a permit required to assemble peacefully?" Mr. Bryant asks. "If a permit is requested, is one always granted? Or can there be an attempt to deny our lawfully allowed rights?"

"You don't have a permit!" Officer Flanagan says, his eyes flashing anger, his face turning an even darker shade of red. "Now move along!"

"Are you familiar with Mr. Bull Connor from Birmingham, Alabama?" Mr. Bryant asks, his voice rising. He points to the cameras that are recording all of this, as are the reporters who are feverishly scribbling their notes. "I'm sure every one of the media members assembled here knows that name, as do I and at least all of the adults assembled here, if not also many of these fine young men and women." He points behind him to the mothers and the NAACP members, who all nod, and then to all of us students. I nod hard and fast.

Mr. Bryant continues, "Some of us marched against that man and others down south, who also tried to invoke the need for a permit, and then launched attack dogs on us and directed fire hoses spewing water so hard it knocked grown men to the ground. Are you going to claim brotherhood with the likes of Bull Connor? Are you going to claim brotherhood with Cecil Ray Price, deputy sheriff in Neshoba County, Mississippi? A member of the Ku Klux Klan. Complicit in the murders of James Chaney, Andrew Goodman, and Michael Schwerner."

"Enough!" Officer Flanagan removes his billy club from a strap on his waist and slaps it against his palm. "I'm not going to debate the issue with you! Move along or face the consequences!"

I feel like my eyes are about to pop out of my head. My pounding heart is in my throat. A sour taste forms in the back of my throat.

But Mr. Bryant remains cool as a cucumber.

"If you are prepared to violate our right to free speech and do so publicly while the rest of the world watches"—Mr. Bryant points theatrically to the cameras and reporters—"then we are prepared to suffer the consequences."

Officer Flanagan hesitates. A group of the students off to our right, perhaps ten in all and all of the white kids who'd been clowning for the cameras, back up quickly, one step after another. One bolts for the school, then the others follow.

But the rest of us do not move.

Somewhere far in the distance, a car horn honks. A laughing woman exits Mandee's Pizza, stares at the police cars and hurries away. A cold sweat breaks out on the back of my neck. I can almost feel that billy club crashing down on my head.

Officer Flanagan turns to the TV cameramen, still filming. "Turn those off!"

As if in answer, one reporter doubling as his own photographer steps up and takes Flanagan's picture. Then Channel 4's John Ahern faces his camera and says, "We're being told to turn these cameras off, but we will not comply. The public has a right to see what's happening here and Channel 4 will deliver it to you."

The tall officer behind Flanagan taps him on the shoulder and whispers in his ear. Officer Flanagan grits his teeth, exhales loudly, and nods. The tall officer, Officer Murphy according to his gold name badge, steps forward. He has dark eyes, an angular face, and thin, bony hands.

"We will allow you to remain here so long as you remain peaceful," he says. "If, however, you fail to do so, you can expect to spend the evening in jail."

"Thank you, Officer," Mr. Bryant says. "We will not disappoint you."

*

Within minutes, we face our first test. Joe Thurman emerges from the school's front doors. Wearing only his gray LEHS warm-up suit and sneakers, he hesitates, standing beside one of the ancient-style, three-story-high concrete columns, looking as if he's about to turn around and go back inside. I nudge Charlie, who's standing beside me, and nod toward Thurman.

Charlie draws in his breath sharply. He calls softly to Jamaal, then to the other players, who are sprinkled throughout the crowd, and points out the traitor. Not only is Thurman the only black player still on the team, the only one on *the other side*. He also claims, and this is far worse, not to have heard Abram's use of the epithet. Says he was talking to someone else, and didn't hear a thing.

Which is impossible, of course. No one talks during a Coach Abrams practice, not while he's talking, and especially not while he's yelling.

Thurman heard it. Heck, Helen Keller could have heard it. A construction worker using a jackhammer could have heard it. The Rolling Stones could have been performing "Paint It Black" at full volume and still have heard it.

Thurman is just covering up for Abrams. I get that Thurman is in a tough position. He's playing for a college scholarship next year. He's playing for his basketball life. He's playing not to go to Vietnam.

I get all that. I get that it's too big a sacrifice for him to quit the team and unify our protest. But I don't see how he can cover up for Abrams, lie for him, and still live with himself.

And I'm not alone. The crowd begins to murmur as Thurman approaches, head down as if he's studying the cracks in the walkway. A soft but distinct chorus of boos emerges and then grows louder. All the cameras point his way. The reporters all perk up.

"Think he's come to join us?" Charlie asks bitterly.

Thurman goes straight to Charlie. "Hey, man, can we talk?"

The boos fall silent, perhaps because everyone wants to hear what's being said.

"Sure," Charlie says, his face hard. "What you got?"

"Privately. Away from here," Thurman says. He gestures toward the rest of the crowd and the TV cameras, who are recording the exchange.

"Joe, what do you think of all this?" Tomisetti, calls out.

Thurman shakes his head, and closes his eyes. To Charlie, he says, "Just us. You, me, and the rest of the players. Nobody else."

As those of us with placards hand them off to others, Charlie turns and tells everyone, most notably the media but also the adults and the other students, that we just need a little privacy, we'll be just a short distance away, and we'll be right back.

"If you follow us," he says, looking at the TV cameras and reporters, "we'll have to go inside the school, where you aren't allowed. So just give us a few minutes." He motions for us players to join him, and together we walk with Thurman halfway back toward the school entrance, stopping beside the flagpole that rises forty feet in the air, but this time of day holds no flag. We form a circle around him.

"Listen, I don't really want to be here," Thurman says. "I'd rather be doing wind sprints up and down the court with no breaks for twenty minutes." He sees me for the first time, does a double take, and adds, "I'd rather lose a free throw shooting contest to the midget."

He chuckles, but no one joins in.

"Look, I'm in a no-win situation here, but I've got to say it anyway." Thurman folds his arms and shivers. His eyes dart from one of us to another. He licks his lips. "Coach Abrams asked me to talk to you guys. 'Cause I'm the captain. He's asking for you guys to drop the protest."

"*What*?" comes the reply, almost in unison.

"Hear me out," Thurman says. "He says if you'll drop the protest, he'll take you all back next year, the slate wiped clean. No hard feelings."

"No hard feelings? Really?" Charlie says bitterly. "Why shouldn't we have hard feelings?"

"You know what I mean," Thurman says.

"So if we get off his back, he'll let us come back next year and be treated the same way all over again," Charlie says, his voice rising in anger. "Why did you even bother coming out here with this crap? What's wrong with you?"

"What are you, his slave?" Jamaal says.

"Come on, man," Thurman says, hands out in a what-am-I-going-to-do gesture. "I'm the captain. I gotta do what he says."

"I'm serious," Jamaal says. "Abrams ain't got the balls to come out here himself, so he send you to do his dirty work."

"He ain't never coming out here," Thurman says. "He crazy, but he not that crazy."

"So he send you out here to do what he's not willing to do himself," Jamaal says. "How's that different than a slave cleaning a white man's toilet? You doing that for him? You clean Abrams' toilet? You bow your head to him, say 'Yes, massa'?"

Thurman turns to leave. "I didn't want to do this. I knew this would happen. But Abrams forced me to. He didn't give me a choice."

"We all got choices," Charlie says.

"Face it, man," Jamaal says. "You just a Tom."

Thurman recoils, as if he's been slapped.

"You been one since you heard the man call what we do 'nigger basketball' and decided to stay with him instead of walk out with us," Jamaal says. "And even worse, pretend you didn't hear him so when the newspaper man ask you, you got nothing to say. Let that white man call us a bunch of liars."

"It ain't that easy," Thurman says.

"You been a Tom since then," Jamaal says. "Today you just made it more obvious. You the whitest black man I know. The goddamned midget is blacker than you are."

I feel sick to my stomach. Six months ago, I wouldn't have understood that Jamaal just gave Joe Thurman one of the worst insults possible to a black man, or in Thurman's case, a young black man. Based on an old book from slavery days, *Uncle Tom's Cabin*, a "Tom" refers to a black man who is a traitor to his race.

Does Thurman deserve that? I can't forgive him for pretending not to hear what he had to hear, but when we walked out, he was faced with an impossible choice. Be branded a Tom for staying with the team or quit and give his college career the death sentence. And if his parents can't afford to send him to college without a basketball scholarship, then a year from now he'll be heading to Vietnam.

Is that the sacrifice we're expecting him to make? It makes me sick just to think of it.

But I'm the white kid. I didn't even know what a Tom was a few months ago. I haven't lived what they've lived. Who am I to say who's a Tom and who isn't?

But I feel awful. Just awful.

Yeah, Thurman came out here with an offer that was really an insult to us all. I'm sure he hated the very idea of talking to us. That's why he lingered by the front doors, and almost turned around and went back in. But he couldn't defy Abrams, could he? He'd stuck with the team—he made his fateful choice when he didn't walk out with us—so now he couldn't refuse his coach. He was too far down his chosen path, this close to a college scholarship, to turn back now. It was too late, wasn't it?

Maybe not, but I just feel sick about this. Just awful.

And then Thurman makes it worse.

"I knew this wouldn't work," Thurman says. "I told Abrams that. So he said to tell you guys that you better leave before five o'clock. Don't be here at five o'clock, or you'll regret it."

"What's that, some kind of a threat?" Charlie says, anger dancing in his eyes.

"Hey man, don't shoot the messenger," Thurman says, stepping back with his hands out in a back-off gesture. "I'm just telling you what he told me. I got no idea what it's supposed to mean."

"We ain't going nowhere," Jamaal says. "So Tom, why don't you run home to your massa."

Thurman winces. Pain is etched on his face. "I wish I could be out here with you guys. I really do. But..." He trails off, shaking his head, unable, or perhaps unwilling, to finish explaining himself.

"Do what you gotta do," Charlie says, coldly. "We ain't leaving."

Thurman turns to go, but before he gets ten feet from us, Jamaal adds one final insult.

"Man, I remember when that guy had balls."

CHAPTER 23

All of us players—*former* players, I have to remind myself—return to the crowd on Goodridge Street, and in fairness to everyone, media included, let them know about the five o'clock ultimatum. We explain that we don't know what it means. It may just be a cheap threat to get us out of the way long before the two thousand or so fans show up for the seven o'clock varsity game against Swampscott, always a top rival and one that helps fill up the stands with many of its own supporters. Or perhaps assuming there are only seven protestors like last time, not close to fifty and including three representatives from the NAACP, Abrams is hoping he can intimidate everyone into leaving so there's no story for the six o'clock news and then again at eleven. Or even better, the story is that we all left with our tails between our legs. That makes sense to me

No matter what Abrams was thinking, though, the ultimatum is a bluff. What else could it be? It's not like a bomb is going to go off or anything.

But the threat works, at least in part. The crowd thins considerably. Most of our classmates, including Janice Downing and Mike Mitchell, stream inside to call their parents for a ride or climb into cars of juniors and seniors who have their license. Janice stops by and says she was leaving anyway, she could only be here for a short while to show her support, and I believe her.

But I don't believe Tim Peterson, who chickened out before and now can't look any of us in the eye while saying he was going to have to be home by dinner anyway. It's the first he's spoken of it, and he also heads inside to call for a ride that presumably would already be coming to get him before his precious dinner, if he weren't lying his cowardly butt off.

But then J.P. Clayton, one of our two senior former players, calls out to him, and says he's got his car and he'll give him a lift. Before we know it, the two of them are joined by Ray Thompson, leaving just Willie Jenkins in addition to Charlie, Jamaal, and me.

We're practically on our own again.

And when our classmates see three players leaving, all but five of them go, too. Where before there weren't enough placards to go around, now everyone has one and we've made multiple trips to Mom's car to stack the extras in her trunk.

"Rabbit," she says, "should we leave?"

"No!" I say. "Abrams isn't going to win that easily. He's just a bully. I'm not scared."

That's only half a lie. Yes, I am scared at least a little, but that's really only because of the uncertainty. He can't do anything to us. Why be afraid of the bogeyman?

The police certainly don't appear worried. It's not like they've called in backups. In fact, they've moved their two cruisers inside the semicircle drive to minimize traffic disruption. Two officers, including the combustible Officer Flanagan, stay with the cruisers, keeping the blue lights flashing to remind us they're here, while the tall, peacemaking officer, Officer Murphy, and his partner eye us with no extra concern from the opposite side of Goodridge Street.

There's really only one good result of the ultimatum. It seems to have prompted much of the media, reporters and TV camera crews alike, to stick around. Their flurry of activity had fallen off to nothing, so they'd been openly talking of wrapping things up, having gotten all they needed. Now, however, they don't want to miss something their competition gets. If there really is something to Abrams' threat, what's another hour?

Tomisetti, however, leaves before I get to give him a piece of my mind. That's a shame because I certainly had a few choice words ready for him, but it sounded as though Mom handled that task pretty well all by herself. And I'm sure he had no reason to stay. He'd made up his mind what to write before he even got here.

The sun sets around 4:30, and darkness falls. The TV camera lights stay off; there's nothing to film right now. Irregularly spaced streetlights on the other side of Goodridge cast a meager yellow glow but the darkness remains. We can see the outline of the oak trees that dot the snow-covered area between the street and the semicircle curving up to the school and then back away from it, but we can barely make out faces just fifteen feet away and again have to use flashlights to illuminate our placards.

Cars drive by, their headlights piercing the darkness. From a few of them, passengers jeer, once with the worst racial epithets, but most cars park along the street and down the side streets, further and further away as time passes, and their occupants walk past us into the game. Most ignore us, looking the other way or studying the ground. A few give us the finger or tell us what horrible human beings we are. At first, my pulse begins to race every time another spectator approaches, but after a while, it all feels commonplace.

The only true tension comes from wondering what might happen at five o'clock.

The temperature falls. Three more of our classmates call it quits, leaving only two girls, Tina Oakley and Kelly Summers: Tina short and slight; Kelly, a bigger girl. I thank them for staying. They nod somberly. We all keep pacing back and forth from one tip of the semicircle drive to the other, chanting our slogans and checking the time, but the sidewalk feels deserted now. What was once more than fifty protestors has dropped to only thirteen.

I'm not superstitious, but having exactly thirteen protestors feels unlucky, so I'm not exactly heartbroken when Willie hands his placard to Charlie, who already has one, and says, "Sorry, man, but I've had enough," and walks off to his car parked behind the school.

It's disappointing, but we still have a solid dozen remaining: the three moms, Mr. Bryant, the three NAACP representatives, Tina, Kelly, Charlie, Jamaal, and me.

The Dirty Dozen, I say to myself, a silly thought just to amuse myself—I haven't seen the movie—and fight off my growing unease about the impending five o'clock deadline.

Then a shocking arrival makes us thirteen again.

Anna.

*

I don't see Anna emerge from the shadows until she's practically on top of us, just thirty feet away, walking briskly past a gnarled, leafless tree on her left, wearing her bluish-gray wool coat and new black shoes. Her shoulder-length blonde hair pokes out from beneath her bright white hat. She's carrying two textbooks in one gloved hand held against her chest and her black flute case by her side in the other.

She smiles when she sees me and comes running. She shifts her books into the crook of her other arm and as I hold my placard out away from my body, gives me an awkward, but wonderful, hug. I wrap my free arm around her. I breathe in the fragrance of her perfume—citrus this time— and the clean smell of her hair. After all our imaginary hugs, I'm reminded once again how much better the real thing is.

It's so wonderful, I momentarily forget everything else. Most of our supporters leaving, the looming deadline, even where I am. It's all just the two of us.

Then a photographer's flash goes off. We both stiffen, and Anna pulls away. She relaxes when she sees that we were not the subject of the shot, but I don't relax. Not because our group has suddenly grown back to the unlucky number of thirteen. I don't believe in any of that.

But I halfway believe in Abram's five o'clock deadline, and Anna has chosen to show up less than ten minutes away from it. I still can't imagine what we have to worry about, but this is the most horrible timing possible. If something does happen, I sure don't want Anna involved.

"I didn't expect to see you here," I say. Anna has band practice just about every school day, either for the entire orchestra, or a small, eight-person jazz group, or an even smaller group of just four that plays chamber orchestra classical music. After practice, she has to go straight home. And given her father's view of me and the protest in general, I never expected Anna to even think about joining us.

"I wanted to come and support you. You and your friends and the cause," she says. She twitches her mouth to the left and then to the right, announcing, I'm guessing, that she's uncomfortable with what she's about to say. "So I told my mom a little white lie. Actually, not so little." She grimaces. "I told her I was going to the basketball games, so I wouldn't need a ride until late." She takes a deep breath. "I *never* lie to my mom, and I can't say I feel comfortable about making this exception, but my brother's going to the movies with some girl, so I don't have to worry about him, and I didn't know when I'd get another chance to support you." She smiles. "So I'm here."

Out of the corner of my eye, I see my mom looking on twenty feet away, eyebrows raised, before she turns quickly away. She hasn't said anything, but she knows I haven't been calling Anna, and probably guessed we were done with each other. Puppy love and all that.

I motion Mom over and introduce the two. They say all the right things and smile, seeming to like each other right away.

"Mom, you can't say anything," I say.

She frowns. "About what?"

"About Anna and me. And about her being here."

"Oh."

"Her father is like Dad. He doesn't like me."

Mom frowns. "Your father has his problems, but you can't say he doesn't like you. He cares for you very much. He loves you."

There are times I'd debate that, perhaps with the smart-aleck comment that he has a funny way of showing it. But now isn't the time, and I know what she means.

"What I meant is, he thinks like Dad. He thinks like Tomisetti. That I'm an awful person and all of this is wrong. He's forbidden Anna to have anything to do with me. And he'd certainly go through the roof if he found out she's here."

I glance at Anna, beside me, and she nods somberly. "He'd ground me for life."

"We aren't doing anything wrong," I say quickly, "but her father wouldn't see it that way. So I need you to keep this secret." I give Mom a weak smile. "Remember, we're a team."

Mom sighs. "Rabbit, sometimes I don't know what I'm going to do with you."

"You're going to love me," I say, and she shakes her head and laughs.

"Anna, let me take your books and flute case—Rabbit says you're amazing—and I'll put them in the trunk of my car. You can get them when you leave."

"Thank you," Anna says, and hands over her books and flute case.

"Is that a yes?" I ask my mom, knowing the answer. "You'll keep the secret?"

Mom rolls her eyes. "Of course, I'll keep your secret." She motions her head toward the TV cameras and reporters. "But watch out for them. They won't be so cooperative." And she heads off to the car, shaking her head.

"Your mom seems nice," Anna says.

"She's the best." I say. I walk us thirty feet back toward the school, away from the crowd and into more of a cloak of darkness. There are four bright lampposts just outside the front doors, but there aren't any others between them and the streetlights on the other side of Goodridge. "And she's right about the media. Don't talk to any reporters and if the TV cameras start filming, duck down or turn away. Don't show your face."

"Okay."

"In fact, it might be best if you leave now."

Her eyes widen in surprise and hurt. "Why?"

Five o'clock is just minutes away so I quickly summarize everything from Officer Flanagan slapping his billy club menacingly against his palm to Joe Thurman relaying Abrams' ultimatum and implied threat.

"Maybe you should leave with me," she says. "All of you should leave."

"Abrams isn't going to win that easily," I say. "What can he do to us that he hasn't already done?" I shake my head. "I'm not leaving. But I might feel more comfortable if you did. I appreciate your support, I really do, but if something does happen, I don't want you here when it does."

"If something does happen," Anna says, "I don't want *you* here when it does."

We're at a stalemate.

*

The five o'clock deadline comes and goes.

Nothing.

I start breathing easier. I wave away a short, bearded reporter from the *Herald Traveler* who approaches Anna, saying that she doesn't want to talk, and though he frowns, he accepts it, and no one else follows. I suspect that if she were an adult, or if the reporters didn't already have all the material they need, he and others wouldn't stop so easily. But it's clear that most of the reporters, if not all, have just been waiting for the promised five o'clock fireworks, and now that it's ten after, they're glancing at their watches in annoyance and deciding how much longer they're willing to waste.

None of the TV camera crews are filming right now, which eases my mind about Anna being found out. They're just standing around, each channel's reporter and cameraman casually waiting beside their hooded cameras on their tripod stands. If nothing else happens, they're probably just waiting for the six o'clock news, though Channel 5 and Channel 7 may wait until Channel 4 leaves first, since both of them got scooped the last time.

The tension in the air that led up to five o'clock plummets with every minute. The seven adults are still walking single file, shaking their placards and chanting, but the six of us students have broken off into twos: Tina and Kelly in front, Anna and me in the middle, helping to shield her from the cameras at least a little if they turn on, and Charlie and Jamaal in the rear. We're close enough to each other, almost on each other's heels, that we're chatting with each other more than chanting.

I make a wisecracking comparison between Abrams and the Big Bad Wolf in the children's fairy tale, and say in exaggerated fashion, "I'm gonna huff, and I'm gonna puff, and I'm gonna *bloooow* your house down." I proclaim, unnecessarily, "But he ain't blown our house down!"

Charlie compares Abrams to a bully who's all bluster, but when put to the test, can't fight worth a lick.

Jamaal tells us about his father marching with Dr. King in Selma. We listen reverentially. Then perhaps inspired by the story, Kelly begins to sing, "We Shall Overcome." She has a beautiful, strong soprano voice, and the message almost moves me to tears as I think of all the other marchers who have sung that song, paying the price, sometimes dearly, for what they believe in. Soon, we're all joining in with Kelly, which isn't so good musically because none of us guys have very good voices—Charlie's is particularly bad, almost every note off tune—but it brings us even closer together in spirit.

We barely notice the convoy of four cars and two pickup trucks that turn onto Goodridge from Chestnut Street, pass us moving left to right, and park a few hundred yards down the street on the opposite side. We keep singing, assuming these are just fans showing up for the game, presumably from Swampscott since they're arriving together.

We could not have been more wrong.

*

There are maybe twenty or twenty-five of them, all just vague outlines in the darkness, approaching the school along Goodridge Street. We're walking in their direction, thinking nothing of it, the six of us teenagers side-by-side, in front of the single-file adults behind us. We're not quite to the midway point where the walkway to the school meets the sidewalk, singing and holding our placards, fighting off the cold in our fingers and toes.

I suspect we're all relieved that it's now 5:23, well past the deadline. I know I am. Abrams' threat was the bluff that we thought it was. Still, it made me a little uneasy.

I barely notice the approaching fans until half of them break off and walk stiffly down the semicircle drive off to our right while the rest stop short of it and just stand there, hanging back. That's odd. Why aren't they all going into the game?

What are they doing? I tell myself it doesn't matter. I just have the jitters from Abrams' threat. No need to get all melodramatic.

But what are they doing there? They're clustered together almost two hundred feet away, directly ahead of us, just standing there.

I tell myself not to be a nervous Nellie. There's obviously a good explanation.

We keep walking. The cluster of fans is now a hundred and seventy-five feet away. A hundred fifty.

"Slow down," I say softly. Tina and Kelly turn around and look at me quizzically, while I hold out my arm to hold Anna back. Charlie and Jamaal almost crash into us from behind, the poster board top of Charlie's placard tapping me in the head.

"What's the matter?" Anna says in barely more than a whisper.

"I don't know," I say. "But something feels wrong about those people up ahead." I say "people," not "fans," because they're not looking like fans to me anymore. They're wearing dark winter jackets and black ski hats like any other fans, and like most of us. But there's none of the joviality of fans before a game, none of the playful banter and laughter.

A hundred and forty feet away. Standing there while we come slowly closer. A hundred thirty. A hundred twenty.

They're hanging back in the shadows, shrouded in darkness. If they came forward just twenty or thirty feet, they'd be more visible, illuminated at least a little by the corner streetlight on the other side of the street. I glance that way and see the sign for the side street.

Graves Street. A shiver runs up and down my spine.

When we get a hundred feet away, I say, "Let's stop here."

I'm spooked. I don't want to get any closer, but I also don't want us turning our back on them either. Which leaves standing there, doing nothing.

Then, just as the adults close in behind us, a light goes off in my head. I burst into laughter. I am such an idiot. Such a 'fraidy cat.

All around me, my friends look at me like I've gone insane. Even Anna.

I gesture toward the outlines in the darkness a hundred feet ahead of us.

"Abrams had me spooked," I say, shaking my head, bemused at my foolishness. "I thought those people up ahead meant us harm. But they *support us!*"

Everyone frowns. Anna says, "How do you know that?"

"They think this is like a picket line, like when a union strikes," I say, smiling broadly. "Their friends didn't care so they went into the game." I gesture off to our right where the other half of their group headed down the semicircle to go in to the game. Then I point at those that remained behind. "These people are trying to decide whether they can, in all good conscience, cross our line."

"But that isn't what we're trying to do," Charlie's mom says from behind us.

"I know, but they don't know that," I say. "We just need to tell them."

I stride forward confidently, past Tina and Kelly, my heart brimming with gladness. A group of Swampscott fans has actually been considering going back home to honor our plight. I'm stunned at the gesture. We'll have to invite them to speak to the reporters and TV stations. This is great!

Eighty feet away. Almost to the Channel 7 crew. I smile and wave to the group in the shadows.

One of them at the front yells something and in unison—

—they pull down their black ski masks, covering their faces. All but two wide holes for their eyes and another for their mouth.

I stop. My blood runs cold.

They charge.

Suddenly, beneath the meager yellow glow of the streetlight, I can see all too well what they've been holding stiffly by their sides, hidden in the shadows.

Baseball bats.

"*Run!*" I yell, whirling. "*Run!*"

I crash into Tina and Kelly.

"*Baseball bats!*" I yell, and try to turn Tina and Kelly around and get them moving. I drop my placard, grab Anna's arm, and pull her forward. "*They've got baseball bats! Run!*"

We're all screaming and yelling and running, stumbling in the darkness, tripping over discarded placards, and crashing into each other.

TV camera lights blaze on, blinding us with their brightness.

"Request backup! Repeat, request backup!" Officer Murphy yells somewhere off to our right, presumably into a walkie-talkie he must have pulled from his belt. He yells some code number, then repeats his command. "Request backup! Repeat, request backup!"

Then he and his partner are yelling at our pursuers, "Police, stop! Police, stop!"

Over and over, in higher registers of panic.

"Police, stop! *Police, stop!*"

I slam into Charlie's mother, and knock her over.

"Sorry!" I yell, and yank her back onto her feet, sure we'll be feeling the hot breath of our pursuers on the back of our necks in seconds, sure those baseball bats will be splitting our heads open like melons.

Screaming and yelling erupt all around us. Panic fills the air. I grab Anna's hand. See her terrified eyes.

"Inside the school!" I yell, then spot my mom, just a few feet to our left. I yell to her as well. To all of our group. "*Inside the school! Get inside the school!*"

We cut across the crusted snow—we'll never make it to the walkway, we've got to cut across the diagonal—and as the snow crunches beneath our feet, and we leave the TV camera lights behind and move into increasing darkness, I stop dead in my tracks.

Struck with horror.

I see now where the other half of that group went when they split off from the others that stayed behind. They went down the semicircle drive, outflanking us, cutting off our path to the school, some of them going further and getting behind us as well.

We're trapped.

They race at us now through the darkness across the crusted snow, dark ski masks pulled down over their faces.

Waving baseball bats of their own.

CHAPTER 24

I look all about the darkness in wild panic. The burning taste of bile fills the back of my throat. Our attackers are coming at us from all directions: the half of them that hung back in the shadows are charging from the direction we were walking toward, right into their ambush; some of the others, the ones that outflanked us, from off to the right, by the school; and the rest of them that raced even further along the semicircle are now charging from behind.

We're trapped. Caught in their three-pronged, pincer-like grip. Closing in from all sides.

All sides but one. We have only one route of escape. Back out to Goodridge Street, cross it to the other side, and down a side street.

Maybe even *Graves* Street.

"This way!" I yell to Anna, and point to Goodridge, to the TV camera lights.

She slips and stumbles in the snow, almost falling. We barely get ten feet before she slips and stumbles again. Her new shoes can't handle the ice-crusted snow. She realizes it at the same time I do, and yanks them off.

Still holding them, she runs for the street with me in her stockinged feet, toward the blinding TV camera lights.

"Go down a side street!" I yell. "Keep running and don't stop!"

Anna looks at me in horror.

"I can't leave you!" she cries.

"Get safe! I've got to find my mom!"

"Rabbit!" she cries.

"*Go! Please!*" I beg.

She doesn't move. Looks like she can't.

Something deep within me comes up with the words. *"If you love me, go!"*

Even in the darkness, I can see the pleading in her eyes.

And then she races for Goodridge and beyond.

*

Before I can find my mom, an attacker finds me. I stumble right into his path.

I'm crashing through the snow in a blind panic, wishing I could help *all* my friends and the other adults, but knowing I have to find her first. With the blazing brightness of the TV cameras well behind me back out on the street, the darkness is thick. I can only make out vague shapes and outlines of people and trees.

And baseball bats.

I shield myself behind a tree to avoid being spotted by one attacker who turns off in the other direction. I move back closer to Goodridge, hoping my mom heard my directions sending Anna that way and followed them, too.

Not here.

I turn back toward the school. I rush through the snow, fear filling my heart, and—

He steps out from behind a tree. Only fifteen feet away, waving his bat. Little more than five feet away before I come to a skidding halt. A black ski mask covers all but his eyes and mouth.

He laughs the most hateful laugh I've ever heard. It chills me to the bone even as it sounds vaguely familiar. He's got six inches on me and maybe forty or fifty pounds.

Plus, of course, the bat.

His eyes are filled with raw hatred. Perhaps that's all in my head. In fact, it must be. In this darkness, there's no way I can really see anything even this close, looking into the three-inch-wide by one-inch-high slits cut into his ski mask. But I sense it just the same. He hates me with all of his heart.

He waves the bat, and laughs.

I back up toward Goodridge Street, the ice-crusted snow crunching beneath my feet. A tree is ten feet behind me, its leafless gnarled branches twisting toward the sky, its trunk not more than a foot in diameter. It can be a useful barrier if I can lure him to it.

"Please leave me alone," I say, crouching to make myself look even smaller, trying to sound even more terrified than I really am, if that's even possible, to lure him on.

He laughs and moves in for the kill, waving the bat.

I back up and plead. He's bigger and stronger than me and he's got a baseball bat in his hand while mine is empty. But maybe I'm smarter.

I back up until I can touch the tree with my left hand. My attacker is right-handed—he's been holding the bat in his right hand all along—and now the tree trunk is in the path of his swing.

He closes in. I take one more step back and—

I attack.

I lunge at him. I hook my thumb into the ski mask's opening for his mouth, scraping my thumbnail across his lips, while I grasp the ski mask's fabric firmly with the other hand and twist it as hard as I can.

I slide the mask far enough askew that the eye outlets now point out sideways. I've effectively blinded him.

He flails wildly with his bat, but it only hits the tree trunk beside me with a hollow *thunk*.

He pulls at his ski mask, trying to yank it off, but it snags partway up his face, exposing only his mouth, chin, and half his nose.

I've only got a split second left of my advantage. I've never been in a fistfight before in my life, so I don't really know what I'm doing. And he's still got the bat in his hand.

So I fight dirty. I know it's a cheap shot, but I take it anyway.

I clench my fist, wind up low, and drive the hardest uppercut punch I can throw right where it hurts, between my attacker's legs.

My knuckles connect with his privates—bull's-eye!—and for an instant I think I'm going to drive them all the way up his body, through his throat, and out his mouth. The first regurgitated genitals in history. But my fist hits solid bone and goes no further.

He exhales a loud *ooof!* and then howls in agony. He staggers back, but I'm right on him. As he doubles over, I wind up for another uppercut, the hardest one I can throw.

This time, my fist drives into his nose. I hit it dead on. It breaks, the bones compacting with a sickening crunch. Blood spews everywhere.

I instinctively jump back. But then I spring right back at him as he staggers backwards again, both arms flailing, the one with the bat swinging wildly through the air.

He falls onto his back. I jump onto him, pinning his right arm, the one with the bat, with my left knee, and my other knee on his chest. Blood gushes from his nose.

"Please," he begs in a gurgled choke that again somehow sounds familiar.

I yank the bat out of his hand. I pull the ski mask off his face.

Jimmy Keenan.

I freeze, unable to believe my eyes. My old tormentor, back to finish off what he couldn't do a few months ago. Hating me then for taking his starting position on the football team and God knows what else, he lured me outside during a school dance, and with his two goon friends, Jerry Soucy and Luke Scanlon, proceeded to beat me with a baseball bat just like the one I hold in my hand now. They'd have gone all Louisville Slugger on me until I was dead, unconscious, or at least no longer able to play football. The only thing that saved me was the fortunate intervention of Coach Callahan, a chaperone at the dance who'd seen me go outside. Keenan, Soucy, and Scanlon had been kicked out of school and, I thought, out of my life.

"Please," Keenan begs again.

He still has the blue eyes and the curly, golden-blond hair that drove girls wild, but none of them would be swooning over him now. Blood covers not only his face and crooked nose but also the snow on the ground beside his head and, I realize belatedly, my fist. I even taste it on my lips, though that may all be in my head, too. Just in case, disgusted, I turn my head, and spit in the snow. The coppery smell of his blood fills the air.

I remember Keenan's foot on my chest those few months ago, pinning me down, and with that insane gleam in his eyes saying, "You don't deserve to live another second." I was terrified. He was crazy enough to kill me. He laughed and said, "Bet you can't score any touchdowns with a broken leg," and then tried to prove his point. He swung his bat like an axe into my thigh. Excruciating pain like none I'd ever felt before shot down my leg and exploded up into my brain.

As I get to my feet now, I feel the primal urge, for just the briefest of instants, to pay him back. An eye for an eye. Show him no more mercy than he showed me.

But I won't do it. I'm not like him, and I'll never be.

"Stay there!" I command him, stabbing my finger in his direction.

I'm about to threaten what I'll do if he doesn't, when I sense his gaze shift to something over my left shoulder.

I dive to my right just as a bat slices through the air, passing through where I was just an instant earlier. I roll through snow and pop up to my feet, backpedaling one step, then two, then three as if I'm a cornerback again trying to cover a split end.

My new attacker easily tops six feet, maybe six-two or -three with broad shoulders. His dark eyes peer menacingly out at me through the slits in his black ski mask. He waves his bat at me, then proves he's no fool. He steps to my left, trying to angle me toward Keenan, who, still groaning, rolls onto his side that faces me, and spits blood in the red-splattered snow. But I match the attacker, stepping to the left, too.

Keenan rocks onto his elbows and knees. Blood streams from his nose. He points at me and says in a wet, choked snarl, "Kill him!"

Only now do I hear sirens, wailing both from the direction I'm facing and from behind. Have they been screaming their warning for a while now, and locked in a life-and-death struggle, I didn't notice? I suspect they have. The ones from behind and just off to the left sound very close and loud, and are getting closer.

The attacker again moves left, still trying to outflank me, but I again match him.

I'm about to make a run for it when deafening gunshots ring out, one right after another.

Boom. Boom. Boom. Boom.

It's close and unmistakable. These aren't cars backfiring. These are guns. Loud ones.

Four of them.

Close.

The attacker freezes. His dark eyes widen. He glances over his shoulder, and drops his bat.

"*Over!*" he yells. "*Over, over, over!*"

Something in his voice sounds familiar, but with just the one word I can't place it, nor do I really try. My mind is locked on the gunshots.

"*Over!*" he yells one more time, then drops his bat and breaks for it.

He makes a beeline, away from me and the school behind me, diagonally to the right. Toward the vehicles he and the other thugs arrived in.

I'm still in shock at the gunfire.

Guns. Four of them.

Fired.

Close.

Keenan staggers to his feet, takes three steps, and tumbles back onto the snow-crusted ground.

The other attacker has forty feet on me, headed to his getaway, before the awful realization sparks me to action.

He's going to get away with this.

Red-hot, molten anger erupts within me—*he is* not *going to get away with this!*—and my legs begin to move.

I'm after him. I'm wearing a thick winter jacket and dress pants that aren't made for speed.

But I am.

He is not going to get away with this.

This piece of vermin is *not* going to get away from here. Not going to get away from *me*. He *will* pay.

I can't remember ever losing a race. I'm not going to start now. Head start or no.

I pump my arms and legs. Faster, I tell myself, faster! But I stumble through the crusted snow, my arms flailing, my feet slipping. I'm making up almost no ground. He's going to get away.

No, he isn't.

I break through to the shoveled sidewalk. Past the Channel 7 TV cameras that shine brightly. Now, I'm moving. Faster! Faster!

He's already slowing. He looks back over his shoulder. He's so surprised to see me after him, he almost falls.

My mind flashes back to the football season when I returned nine kicks for touchdowns. I always outran my pursuers, forcing my legs to move faster and faster. Now, the roles are reversed. The pursued becomes the pursuer. But the secret remains the same.

The faster guy wins.

I'm the faster guy.

I close to within twenty feet.

Fifteen.

He looks back when I get to within ten, and that gets me to just five feet back almost instantly. Behind his black ski mask, his eyes widen in disbelief. He looks to his getaway car. It must be one of them just ahead.

But he knows he isn't going to make it.

Three feet. Two feet. One.

I launch myself at his legs—a little guy always has to go at the legs—and I take him down with a textbook tackle.

He slams down hard onto the sidewalk. *Ooof!*

No end zone for the bad guy.

But then he whirls on me, and despite having no leverage with me on top of him, slugs me in the side of the head.

I hadn't expected that. Hadn't thought that far ahead.

He slugs me again, and I see a few stars. That one hurt.

But he is not going to get away with this.

I hear gasps for air and thundering footsteps from behind. I fear, no, I *know*, that this thug's friends are approaching, and one is sure to have a Louisville Slugger with my name on it.

My skull's name on it.

But my brain can think of only one thing. *Not going to get away with this!*

I hook two fingers into one of the thug's ski mask eye slits and another two into the mouth and yank it sideways.

It works. He's as blind as Keenan was when I played the same trick. But it really doesn't work at all.

The thug wraps his powerful arms around me, putting me in a bear hug, and rolls until he's on top. Even blinded, he's just too much bigger than I am for me to stop him. He struggles to get to his knees, but as he does, I reach out and grasp hold of the top of his ski mask.

It pulls free in my hand.

My jaw drops. I can't believe my eyes.

For a split second, I think it's Coach Abrams himself.

And then I realize it's his brother, Delvin. He was there at the practice where it all blew up. Where Coach Abrams exposed himself publicly for being exactly what so many of us already knew him to be. I can still hear Delvin Abrams' words in my mind.

"Let 'em go," he said dismissively, his proud chest thrown out. "You're better off without the whole lot of 'em."

Well, I'm not letting him go. He's not getting away with this.

So when he breaks off his hate-filled glare, and tries to sprint for his car, I launch myself again at his legs, wrapping my arms around them, pulling them tight.

He struggles, and punches me in the head, catching me a good one between the eyes. But I'm not letting go.

He is not going to win.

As a squadron of police cruisers come screaming down Goodridge Street, sirens blaring and blue lights flashing, I take Delvin Abrams down one last time.

And in taking down his brother, I take down Coach Abrams.

EPILOGUE

Within an hour, the School Committee puts out a press release saying it is calling an emergency meeting for the following evening. It will be a closed doors session with only the committee members, Coach Abrams, and the seven players in attendance.

But that doesn't wash.

The attack with video footage leads the eleven o'clock news on all three Boston channels. Images of ski-mask-wearing thugs, directed by the coach's brother, swinging baseball bats at defenseless high school students and adults needs no commentary to provoke outrage. But it comes anyway, blistering and bold from our version of Dr. King, Mr. Bryant, who himself suffered a broken arm in the attack.

"If the Boston area is to prove itself different from Selma, Alabama, and Neshoba County, Mississippi," Mr. Bryant says, "then it must stand up now and reject not only this violence, but the hatred and prejudice that spawned it."

The next morning, a story appears on the bottom of the front page of the *Boston Globe* under the headline BAT-WIELDING ATTACK ON LYNN STUDENTS.

Not the front page of the Metro section.

The front page itself.

Of the *Boston Globe*.

The story says that nine of the thugs were arrested, most notably, Delvin Abrams, brother of the basketball coach, and there's an active investigation to identify and arrest the others who successfully fled the scene. It lists by name and address the others who were arrested, except for one unnamed minor. That has to be Jimmy Keenan. I saw him loaded into the back of a cruiser.

I recognize only one of the other names, but it stuns me: Rick Cassidy's father. It's shocking all by itself. Tragic and appalling. Then I realize the attack occurred during Rick's JV game. Somehow it seems even sadder that the father was willing to miss the enjoyment of watching his son play to act out the terrible evil inside his heart. I think of Rick's casual cruelty and raw bigotry, formerly inexplicable, and now they make at least a little bit of sense.

Like father, like son.

I recoil from that phrase, and swear it will never, ever, *ever* be applied to me, but it's hard to argue against this connection.

The *Globe* story also describes the beatings, mostly to the arms and ribs, causing broken arms to Mr. Bryant and one of the men from the NAACP, a broken wrist to Charlie's mother, and rib fractures to half a dozen of our group, including Kelly Summers, Jamaal, and his mother. The story quotes a police spokesman saying that the injuries undoubtedly would have been even more extensive, and potentially fatal, had not additional officers arrived on the scene and had not Officer Robert Murphy, after all other options had been exhausted, fired four warning shots, which prompted the attackers to flee.

But most damning for Coach Abrams is not the many arrests or the injuries. It's the recounting of his threat, relayed by Joe Thurman, that if the protestors did not disperse before five o'clock, they would suffer the consequences. With Abram's own brother leading an attack shortly after that deadline, the coach's protestations of ignorance fool no one.

By noon, knowing he's about to be fired, Coach Abrams resigns.

*

The next day, Coach Silveri, the JV coach, and Coach O'Donnell, coach of the freshmen team, are named interim varsity coaches. They'll share that position while still running their original teams. Their first act is to invite all seven of us back onto the team.

We all happily accept. Charlie and Jamaal go straight to JVs. Charlie, who avoided major injury by using the sturdy wooden post of his placard to fend off multiple attackers, instantly dominates the JV level. After two contests where he's once again a man versus boys, he's elevated to the varsity. Jamaal's rib injuries, however, are so severe they inflict stabbing pain when he so much as tries to run up the floor. He misses all but the final three games of the season.

For all of us—except, I suppose, Jamaal until he gets back into action—it feels good to be part of the team again. Running the fast break. Hitting the open man for an easy basket. Sinking a fifteen footer, and hearing the net go *swish*! Grabbing a rebound. Hitting one free throw after another. Stopping the other team's top scorer. Running a pick-and-roll to set up a layup.

A gaping hole in our lives has been filled.

But there's no Hollywood ending.

None of our teams win a championship. In fact, there's plenty of friction on the varsity between some of the white and black players, especially from the white players who lose their starting positions, or most of their playing time, to Charlie or to the returning Willie Jenkins and J.P. Clayton. Others resent the fame the black players received "after walking out on us."

And although Joe Thurman earned back a lot of our trust, and some of our admiration, when he confirmed what everyone knew, that Abrams had issued the five o'clock threat, Thurman would never again be best buddies with Willie, J.P., Charlie, or the rest of us.

We're not one big happy family. But we're all back together, one way or another.

I have some good games and some bad ones. With Jamaal out of the picture on the freshmen team, I'm the starting point guard. I play a lot, have fun, and improve, as do my teammates. We do okay considering that our two stars, Charlie and Jamaal, are no longer there to carry us.

But there's no magical last-minute victory like there was on the football field on Thanksgiving Day. I don't make a miracle shot at the buzzer. The freshman team falls just short of a .500 record in our games without Charlie and Jamaal. Jamaal helps the JV team win two of the three games he plays, but that's only three games. And with Charlie's addition, the varsity recovers from its disastrous record, but still falls in the second round of the state tourney.

No Hollywood ending.

But we won something more important than a contest between two teams. As much as we all love to win those games, and hate to lose them, those victories pale in comparison to defeating injustice and bigotry. We ensured that for this year and in the years to come, all players will have at least a chance to be treated fairly with no regard for the color of their skin.

We won that one.

That's the biggest win of all.

*

At home, things could be better. They could be worse.

On the night of the attack, my father arrives home from work having no idea what has happened. He's been freezing us out these last few days, refusing to speak even a single word to either Mom or me since watching the coverage of the first protest.

It's been a four-day silence. I've been counting.

On this night, he enters the front door, takes off his coat, and seems prepared to sit down to another awkward dinner, stone-faced and drained of all emotion, staring down at his plate so he doesn't have to look at us, mechanically shoveling in his food. Tonight, it's leftover meatloaf and potatoes because Mom didn't have the time, or the energy, to make something fresh. The aroma of the meatloaf is in the air and has me salivating, but it isn't ready yet, and Mom has things she needs to say.

"Andre, sit down," she says, and points to his accustomed place at the head of the dining room table. He looks at her in surprise, presumably wondering who she thinks she is to order him around. But it's not enough to break his stone-faced silence. We sit down, my father on the left and Mom on the right, and she recounts her harrowing escape.

Unable to find me in the darkness, she stumbled aimlessly through the snow, calling out my name, panic rising deep within her chest. Suddenly, she sees the outline of a bat-wielding attacker coming at her. He seems big, but she really isn't sure. He may be thirty feet away, or forty or fifty. She doesn't know that either. All she knows for sure—all she sees—is that bat waving through the air.

And he's coming right at her.

She screams and runs. She's running toward Goodridge Street and the faint glow of yellow light coming down from the streetlights on the opposite side. She runs, slips for just a moment, and then she keeps running again.

She knows she can't escape him. She hears the sound of his heavy breathing—his panting!—right behind her. He's right on her heels.

She glances back, knowing it's the wrong thing to do. She's sure to stumble, sure to fall into a clump if for no other reason than sheer terror, but she can't help herself. She looks back.

And he sees her face.

He's only a few feet behind her, his black ski mask snug against his features. His bat is raised, poised to deliver a crushing blow. She can almost sense a smile of pleasure and anticipation behind that mask.

But he sees her face, and stops. He stares at her, disbelieving. Drops the arm with the bat limply to his side. He swears angrily, his white teeth bared like fangs, visible through the mouth-sized hole in the mask.

And he turns to seek another target.

"He saw that I was white," Mom says now. "It's the only possible explanation. I couldn't figure it out at the time, but it's the only thing that makes sense. He was there to beat black people."

Then I tell my story, and how my attackers, Jimmy Keenan and Delvin Abrams, knew me personally. I didn't need to be black for them to hate me.

When I finish, my father stares, ashen-faced, at the two of us, looking at Mom, then me, then Mom again.

"I'm relieved both of you weren't hurt," he says, his first words to us in four days. "You were lucky. Very lucky." He breathes noisily in through his nose "Rabbit, I know I said a few days ago that I hate you. I regret that. I don't understand what's happened to you, but I don't hate you. I was just angry. I care very much for both of you."

He takes in another deep breath, and shakes his head. "But I'm upset that you both put yourself in that position. Especially you, Marie. What were you thinking of? Rabbit's got a mind of his own. These days, I can't control him anymore than I can control the weather." He gives me a hopeless, unhappy look, as if he's given up on me.

He turns back to Mom. "But I never would have expected this kind of defiance from you. I suppose I should have, based on your recent behavior." He says the words bitterly, anger flaring in his eyes. "You know how important appearances are at my job. If I can't control my own wife, then how can I be trusted to control an entire division of the company? And yet, you're not only protesting out there with the rest of them, making a damned fool of yourself, but you even made the signs!"

He throws his hands out wide, palms up, perplexed at her treachery and demanding an explanation.

A heavy silence fills the room. Mom purses her lips. She seems to be weighing her options. I badly want to speak up, but this time it's as though I've passed the ball to her and she needs to sink the open shot.

She gets up from her chair, leaves the table without saying a word, and steps into the kitchen. She's only gone for a minute or two, but it feels like a lifetime. We watch her from the dining room table as she pulls the meatloaf out of the oven and sets it on a platter. I race to the kitchen to help. Together, we bring the meatloaf, potatoes, and peas to the table. I sit down, but she remains standing. No one touches the food. She folds her hands in front of her dark brown dress. She looks at my father. The two lock eyes.

"Andre," she says, softly but firmly. "I'm not yours to control."

"You're my wife!"

"On matters such as these, I will follow my conscience."

He looks at us dumbfounded. "You two are just going to do whatever you want, regardless of what I say?"

Mom straightens her back, and tilts her head upward. "We are going to follow our consciences."

"No matter what I say?" he asks, his voice growing shrill. "*Regardless of the impact on my job?*"

I'm dying to tell him what he can do with his stupid job, but even I know this is a time for me to hold my tongue.

"Andre," Mom says softly, "we have to follow our consciences."

And that closes the issue.

My father's shoulders slump, and we finally dig in to the meatloaf, potatoes, and peas. My father dejectedly picks at his food, but I make up for him. I eat three helpings.

The attack is the lead story on the eleven o'clock Channel 4 news. Even though it's past my bedtime on a school night, we watch it silently together, my father in the tan lounge chair and Mom and I on the sofa. We're all in our pajamas and slippers, my father in his dark bathrobe, my mother in her white one. Our eyes remain glued to the black-and-white screen. The volume is turned up so there's no difficulty hearing the anchorman narrate the story.

My father recoils at the video footage of a masked attacker beating a fallen Jamaal in the side with his Louisville Slugger. The blood drains from my father's face. It's as if he needed to see it for himself to believe it.

When the news cuts to a commercial, he gets unsteadily to his feet.

"Good Lord," he says. "You two were so very lucky." And then he goes to bed.

As the succeeding days pass, his anger and resentment don't totally disappear, but they do drop considerably. It seems the bosses at work he is so desperate to impress have fallen in line, at least a little, with public opinion. Our attackers, or perhaps it was their bats, turned us protestors into, if not totally sympathetic characters, then at least acceptable ones.

Even Tomisetti is forced to paint us players in a somewhat different light, focusing on our return to the team and what a good thing that is, while falling silent as to how we're all a scourge to society.

So my father doesn't have to be ashamed of Mom and me after all. At least, not much. He doesn't have to take us down the path of Mutually Assured Destruction. He remains bitter and distant, but it could be worse.

If I'm tallying everything in my life as either a win or a loss, I have to consider my relationship with him to be a loss. Perhaps a resounding, soul-crushing loss.

But I'm going to consider it to be a contest that's far from over.

On my bad days, I'm ready to throw in the towel. I just don't care. The scoreboard says there's no hope. Why bother? I'm better off without him. And at least I have my mom, the best mom ever.

But on my good days, I'll tell myself that a comeback is still possible, no matter what that scoreboard says. In the words of Yogi Berra, "It ain't over till it's over."

I'm going to cling to that.

*

I'm certainly going to cling to Anna. Not literally, of course. But in my mind, I hold her hand as we walk together to classes, and we share hugs that are entirely in our minds.

It's not as good as the real thing, of course, but she thinks her father might ease up a bit soon, and we can get back to really going out. He still doesn't like me, but he might not hate me as much as before. Fortunately, Anna was never identified in any of the news reports as being at the protest. Mom retrieved her flute and textbooks for her, then while all the rest of us were being interviewed by the police and media, Anna snuck undetected back into the school and into the basketball game to maintain her cover. Which is a very good thing. If her father knew that she was briefly marching with us, I might never get out of his doghouse.

But there's hope. Anna and I care about each other. That isn't going to change.

Even if we can't officially go out, she's still my girl.

Well, more than just my girl.

The morning after the attack, before homeroom, we're standing together in front of her locker, she in a pretty, navy-blue dress and me in a dark blue dress shirt and black slacks. She's empty-handed; all her books are in her locker. She takes the two books I have in my hand, and stacks them in her locker on top of her own. She looks up and down the hallway, half-filled with other students walking in both directions, talking and laughing. Others are at their lockers, but none close to us.

"What are you doing?" I ask.

"Did you mean what you said when you told me to run last night?" she asks expectantly.

"Of course," I say, not understanding what she's getting at. "If you'd stayed, we probably would have both gotten beaten senseless."

Her shoulders slump. She looks deflated. She asks, "What's the one thing you said that finally got me to run?"

I draw a blank. This is clearly important to her, but all I remember is the sheer panic I felt that our attackers would hurt her and my mom and my friends. And all our supporters. And me, too. All I remember is the terror that gripped my heart.

"You don't remember, do you?" Anna asks with a dejected look that's making me feel bad.

"I was so scared for you," I say. "I—"

And then it hits me. Hits me like a baseball bat over the head. It hadn't been something I'd consciously meant to say at the time. It just burst out from deep inside me. Forced out by the panic.

"I said, 'If you love me, go!'"

Anna brightens. A smile creeps across her lips. "And did I go?"

I nod, a lump forming in my throat.

She looks at me so sweetly. "That was probably the only thing you could have said to get me to leave. So you know what that means."

I sure do.

Anna loves me! She loves me!

Anna loves me! Anna loves me! Anna loves me!

The words, no, the *knowledge*, floods over me. It's like a tidal wave crashing over me, knocking me down, rendering me speechless. I'm so deliriously happy, I can't speak. My throat feels like there's a basketball in it. I can't swallow.

It's only when she blinks and the first hint of hurt comes into her eyes, that I realize she's interpreting my silence as rejection.

As if I could ever reject her!

But I quickly nod furiously. *Yes, yes, I know. I know you love me, and it makes me so very, very happy, and—*

Finally, I dislodge the basketball from my throat, and say the words I've wanted to say for so very long, words that wipe out that earliest hint of hurt in Anna's eyes.

"I love you!" I say, and mean it with every bone in my body. Mean it with every pounding beat of my heart. Mean it with everything in me. "I love you, I love you, I love you!"

"Oh, Rabbit!" she says, her eyes beginning to well with tears. "I love you, too!"

She glances up and down the hallway, then throws herself into me, wrapping her arms around my neck. I wrap my arms around her waist. I smell lilacs and the sweet scent of strawberries in her hair. I feel her heart beating furiously against mine, although perhaps that fierce hammering is coming from my own heart, overflowing with joy and happiness.

"I love you so much!" we both say at the same time into each other's ears. "So much!"

We pull apart from each other. I look into Anna's soft brown eyes, and see there's a twinkle in them just for me. She's the most wonderful girl ever. She loves me. And her eyes twinkle. Just for me.

I am the happiest guy on Earth.

The Rabbit Labelle Saga

Offside
Offensive Foul
Bottom of the Ninth (forthcoming)

Acknowledgements

Thanks to the many friends who helped me get details right. I imposed often on Jen Mahoney, Charlie Mahoney, Dave Grazewski, and John Bingham, and they always came through for me. The questions also flew at Mary Winston McCarriston, Matt Muise, Paula Carson Fallon, and Colleen Lowery Crosby, and I always got the answers. I should probably list the entire Lynn English Class of 1974 to avoid leaving someone out, but these other friends also helped whenever asked: Brian Bagley, Cathy Cole-Adams, Cyndi Cumminsky, Mike Amenta, Nancy DiCesare, Robin Daly, Jim Tidmarsh, and Marie Gheringhelli McDermott.

To my awesome team of first readers, who once again provided me with great insights, and to my editor, Dayle Dermatis, whose expertise caught countless mistakes. Any typos or errors that remain are entirely my own fault.

To all my friends and family, for their love and support.

But most of all, to the Best Wife Ever and the love of my life, Brenda, whose support borders on the insane. I am so very, very lucky.

About the Author

David H. Hendrickson's first novel, *Cracking the Ice*, was praised by Booklist as "a gripping account of a courageous young man rising above evil." He has since published five additional novels, including *Offside*, which has been adopted for high school student required reading, and most recently, Offensive Foul.

His short fiction has appeared in Ellery Queen's Mystery Magazine, *Heart's Kiss*, Pulphouse, and numerous anthologies, including over a half dozen issues of Fiction River. His story "Death in the Serengeti" was selected for *Best American Mystery Stories 2018*.

Hendrickson has published over fifteen hundred works of nonfiction, most recently his first book for writers, *How to Get Your Book into Schools and Double Your Income with Volume Sales*, and also *Travis Roy: Quadriplegia and a Life of Purpose*. He has been honored with the Joe Concannon Hockey East Media Award and the Murray Kramer Scarlet Quill Award.

Visit him online at http://www.hendricksonwriter.com.

A Special Request from the Author: Word of mouth is crucial for any author to succeed. If you enjoyed this book, please consider leaving a review where you purchased it. Even if it's only a line or two, it would make all the difference and would be very much appreciated.